Shattered

Unfinished Business
Book 4

Juanita Kees

Published by Juanita Kees (Kees2Create)

eBook ISBN: 9781763632431

Paperback ISBN: 9781763632448

Cover Design Copyright © by Paradox Book Cover Designs And Formatting

Shattered

Juanita Kees

She's a stranger to the outside world. He's seen far too much of its dark side. As tragedy unleashes terror on the farm, can Bridey and Cole work together to bring peace and love to Mindaleny Ridge?

Bridey McCaffrey's life has never been perfect. All she's ever known is control. Under strict rules, she is isolated from the community, a prisoner at Mindaleny Ridge. But as tragedy strikes on the farm, a new nightmare unfolds for her and her three children. When she receives a mysterious call for help, what is uncovered will open the doors to hell. It will take all her remaining strength and courage to keep herself and her children safe.

Sergeant Cole Delaney is looking forward to some quiet, small-town policing, until he realises that secrets run deep in the town of Moonie River. And the family living out at Mindaleny Ridge appear to be a magnet for trouble. He's no longer arresting goats for chewing up Mrs Lee's petunias or breaking up fights over a poker game in the park. There is something far more sinister going on in his town. And his growing attraction to Bridey makes him even more determined to keep her and her young family safe.

Together, Cole and Bridey follow a trail of murder and manipulation to catch a killer. Can they end his reign of terror to find happiness together before it's too late?

About the Author

Join me on this wild, suspenseful, thrilling ride through small towns to catch bad guys, solve crimes, and find happy ever afters.

Juanita escapes the real world to create emotionally engaging stories steeped in crime, suspense, mystery, and intrigue. Her books are set in dusty, rural outback Australia and on the NASCAR racetracks of America. Her small-town USA and Australian rural stories have made bestseller and top 100 lists. Juanita also likes to dabble in the ponds of fantasy and paranormal with Greek gods brought to life in the 21st century.

Juanita graduated college with distinctions and a diploma in Proofreading, Editing and Publishing in 2011 and started her freelance writing business, Kees2Create Words. As a developmental and structural editor, she assists writers to polish their manuscripts for submission. In 2012, she achieved her dream of becoming a published author and now has multiple novels on the market.

When she's not working, writing, editing, or

proofreading, Juanita enjoys travelling to discover new worlds for inspiration. Mother to two handsome heroes and partner to a car enthusiast, Juanita also has a passion for fast cars and country living.

Juanita loves to talk books with readers and would love to connect. Contact her via:

Website:

https://juanitakees.com/contact/

Kees2Create Words Editing:

https://kees2createwords.com/

BookBub:

https://www.bookbub.com/authors/juanita-kees

Newsletter:

https://kees2createwords.substack.com/embed

Goodreads:

https://www.goodreads.com/author/show/6454477.
Juanita_Kees

Book Love Book Club:

https://www.facebook.com/groups/
607880523038543

Note of Caution from the Author

This book contains references to life experiences that some readers may find unsettling. While all care has been taken to treat these sensitive matters with empathy, care and respect, readers who may have experienced miscarriage, domestic violence, manipulation, suicide, or religious abuse may find some scenes confronting. Please read on with caution if you are affected by any of the above.

Chapter One

Bridey's fingers moved from the edge of the laundry basket to touch the tender bruise on her cheek. She'd better hurry to get Thom's lunch on the table. There'd be trouble if he came in earlier than usual.

Mid-afternoon sun streamed in through the kitchen window as her gaze roamed over the farm. Where fields of healthy crops might once have thrived, they now struggled to grow. Barren dust had replaced healthy soil, scattered with the remains of seedlings that had given up the struggle to survive. High up on the ridge Mindaleny was named for, gum trees flourished despite the dry below.

She wondered, as always, what lay beyond that ridge, as she turned to check the heat under the soup pot. It would only need a little warming up. Enough for one. Even if there was more, Thom would eat his fill before anyone else would be allowed to eat. The boys would have the leftover bread with Vegemite for lunch.

The back door slammed open. Bridey's heart sank as heavy boots stomped along the wooden boards, shaking the floor beneath her feet. Too late. There'd be a dirt trail to clean up, but it didn't matter. Saying anything would only cause more of a scene. Her shoulders tensed as the footsteps halted in the doorway and the smell of stale sweat drifted in.

'God damn it, Bridey, you can't even do a simple thing like have lunch ready on time. You're bloody useless!' Thom's hands gripped her upper arms hard as he turned her to face him. There'd been nothing gentle about his touch. Ever.

She dared not argue when the smell of whiskey lay on his breath. Bridey swallowed the urge to gag and willed her stomach to settle. Would the time ever be right to tell him she was pregnant again? She couldn't put it off for much longer.

'I'm sorry, Thom. I'll try harder.'

'Bloody oath you will. You'd better make sure you're not late with my lunch again. I've got enough on my hands trying to put food in your mouths. The least you can bloody do is have my lunch ready on time.' He pushed her away to lift the lid on the soup pot. 'What is this slop? Do you expect me to eat this shit?'

Bridey staggered back as he raised his hand, the soup lid gripped in his fingers. Behind him, the children hovered in the doorway, poised to run if he looked in their direction. The twins stared at them, wide-eyed and terrified, their older brother between them. They knew what the outcome of an argument would be.

At six, Alex stood a head taller than Garrett and Shaun, far too wise for his age. He'd seen and heard too much in his short lifetime.

'Please, Thom. Not in front of the children.'

'Not in front of the children.' He mimicked her, his mouth pulled in a cruel taunt. 'Here's an idea! How about I send the little buggers away, huh? Give them to the New Lord. He'll sort those little shits out. Some bloody brides you turned out to be. If I knew that bastard was giving me a useless whore who can't even cook, I would have told him I'd pick one out myself.'

Bridey hung her head. Any response would only result in an unpleasant scene that would escalate out of control faster than a wildfire in dry bush. If Thom carried through with his threat to send the boys to the monster of a man who ruled their lives, her beautiful children would be destroyed by the evil he represented.

Thom leaned in, his face ugly with a rage he didn't care to control as he tossed the lid on the floor and threw the pot over on the cooktop. Bridey reached out to stop it falling onto the kitchen floor, scalding her hand.

Thom picked up the half empty bottle of whiskey off the bench. 'Make yourself useful. Go buy some more fucking whiskey. And don't even think about running again because, by God, I will find you and you will regret it.' With another hard push that sent her hip crashing into the sharp edge of the table, he stormed out of the house, slamming the door behind him with a rage that made the walls shake.

Through the window, Bridey watched Thom swig from the bottle as he weaved his way down the path back to the barren fields, the burn on her hand stinging. The empty bottle smashed to the ground and shattered against a rock. He ignored the spray of glass and pushed through the gate, letting it slam shut behind him.

Another baby was the last thing they needed. Not that she'd had a choice. It was her duty as his wife to serve him, and if she conceived while submitting to his needs, well then it was her own fault. Thom hated condoms, and the New Lord had banned the use of contraception for all the brides. Hadn't the New Lord already expressed his dissatisfaction that she'd only produced boys so far?

Bridey had spent the last week wishing the test

she'd bought at Mrs Lee's shop hadn't presented two positive pink lines. Another baby would only make things worse ... if it survived the beating she knew would come later.

She placed a protective hand over her belly, praying that she had enough strength to continue to bear the brunt of his anger to protect her children from it. Running away was futile. The last time she'd tried, he'd beaten her so badly she'd ended up with a fractured eye socket and threatened to set fire to the car. With her and the children in it.

He was always sorry after. Sorry that she'd made him do it. Sorry that she was incapable of just about everything. She'd deserved what she got for trying to leave him when he gave her and her brood a home to live in. He was the provider. She was the burden he dragged around like the rotting potatoes he'd unearthed from the ground.

As he disappeared out of sight, she rushed to gather up the boys, hurried them outside, and bundled them into the back seat of Thom's father's old Valiant station wagon. At least he hadn't hit her with the bottle or the pot lid.

'Quickly now, boys. We can't stay out too long.'

'Do we have to come back, Mum?'

Alex's quiet question tore at her heart. 'Yes, we have to come back.'

'Why?'

'Because we have nowhere else to go.' She wished they did. That she could take the children and disappear. Approach strangers for help to escape. But Thom would come looking for her, and he'd bring the wrath of the New Lord with him. Survival in the world outside of the isolation of the church would always remain a mystery. She'd lived with the Children of the New Lord all her life, their every move kept secret from the Unchosen.

Bridey cursed the sting of tears as she secured their seat belts and closed the car door. Could their life be different if Thom stopped drinking? She hated fuelling his habit, but the consequences of not stocking up his supply would be a lot worse than ignoring his orders.

As she drove into town, the boys were more subdued than usual. No excited chatter from the back seat, knowing they would get their rare ice cream treat at the shop. Bridey sighed. The older they got, the more they'd understand, and the less she'd be able to protect them, especially if Thom followed through on his threat to send them away. She didn't want them to grow up the way she had. In her care, they at least had some protection.

Thirty minutes later, Bridey pulled up in front of the small grocery store. She opened the heavy car door as the boys released themselves from their seats and climbed out onto the pavement outside the shop. Alex slipped his hand into hers, squeezing her fingers.

'We'll be fine, Alex.' She hoped her smile would appease him but they both knew the day wasn't over yet and the night was yet to come.

~

Cole smiled as he strode toward Mrs Lee's grocery store that doubled as the newsagency and post office, a combination so common in small towns. His city colleagues had taken bets that he'd be bored within a week. After working the drug squad in Perth for ten of his fifteen years on the force, he'd relished the thought of less exciting policing in a quiet small town. Today, his biggest case would be to catch the culprit who'd used the last of the coffee in the jar and hadn't replaced it.

Bored? Not a chance. Three weeks into his new position as sergeant-in-charge at the Moonie River police station, and he was having a ball. He'd broken up a half-hearted brawl over a card game in the park and had taken a stray nanny goat into custody for chewing up Mrs Lee's prize petunias. Chewy now had a job mowing his overgrown backyard at the house attached to the station. A part of him kinda hoped no one would come forward to claim her. She was growing on him.

Ahead, a mum shepherded three boys onto the pavement outside the Moonie River General Store and Post Office. He hadn't seen them around before, and he'd pretty much met everyone within a ten-kilometre radius. Most likely she'd come into town from one of the farms. Cole stepped up his pace to hold the fly screen door open for them. He caught a startled look from the three boys as they huddled closer to their mum.

She threw him a quick nervous glance as she placed a protective arm around the eldest boy. 'Thank you.'

'My pleasure.'

He had a fleeting moment to study her before she guided the boys ahead of her through the door. Auburn hair — straight and long — secured into a ponytail and covered with a blue headscarf. A thin face, curved lips, sad blue eyes, and an ugly bruise that marred otherwise perfect skin.

A knot tightened his stomach. He'd seen bruises like hers too many times before. The fly screen banged shut behind him. The woman ahead of him flinched. Whoever she was, she walked on shards of glass.

Cole made his way to the aisle that carried tea, coffee, and sugar, pretending to study the selection available, his attention on the woman and kids. Body language never lied. No way could he ignore that all of them were a little jumpy and out of their comfort zone. She was older than he'd thought at first. Maybe mid to late twenties. Skinnier than was healthy. The boys were clean and groomed, no sign of neglect or harm.

'It's all right. Off you go. One ice cream each. I'll be right here at the counter, picking up the mail from Mrs Lee.'

The soft reassurance in her tone seemed to be enough for the boys. The younger twins headed for the ice cream freezer, their older brother following behind them, constantly looking around him as if he expected to be blind-sided and wanted to be sure he saw whoever was coming. A big responsibility for a boy who hadn't even reached double digits in age yet.

Cole picked out a glass jar of instant coffee and flicked his gaze over the label as the young woman approached the counter.

Mrs Lee's happy smile lit up her face. 'Bridey! We haven't seen you in a while, dear. I've got a pile of mail for you. I said to my Ed that if you didn't come in this week, I'd get him to run it out to Mindaleny Ridge for you.' She turned to retrieve a bundle of envelopes wrapped with a rubber band. 'That's a nasty bruise on your cheek. Is everything all right?'

'Of course.' Bridey touched her cheek. 'I wasn't

looking where I was going with the mop and walked into a door.'

'Mmm...' Mrs Lee studied the young woman for a moment before she smiled and patted her hand. 'I've always said housework is dangerous.' Mrs Lee handed over the bundle of mail, her smile fading as she covered Bridey's outstretched hand with hers. 'Take care of yourself and the boys, my dear. Life is precious. If I can help in anyway, all you need to do is reach out.'

Cole's interest piqued. He needed to pay more attention to town gossip. How many times had the young mum come in with fist-sized bruises and excuses for them?

Bridey's back and shoulders tensed. 'We're fine, Mrs Lee, but thank you. It was just a moment of clumsiness on my part.'

'I understand, dear.' Mrs Lee nodded in Cole's direction. 'Have you met our new officer-in-charge?' She waved him over. 'Sergeant Delaney, come over and meet Bridey McCaffrey.' She gave her attention back to Bridey. 'This lovely young man took over from Pete a few weeks ago.'

Cole approached at a relaxed stroll. At six-foot-five and a hundred-and-seventeen kilograms of gym-toned muscle, his size had once been an intimidating weapon. He didn't need to be that cop anymore and Bridey appeared to be intimidated enough.

He held out his hand to shake hers. 'A pleasure to meet you.'

She hesitated a moment then placed her hand in his briefly before withdrawing it again. Clean, unpainted, trimmed nails. Working hands with a plain wedding band on her left-hand ring finger. No other jewellery, but the back of her right hand sported a fresh burn mark.

'Hello, Sergeant.' Turning back to Mrs Lee, Bridey opened her purse and pulled out a twenty dollar note. 'That's for the ice cream. Thank you for holding onto the mail for me.' She handed over the money. 'Please put the change in the collection box for the bush fire appeal.'

'Thank you, dear. That's truly kind of you. Are you sure, though?'

'Yes, yes, of course.' She gathered the boys together. 'Alex, Garrett, Shaun! Quickly now. One more stop on the way home. You can finish your ice cream outside. Thank you, Mrs Lee.' She nodded at Cole. 'Goodbye, Sergeant Delaney.'

'Goodbye, Bridey.' He smiled down at the boys who stared at him with solemn eyes, melting ice cream running down the sticks and over their fingers. Cole reached for three serviettes from the counter. 'Here you go, take these with you.'

Alex reached for the serviettes with a murmured

thanks and handed one each to his brothers. In a normal situation, he would have thought that was because Bridey McCaffrey had raised her boys to look out for each other but, judging by the fear in the boys' eyes, he doubted their situation was normal. The family hurried out of the shop and headed for the Liquor Inn attached to the pub across the road.

Mrs Lee released a long sigh. 'That poor girl.' She shook her head. 'That money she told me to put into the collection tin would have come out of her weekly grocery allowance.' She reached over the counter to place a hand on Cole's arm. 'Bridey only ever uses cash, and never has more than a twenty dollar note to spend in here unless she's picking up her monthly supplies. No credit card and I've never seen her use the auto teller. Her Thom is a mean bastard. He's been banned from the pub for getting into fights, and pretty much banned from coming into town, so he sends Bridey in. His parents own Mindaleny Ridge. One day, they took off with their caravan and never came back. Left Thom at the farm. My Ed says they probably couldn't live with the boy anymore.'

'Or perhaps they wanted to join the rest of the grey nomads off on their big adventure around Australia?'

Mrs Lee shrugged as she lifted her hand from Cole's arm. 'They didn't seem to be the type to socialise that way. They didn't mix, seldom came into town unless it was for the mail or supplies. Kept to themselves. And dressed strangely ... There was some gossip around town that they'd left a cult farm in the Blue Mountains and had come out to start one here in Western Australia. There was a man who came out to visit them once — Pastor Camden, I think he said his name was — so it made sense. He stopped in here to ask for directions to Mindaleny Ridge. We had a meeting at the town hall about it. We don't want that kind of trouble in our town.'

'Pastor Camden?'

Mrs Lee shuddered. 'Creepy bloke if you ask me. Cold eyes. I think everyone was relieved when the McCaffreys took off again within the first year. We all just figured they'd decided to move on somewhere else, and no one wanted their cult anywhere near our town anyway.'

'But Thom stayed on. Did anyone think it was odd that he didn't leave with them?'

Mrs Lee shuffled through the mail left on the counter for sorting. 'He was a grown boy. I guess he wanted to stay or maybe he just didn't want to be a part of his parents' church anymore. We all thought he'd settle down and behave himself when he brought home a wife. Instead, he continued to be a menace in town and isn't very nice to Bridey.'

Cole decided to nibble at the bait. The bruises on

Bridey McCaffrey's face and burns on her hand were fresh enough to raise a niggle in his mind. 'What makes you say that?'

'There's not a time she's come in without a fresh bruise or scar. Doc Hamilton is a friend of ours. He doesn't disclose his patients' information, but he has seen to Bridey a few times now. Even reported some of the incidents to Pete, the old sergeant-in-charge before you came along.'

'What did Pete do about the reports?'

'Said there was nothing he could do unless Bridey filed a report or applied for a violence protection order.' Mrs Lee sighed. 'He never took these kinds of things seriously. He said it was between a woman and her man to sort things out or go their separate ways. Claimed he didn't have time to chase down a little tiff between husband and wife that would blow over by nightfall. Frustrated the hell out of Doc when Pete would say that she needed to understand the stress that Thom was under running the farm on his own and be more supportive.'

'It can't be easy for either of them.'

'Drought, rain, floods, pests ... it's not easy for anyone anymore. It's affecting the mental health of our farmers. The black dog has taken down many of our people.' She sighed again. 'I'd like to say he used to be a good boy, that Thom, but there was always something strange about him and his family. And I don't think drinking the way he does helps any. Whiskey changes a man's soul, doesn't it, Sarge?'

Bridey came out of the bottle shop with two bottles of cheap brown whiskey in her hand. She led the boys across the road, their hands linked. Cole waited until the car doors slammed and the engine growled to life before answering Mrs Lee.

'Sadly, yes, drinking often releases a beast.'

And he wouldn't be surprised at all if it was just one of the reasons for Bridey McCaffrey's bruises. Perhaps it was time for him to pay Thom McCaffrey a visit to introduce himself.

Chapter Two

The iron grate rattled under the wheels as Bridey steered the heavy Valiant across the entrance to Mindaleny Ridge.

She rolled past what had once been strawberry fields. Thom had the trench digger out, and instead of planting strawberry plants, he'd dug out a trench where they'd once struggled to survive.

A pile of dirt sat in the bucket, interspersed with dead leaves, and dried up husks of old strawberries, the digger abandoned in the trench and tools strewn all over the ground beside it. Where was he?

Bridey's stomach lurched at the prospect of what might happen if he was waiting for her inside the house. The least she could hope for was that he'd headed out somewhere in the shade outside. The boys piled out of the car as she turned off the engine.

They waited until she'd opened the back door and called out, 'Thom? We're home.' Silence greeted them, so Bridey ushered the boys inside. 'Quickly, boys. Go wash your hands and wait for me in your room until I tell you it's okay to come out.'

A sadness tugged at her heart for what might have been. The boys should be free to be boisterous and noisy, to play in the muddy fields and get as dirty as they pleased mucking around beside a father who loved them. Instead, everyone tip-toed around Thom, terrified of triggering him into an angry outburst. She'd hoped — prayed — for a miracle. That he'd give up drinking, be less angry. That when the boys were a little older, he'd be able to communicate with them better, trust them to help around the farm, take some of the weight off his shoulders. Maybe then peace could come to Mindaleny Ridge.

No point wishing for miracles. The time for wishing was done. Bridey reached for a pan, then opened the fridge to take out the mince she'd defrosted that morning. The boys loved spaghetti bolognaise. Hopefully, there'd be enough left over after Thom had eaten so they could go to bed with full tummies. She chopped the onions and tomatoes for the sauce, added celery for colour, and gathered the herbs and spices for the sauce off the rack on the wall.

Movement outside the kitchen window caught her

eye and a knot clenched in her stomach. But instead of coming into the house, Thom strode into the potting shed at the bottom of the garden, slamming the door behind him. She hoped he'd stay outside, at least until she'd bathed the boys.

A soft breeze blew in through the open laundry door, lifting her hair as she waited, the knot in her tummy growing. How long would he stay outside in the shed before coming inside? How much time did she have to prepare herself for another endless night?

A piece of paper on the edge of the kitchen bench fluttered to the floor. Bridey bent to pick it up. Thom's scrawl covered the page, an untidy mix of capitals and small letters. Angry words pressed hard, the full stops stabbed to make holes on the page. Her heart seized as she read them, her breath catching in her chest.

IM dOne. With YOU. With LiFe. With HIM.

The sound of a gunshot exploded from inside the shed, scaring the cockatoos in the trees into flight.

'Dear God, Thom.' Clutching the letter in her fist, she ran out the laundry door, down the back steps, her heart pounding as she screamed his name. 'Thom!' Reaching the shed, she hammered a fist against the hard wood, torn between wanting a response and hoping she wouldn't get one. 'Thom!'

Silence. The reality of what he'd done sank in. Her

knees buckled. She sank to the hard, dusty ground. Disbelief rushed in, battered her in waves. She'd never wished him dead. Not even at the worst times when she'd thought she wouldn't survive his punishment. All she'd wanted was for him to stop. Stop drinking. Stop the beatings. And now he had.

'Mum?' Alex's cautious call reached her from close by, terror in his eyes.

'Stay away, baby. Keep your brothers away. Everything's all right.' She scrubbed at the burn of tears and breathed through the panic that preceded realisation. He couldn't hurt them anymore. 'Go inside, quickly now.'

Her stomach churning and nausea building in her throat, she waited until Alex and the twins had gone inside before opening the door barely wide enough to peer through the crack. Thom lay face down on the floor of the shed, blood turning the grey concrete pad dark red.

Her hand slipped from the door. It squeaked shut and she leaned back against it. Tears slipped down her cheeks, the ache in her chest intensifying. A multitude of emotions that ranged from relief to sadness and regret washed through her. 'Jesus, Thom,' she whispered.

Numb, Bridey hauled herself to her feet, willing

the bloody scene etched into her vision to go away. Up the laundry stairs and into the kitchen, she lifted the receiver on the phone on the wall and dialled the triple zero number for emergencies taped above it.

'What is your emergency please?' The impersonal tones of the operator leeched into her mind.

Sinking to the floor, she forced out words. They rang empty in the silence of the kitchen as three pairs of eyes watched her from the doorway. 'Police ... and ambulance.'

'Can you please state your name and address, and the nature of the emergency?'

'Bridey McCaffrey. My husband is Thomas McCaffrey. Lot 526, River Road, Moonie River. The farm is Mindaleny Ridge.' Tears choked her throat. Hysteria edged the words as the twins climbed into her lap and Alex placed his arms around her neck in a tight hold from her left. 'Hurry. Please come. I have my three children with me and my husband ... has shot himself. In the potting shed.'

The phone slipped from her grip as she gathered her children close, burying her face in their hair, holding them tight as the impersonal voice demanded details she had no voice to give. The suicide note she'd gripped in her hand fell to the floor a crumpled mess beside her as she rocked her children and choked down on the need to cry, to let it all out. She had to be brave, hold it together. For the children's sake.

She stayed that way, blanking out her thoughts, fighting off the battering of regret, relief, and guilt at feeling relief until sirens filled the heavy blanket of air around them.

The urgent thump of boots on the stairs, the vibration of them shaking the wooden floorboards. Different boots from Thom's this time. Sergeant Cole Delaney's gentle hand touched her shoulder. 'Bridey?'

Words jammed in her throat. She tightened her grip on the children and leaned away.

'You're safe now. Are you hurt?'

Bridey shook her head, the sergeant's words reaching her through a fog of confusion and disbelief.

'Is it all right if I get the paramedics to check you and the boys over? To make sure you're not hurt in any way.' His quiet, even tones soothed some of the turmoil inside her.

'Yes.' The twins whimpered in her arms as Alex echoed her response, reassuring them as much as himself. Her darling Alex, always so strong, always taking care of his brothers.

'Bridey, I hate to ask this, but have you been into the shed?' Sergeant Delaney sat on his haunches in front of her, his voice soft and kind, the authority of his presence comforting. So different from Thom. But Thom was dead. They were safe.

The memory of how she'd seen him last swooped in again, crumpling her face, stinging her eyes with tears. She focused on holding the sergeant's gaze to dispel the pictures in her head. She hadn't wanted to see Thom like that, didn't want to remember seeing him that way, no matter how cruel he'd been.

Cole ran a hand over his face. 'I'm sorry you had to see that. Doc Hamilton is on his way over. He'll take care of you.'

'Thank you.'

The words came out on a strangled note, a whisper in the thick silence that hung in the air. Thom was never coming home again. The whiskey she'd bought for him would go unopened. The bolognaise she'd been making for dinner would go uneaten. The cruel, angry man was never coming back. She cried tears of relief that her children would never have to witness their mother being beaten again. Never have to cover their ears to block out her pleas for Thom to stop. Relieved that it hadn't been the boys or herself at the wrong end of the gun.

Sobs wracked her body, uncontrollable and wrenching. She fought and lost against the hysteria building inside her. The sergeant moved and a gentler presence took his place. A soft touch on her shoulder, a soothing voice.

'Mrs McCaffrey – Bridey – my name is Cath. I'm a paramedic with the Moonie River Ambulance Service and I'm going to take care of you and your boys until Doc Hamilton arrives. Can you take deep breaths for me and release them nice and slowly?'

Bridey concentrated on the soothing tones of Cath's voice as she talked her through the calming breaths, her first few attempts ragged and unsteady. She had to get back control. The boys needed her now more than ever.

'Are you and the boys injured in any way?'

Bridey opened her eyes, Cath's face blurred by her tears. 'No.'

'That's good. Can I get you anything? A glass of water? A cup of tea?'

Bridey shook her head. 'No.'

Cath smiled warmly. 'Is there anyone I can call? Any family who could come over and be with you?'

'No one. We'll be fine.' Hysteria threatened to rise again. Calling the New Lord would be a mistake. She couldn't go back to the Children of the New Lord. For her boys' sake. She had to find a way to make it alone now. The baby that grew in her belly. How could she have forgotten the baby? 'My baby ... please ... my baby.'

'Where is the baby, hon? We'll make sure all the children are safe.'

'I'm pregnant. I'm not sure how far along. Maybe six or eight weeks. Maybe more. I don't know.'

Calmly, Cath reached for her bag and extracted some items, placing a stethoscope around her neck. 'Let's start with your blood pressure first then.' She wrapped a pad around Bridey's arm and pumped to inflate it. 'Any abdominal pain, bleeding, or cramps? Back pain?'

'No.'

Cath pressed the stethoscope to the pulse below the pad and listened for a moment. She scribbled down notes on a clipboard before releasing the pressure and removing the blood pressure device. 'You're doing fine, Bridey. Keep taking those deep breaths for me. Doc Hamilton should be here soon. I'm just going to take your temperature.' She held up a thermometer, capped the end with a protective rubber cap and held it to Bridey's ear.

Bridey glanced at Alex, who watched each movement the paramedic made carefully. She squeezed his hand, letting him know it was all right. 'Alex, why don't you take the twins and play a game with them at the kitchen table? Garrett, Shaun, you'd like that wouldn't you?'

Garrett looked at her, his gaze solemn. 'Don't like it when you cry.'

'I'll stop crying in minute, baby, I promise. Take Shaun and go play now. I'll be right here with Cath.'

'Are you sick?'

'No, sweetheart. I've just had a bit of a shock, but I'll be fine. Off you go.' She ruffled his hair and Shaun's too, her eyes never leaving them as they moved away to sit at the table with Alex.

Doc Hamilton strode into the room with the energy of a man much younger than his almost seventy-five years. He'd delivered more than a few Moonie River babies in his time and showed no signs of retiring any time soon. He'd also set her broken wrist and stitched the split next to her left eyebrow and knew far more about what lay behind Bridey's bumps, slips and falls than he'd discuss with anyone, even when she knew he'd wanted to.

Cath recorded Bridey's temperature on the file before standing up to brief the doctor. He nodded and smiled at Bridey and Cath, a genuine warmth in his expression. 'Well done, Cath. I'll take over from here. I think we should take you to the hospital, Bridey, just as a precaution. I'd like to do an ultrasound. Cath, would you please arrange for another ambulance?' He waited until Cath had left before kneeling in front of Bridey. 'How are you doing, my dear?'

'I can't go to hospital, Doc. What about my boys?' Panic clawed at her tummy. If the New Lord found out about Thom's death too soon, she wouldn't have time to hide them. He'd take her boys. Turn them into monsters.

'Your boys will be fine, Bridey, I promise you that. I'm sure I can twist the matron's arm to let them stay in the room with you if we decide to keep you in overnight.' His kind smile filled with warmth. 'She's all bluster and iron will, but underneath it all she's a good egg who knows what's best for her patients. Now tell me how you're really feeling.' He raised an inquiring white eyebrow.

'I'm ... numb.'

'Perfectly understandable. You've had quite a shock. Once we've checked out the little one, I can give you something to help for when the shock wears off.'

The sound of the shot still echoed in her head. She'd always expected that one day she or the children would be at the wrong end of Thom's shotgun. Instead, he'd used it on himself.

'Could I have done something to stop it, Doc? Could I have been a better wife?'

'I know I should give you a more professional opinion on that, my dear, but I've seen first-hand the damage he did.' Doc removed his stethoscope from around his neck and placed it in his bag. 'Thom was a violent man, an abuser who should have had his day in court for what he did to you. What happened here today is not your fault. If a man chooses to beat a woman the way he did you, he can make choices to change his behaviour too. He could have reached out for help, but he didn't. You did what you had to do, and that was to protect yourself and your children. And now you have another little one to look after.'

'How am I going to do that? I have no skills, no idea how to run a farm, no money.' And nowhere to hide.

Thom had taken care of all farm business, kept so much from her. The consequences for asking too many questions too painful to endure. Somehow she had to find a way to keep a roof over their heads.

'One step at a time, my dear. Let's get you checked out first. I promise, you won't have to deal with this alone. I'll be right here for you.'

Sergeant Delaney entered the kitchen, papers bearing the West Australian police logo in his hand. 'We're ready for you, Doc.'

'Thank you, Cole. Could you please stay with Bridey until another ambulance arrives? I don't want to leave her alone after the shock she's had.'

The sergeant nodded and held up a brochure with some reluctance. 'I need to talk to Bridey anyway. If you have any questions, Nick can answer them for you, Doc.'

'Thanks. I'll be back to see you in a short while, Bridey.'

Her gaze followed Doc's path out the door, reluctant to look at the sergeant. Cole Delaney symbolised a finality she'd been blindsided with. A blow she hadn't seen coming. She wasn't Mrs Thomas McCaffrey anymore, she was his widow.

Chapter Three

Cole held out his hand to Bridey. Tears stained her cheeks. Her swollen eyes, pinched lips and reddened nose bore outward testimony to her pain. Inside, she'd be a bigger mess. He knew that feeling all too well. He knew about the sleepless nights that would follow today, pictures burned into her memory of the last time she'd seen her husband. He'd had enough of those nightmares himself to understand the terror they brought with them.

'Can I help you up, Bridey? You might be more comfortable at the table.'

'Thank you.' He caught the whispered words as she placed her hand in his.

Cole helped her up. She'd be stiff from sitting on the floor for so long, and she'd held those kids so tight, he'd bet she'd have pins and needles in her arms.

He sensed three pairs of eyes watching him from the kitchen table. This family had way too much ahead of them, too much to work through, yet despite the fact that Bridey McCaffrey looked like a puff of wind could blow her away any minute, he also sensed an underlying strength that would see her through this. She had three boys to fight for.

Settling her in a chair, he placed the brochure he'd held in his hand on the table beside her. 'I know this is the last thing you want to deal with right now, but this brochure will help you understand what happens next, the rights you need to consider and what you need to do. Take your time. I'll be here if you have any questions.'

Cole moved to put the kettle on to boil and pour three glasses of milk for the boys. His mum had always believed that a cup of tea could cure or comfort almost anything. He placed the glasses in front of the boys. 'Here we go. Drink up, boys.'

Alex looked hard at the glass. 'We're not allowed to drink out of glasses because we break them. We can only have plastic cups. My father says so.' He pushed out of his chair, walked to the kitchen sink, retrieved three plastic cups, and put them down on the table.

No one touched the glasses, so Cole tipped the milk from each glass into the plastic cups. He cast a glance at Bridey. She rubbed her fingers over the cover of the glossy brochure with its nondescript graphic in tones of understated magenta against a grey background. Nothing cheerful about a brochure that dealt with decisions around a death in the family.

'Is Dad coming home, Alex?'

'Not tonight, Garrett.' The boy toyed with his cup.

'Why not? Is he sick?' The other twin sipped on his milk as he waited for an answer. When none came, he asked, 'Is that why Mum's crying?'

Cole swallowed around the constriction in his throat. How did a mother explain to kids so young that their father was never coming home again?

Bridey drew in a breath and let it out with a shudder. 'Your father had an accident, Shaun. He's gone to live with the angels now.'

'Because he didn't love us?'

'Oh, Garrett ... I'm sure your father did love you. In his own way. He just didn't know how to show it.'

'Stop lying,' muttered Alex. 'He didn't care about us. Ever.'

Bridey reached over to smooth her eldest's hair. 'Your father was unwell, Alex.'

'Then why didn't he ask Doc Hamilton to make him better?'

'Because sometimes it's hard to ask for help.'

Alex shoved his milk away, tipping the cup over, the contents spilling over the table. 'I hate him. I'm glad he's dead.'

'Alex!' The pain in Bridey's shout sliced through Cole.

'I hate him. He was mean.' The boy pushed away from the table and ran out the door.

'Alex! Stay inside!' Bridey slid back her chair, terror in her shout, as Cole sprang into action.

'Stay here with the twins. I'll go after him.'

The boy didn't go far. Cole found him on the laundry steps, watching the activity around the shed. The door was closed.

Doc would be inside, filling out a report, receiving instructions from the coroner's office, making arrangements for the transfer to the mortuary in Perth four hundred kilometres away or closer if the coroner agreed there was enough evidence to rule the death as a cut-and-dried case of suicide.

If he'd made his rounds of the farms sooner, met the families in the area, could he have prevented this tragedy from happening? Maybe not this one, but he'd damned well have a plan in place by tomorrow to visit every family farm remaining within his jurisdiction.

He sat down on the step beside Alex. 'I'm sorry about your dad, Alex.'

'I'm not.'

'I'm sure you don't mean that.'

'I do.'

Cole sighed. 'Maybe you do now, but when you're a little bit older, you'll understand the things that made your dad do what he did today. Hating someone eats you up inside, kid.'

'I hate him because he hurt my mum, yelled at us all the time. He was always angry, and he didn't even try to be nice to us. I know he shot himself and I'm glad.' Alex stamped his boots down hard on the step, frustration and anger holding his little body rigid.

A shiver ran down Cole's spine. How much had the boy seen? 'How do you know that? Did you look inside the shed?' The thought of what Alex might have seen made Cole's skin crawl. The scene would be imprinted on his young mind for a long time.

'No. I heard Mum say it when she phoned for the ambulance, but I heard the gun. It was so loud, the birds even flew away.'

Cole breathed out in relief, leaning across to block the boy's view as the shed door opened, Doc came out, and the paramedics entered with a stretcher. Soon the source of the boy's anger would be rolled out into the fading sunlight. 'What's important now is that your mum and your brothers need you. Why don't we go inside? I think you owe your mum an apology and a hug? She's hurting too, Alex.'

The boy's eyes raised to meet Cole's. 'Will the ambulance take him away?'

'Yes, it will.'

'Then I want to watch.'

'Why?'

'Then I know he's gone and never coming back.'

Cole's gut coiled in a knot. Why hadn't Pete briefed him on the trouble at Mindaleny Ridge before he left? How long had it been going on, and how had it got to this point? He weighed up his choices and the consequences of letting a boy so young watch his father's body leave the farm.

Footsteps sounded on the back verandah. Cole looked up to find Bridey and the twins behind them, her gaze focused on the open door of the shed, the twins' faces hidden in the folds of her skirt. Would seeing the ambulance leave help give them closure?

Bridey settled on the step above them, her knees brushing his back, the twins on either side of her. She ran a hand over Alex's hair, reassured him with whispered words, leaning forward to press a kiss to the top of his head.

The paramedics wheeled the stretcher out of the shed. No white sheet of dignity, only the dark, black shape of a body bag. Bridey's stifled sob pierced his heart. Beside him Alex stiffened as if he expected his father to rise from the dead. Cole clenched his hands between his knees to stop himself from reaching out to comfort either of them. He couldn't make this personal.

Another ambulance crossed the entrance to Mindaleny Ridge, the rusty grates rattling under its wheels. One would remove the dead, the other would see to the living. Doc climbed the stairs, his face pale as the doors closed on Thomas McCaffrey and the ambulance rolled away.

'Come along, Bridey. Let's get you to the hospital for that check-up. Cath will ride with you and the boys while the sergeant and I finish up the paperwork.'

Her knees brushed Cole's back again as she stood. 'I'll just get my bag and throw in a few things for the boys.' She held onto the twins' hands. 'Alex, would you like to help?'

'Yes, Mum.' He stood, waiting until Bridey was inside then he looked at Cole. 'I still hate him.'

'I understand, Alex. If you need to talk to someone about it, I'm here. You can trust me.' Even as the words left his tongue, Cole regretted them. He hadn't come to Moonie River to get personally involved, he'd come here to escape that kind of contact. Yet, just like him, for Bridey McCaffrey and her boys, a new life was about to begin.

～

The last time Bridey had been in Moonie River Regional Hospital, she'd given birth to the twins. Doc Hamilton had wanted her to go to the specialist King Edward Memorial in Perth, but Thom had said no. He'd wanted her to give birth at home.

Her thoughts turned to Thom's letter, a crumpled ball in her pocket. She'd picked it up from the floor where it had fallen, clinging to his last words, proof that a part of her life was over, and their future stretched ahead unknown.

Pregnant, a widow, a single mum. The reality of her circumstances penetrated the fog in her mind. With Thom gone, what would happen to them?

Her thoughts went to the brochure Sergeant Delaney had handed her. At some point tonight, she'd have to read it, know what to do next. She'd have to arrange a funeral. If they still lived in the compound, the New Lord would officiate, but if she let him know that Thom had died, it would bring a different hell to her door.

Bridey shivered. The New Lord was a distant threat Thom used to control them. He'd stayed away

36

since the marriage binding. Would he come for them when he found out about Thom, and force her and the children back to the church?

Cath had wanted to wheel her into the hospital waiting room in a chair, but Bridey had refused. Arriving in a wheelchair would only get the town gossips' tongues wagging, and Thom's suicide would already have started a wildfire on their hotline. With every movement, she could feel the eyes of speculation on her and the children.

Doc Hamilton slipped into a chair beside her. 'I got here as fast as I could. You shouldn't have to wait too much longer. I've asked them to shake it up a bit.'

Only an hour had passed since leaving the farm, but the hands on the clock in the waiting room seemed to move far slower. 'Thank you, Doc.'

A radiographer dressed in dark blue scrubs called her name. Bridey stood, the boys and Doc in tow.

'Hello, Bridey, my name is Adele and I'll be doing your ultrasound today.' She glanced at the entourage who followed her. 'I'm sorry, but we can only have the patient in the room.'

Doc smiled. 'Bridey is under my care, and I'd like to be present for the ultrasound, thank you, Adele. The boys have had a scare today, so their mum needs to know they're safe and not sitting alone and afraid in a waiting room full of strangers.'

'Well ... it's not exactly hospital protocol, Doctor Hamilton.' Adele's eyes took in Bridey's tear-ravaged face. 'But she's your patient so I won't argue.'

'Thank you. This is just a routine check.'

'Understood. Come with me then.' Adele led them through the sterile corridors into an examination room. 'The boys can sit over there on the chairs against the wall. Hop up onto the bed for me, Bridey. If you could please push up your blouse and tuck the top of your skirt down below your tummy, we can have a look to see what the little one is up to in there.' Adele waited as Bridey settled onto the bed. 'Comfortable? So, I'm just going to put some gel on your tummy. It's a little bit cold, sorry.' She picked up the transducer probe. 'Ready?'

Bridey nodded, a trickle of excitement breaking through the numbness in her chest. It didn't matter how this baby had been conceived, it was hers and she was responsible for it.

'I'll turn up the sound. Do you boys know what a train sounds like?'

They all stared at her, their expressions solemn, until Shaun made the sound of a train on the tracks.

Adele smiled. 'Yes, exactly like that, just without the toot of the whistle. That's what a baby's heartbeat sounds likes too.' She manoeuvred the probe until she found the sac of fluid in Bridey's abdomen. 'Oh, and would you look at that...' The whooshing sound of a heartbeat filled the room. Adele pointed to the screen. 'There's the baby's head, and that's its spine, and two little arms here. Bridey, it looks like you may be a little further along than you thought.' She fiddled with the keyboard, marked off and entered measurements. 'I'd say you're closer to sixteen weeks based on these measurements.'

'Is it a brother or a sister?' Alex asked.

Adele peered at the screen. 'Mm, I can't quite see that yet, but the baby is healthy and has a lovely strong heartbeat.' She pressed a couple more buttons and the printer churned out a string of images while Adele wiped the gel off Bridey's tummy with a paper towel. 'All done, Bridey. I'll put the images in an envelope and leave them at the front desk for you to take home.'

Home. The word hit like a punch to the gut. Home was a place where bad things had happened today and every time she looked out the window at the potting shed, she'd be reminded of what had happened there. Home was where Thom wasn't anymore. It was just her and the children now. The baby would never know the extent of his cruelty.

Bridey sat up, tucked her blouse back into her skirt, and swung her legs off the table, slipping her feet slowly to the floor. The boys crowded in. She hugged them close.

Doc placed a guiding arm around her shoulders. 'It's almost seven o'clock. The boys will be hungry. How about we pick up takeaway burgers from the Moonie River Pub before I take you all home?'

Home. Where the memory of what had happened today stained the ground at Mindaleny Ridge. Bridey stiffened. What choice did she have but to go home? 'I was making bolognaise ... I can't waste it.' The idea of a meal cooked by someone else tonight beckoned. Counting the money left in her housekeeping jar in her head, she couldn't afford the extravagance.

'My treat. It's the least I can do to help you. It's late and the children need to eat. You need to eat.'

She wavered. Still, Doc had a point, and the boys had to come first. The bolognaise she'd been preparing held no appeal when she knew that every turn away from the cooktop would give her a view that would remind her of what had happened today. 'You've done so much for me already.'

'Then allow me to do this one more small deed, my dear.'

Thom would never have allowed it. But Thom wasn't here anymore. 'Thank you, I accept your kindness.'

'Good. Come along now, let's get everyone fed and settled so you and the baby can rest a while.'

Teetering between numb and terrified of what lay

ahead in the coming days, Bridey followed Doc out into the waiting area and stood at the reception counter in a daze. She rested her hand on the gentle curve of her stomach. Seeing the ultrasound, hearing the heartbeat ... the baby was real, not just two pink lines on a stick. It would take time to process the reality. Four kids. The single mum of four kids.

'Bridey? I just wanted to make sure everything's all right.'

She turned to meet Sergeant Delaney's serious blue eyes. He'd changed out of his uniform, his air of authority still there in the way he wore a pair of jeans and a dark blue T-shirt. He'd showered — his dark blond hair still damp, the scent of soap clinging to his skin.

'Everything's fine. The baby ... is fine.'

A smile touched his lips. 'That's great news.'

Mrs Lee bustled in. 'Bridey, I'm so sorry to hear about Thom, my dear. What a terrible shock for you all. You really shouldn't go back to Mindaleny Ridge alone tonight, so I hope you'll accept my help. I've got a casserole in the oven, and I've made up the guest room for you and the boys.'

'Oh, that's truly kind of you, thank you. But Doc is treating us to burgers ...'

Mrs Lee raised an eyebrow at Doc. 'You want to give the girl burgers when she can have a perfectly good home-cooked meal? I can't let that happen, Bob.' With a warm smile, she turned back to Bridey. 'It's late, dear. The boys will be exhausted and I'm sure you are too. It's a long drive back after such a stressful day. The least I can offer you is a hot meal and a warm bed.'

Overwhelm gripped her heart with cold hands. An unfamiliar house, a stranger's table and a bed that wasn't hers. Her boys in surroundings they may not be comfortable in after the unsettling events of the day. 'I really appreciate your generosity, but I couldn't possibly impose on you like that.'

'It's no trouble at all, and the very least I can do to help. Make this old lady's day, dear. Say yes.' She turned to the sergeant. 'Hello, Cole. Off duty, are you? I've got enough casserole for you too if you're hungry.'

Doc cleared his throat.

Mrs Lee turned to him, rolling her eyes. 'Yes, Bob, there's enough for you too.'

'Good, because a single man could easily starve, you know.'

She prodded his tummy. 'You and my Ed, you'd never starve. Last time I looked, your freezer was still full of leftovers from the poker nights at our place.'

'Well, that's because Ed won the toss at the Valentine's ball back in the day and he got first dance with you, Edna. Otherwise, it would be his freezer stocked with leftovers now.' He turned to Bridey.

'Think about Edna's offer, my dear. I'd be happier with her there to keep an eye on you and the boys tonight. You've had a shock, and Edna makes the best hot chocolate cure for shocks.'

'I can't impose ...' Bridey looked at the sergeant, hoping he'd help.

'I agree with Doc and Mrs Lee. It might be for the best. I'm sorry, Bridey, but I can't get a clean-up crew over to Mindaleny until tomorrow. A little distance might be a good thing, especially tonight when everything is still so raw.'

A sea of emotions crashed in on her. Frustration warred with heartache and exhaustion, nipped at the heels of the terror that had gripped her when the shot had rung out, chased the numbness of shock away. She wanted to scream for everyone to leave her alone, to huddle in a corner with her babies and hide from the world. To smash down the potting shed and the reminder of everything it now stood for.

These people were all being kind, but they were strangers, and her home was her safe haven as much as it was her hell. It was all she and her boys had left. Yet maybe they were right. The memory was still too raw, the pain still too real, and home too sad a place to be tonight.

Bridey turned to Mrs Lee. 'Thank you, I'll accept your kind offer.'

Tomorrow, she'd go home and pick up the pieces of their lives that lay shattered on the ground like the glass from the bottle of whiskey Thom had broken. She would make Mindaleny Ridge a good place to live, erase the bad memories, and create a happy home for her children.

Chapter Four

Cole excused himself from the debate between Ed and Doc over who'd win the wood-chopping title at the fair this year as Bridey wandered out from the guest bedroom, through the front door, and out onto the verandah.

Despite the tastiness of the casserole, dinner had been a subdued affair. Bridey and the boys had eaten little, but that could only be expected. She'd politely refused Mrs Lee's offer of a bath for the boys, a quick wash would be enough, then she'd taken them off to bed.

He gave her a few moments before stepping out behind her, making enough noise so he didn't startle her. She stood, one hand on the rail, the other pressed to her stomach, her face turned upward to the stars.

'How are the boys holding up?' Cole sat down on

one of the old cane chairs with a view up the street. With the house attached to the post office and general store, the Lees had a twenty-four-hour view of Main Street, quiet now, except for a couple of stragglers outside the bottle shop. If they were still around when he walked home, he'd move them on.

'The twins went to sleep right away. Alex took a while to settle.' Bridey moved away from the rail and came to sit in the second chair. 'It's all so surreal.'

'Give yourself some time to process.' Cole swallowed the bitterness that rose in his throat. Who was he to give advice when three years later, he was still processing?

Bridey picked at the material of her skirt, twisting the folds between her fingers. 'I tried so hard not to upset him, but he was always so ... angry.' Slipping her hand into her skirt pocket, she pulled out a crumpled piece of paper and handed it to him. 'You might need this for your report. It's Thom's suicide note.' Her voice quivered. She took a deep breath and released it slowly.

'Thank you. I'll put it in the file.' Cole took the note, folded it, and placed it in his top pocket. 'Thom's death wasn't your fault.' If only he didn't feel like a hypocrite saying it. God knew, he was still trying to stop blaming himself for what happened to Carrie.

Bridey stood and paced the verandah, restless.

Hadn't he done the same thing every night, every day after Carrie had died, the same thoughts blasting his mind? Could he have done something to save her? The difference was that Thom McCaffrey had taken his own life. Carrie's had been taken from her. And that had been on him. A retaliation, a hit, directly linked to a case he'd been working, and he'd lost his wife and his unborn child because some damn bastard had played a game of tit-for-tat.

Who was he to give advice to Bridey McCaffrey? He'd come to Moonie River to escape the nightmare of his role on the special task force. Quiet small-town policing — handing out parking tickets and moving on drunks from outside the liquor store to escape the memory of his wife's lifeless body on their bed, her blood staining their white sheets.

Bridey was where he'd been. She would face that potting shed and see what had happened inside it over and over in her memory. Every God damn day. Would she stay? Would she sell the farm and be free at last? It had taken him three years to sell his house. Three years of sleeping on the couch downstairs because he could never sleep in that room or any other upstairs again. Yet he hadn't been able to part with the memories, close the door or walk away. Until his boss had given him an ultimatum. He couldn't hide behind a desk forever.

'It will be hard going home.' It was only fair to warn her of that.

Bridey's sigh filtered into the silence as she stopped pacing. 'I have no choice. Mindaleny Ridge is the only home I have.'

'You could sell it. Move on.' If Thomas McCaffrey's record was anything to go on, the farm would unlikely have been a place filled with happy memories.

'Where would I go?' Bridey shook her head. 'The boys are already unsettled. I'm not sure if a new start will be the right thing for them.'

'Getting the farm to produce a sustainable income again will be a huge responsibility for you.' Thomas McCaffrey had let things go on the farm and it was clear from her reaction that his wife had known nothing of what he'd been up to behind the scenes. Bridey had suffered enough trauma today, and the file that lay on his desk would stay closed tonight.

'I have no choice. I can't go back to where I was before.' Her words fell so softly between them, he almost didn't catch them. She drew a shuddering breath. 'I grew up in a care home. It's not the life I want anymore. Not for me and certainly not for the boys.'

'A care home?' Cole frowned at the term. 'What kind of care home?'

'Church care homes.'

Shutters descended as Bridey's gaze darted away, her discomfort in talking about her past evident in the sudden tension in her shoulders. The wall that had come down in her moment of vulnerability began rebuilding, blocking him out.

'What about Thom? Will his family take you in?'

'I never met his parents. Thom didn't like to talk about them.'

Cole made a note to look deeper into the McCaffrey family. Had the abused become the abuser? A cycle that had now been broken. With a bit of luck, the three McCaffrey boys would escape that cycle with their father gone.

Every day when he came into contact with cases of domestic violence, he thanked God for the parent he had. His dad — with the patience of a saint — was always available, day or night, always ready to listen and be the voice of reason. Even in those dark days following Carrie's death when Cole had retreated into a shell of frozen loss, thawed only by spurts of red-hot rage and an unquenchable thirst for revenge on her killers.

The frustration of having to trust his colleagues to do their job had almost crippled him. The wheels of the law had turned with excruciating slowness as he'd observed from the sidelines, unable to do anything, his hands bound by conflict of interest.

Had Bridey felt that same frustration as she'd watched her husband spiral into the bottom of a bottle and get dragged deeper into his own net? What kind of nightmare would she and her children have endured if Thomas McCaffrey hadn't chosen to end it?

The cop in him wanted to read that note, those final words. What did a man say to his battered wife moments before he blew the top of his own head off?

Cole checked his watch. The hands had crept close to ten o'clock and it had been a long day for all, especially for the two drunks who still hung around outside the bottle shop. Their conversation looked like it was about to explode into a brawl. Time to attend to other police business. He stood.

'If you need any help at all, Bridey, please call me.' He reached into his back pocket, pulled out his wallet, extracted a business card and handed it to her. 'I can put you in touch with a counsellor to help you and the boys work through this.'

She took the card, her fingers cold as they brushed his. 'Thank you.'

'I'm sorry, but I will have to ask you a few more questions for the report, but that can wait. I'll see you out at the farm tomorrow. To finish up.'

Tears shimmered in her eyes as she nodded, a woman on the edge. He'd been on that ledge, knew what it felt like to travel that dark tunnel before finding light again.

'Night, Bridey.' He wanted to wish her a good night, hoped he might be able to do that in a few months' time when her wounds weren't so raw anymore. She was young, stronger than she thought, and she had her children to live for. She'd survive. Just like he had.

~

Blue and white police tape fluttered in the breeze on the potting shed, tying the door closed. Bridey sipped her tea on the top step of the verandah, the whole scene surreal.

Of all the scenarios that had played out in her head as to how their lives would end, none had been of Thom ending it for himself. She'd lived on high alert for so long, anticipating his every move. Preparing for it. Preparing her children for it. She'd expected him to turn that rifle on them, not on himself.

Ed Lee had brought them home after a comforting yet uncomfortable, unfamiliar night of hospitality. He and his sons had stayed a while to do what they could to clear up the mess Thom had left in the strawberry field. The trench had been filled in and the digger had been put back in the machinery shed along with all the other rusting farming tools. The only evidence left of what Thom had done was a scar on the landscape and the tape that turned a place that had once symbolised new life into one of finality.

A steady trail of strangers had crossed the grate this morning to lay flowers and place candles around the shed. Strangers who'd come to shake her hand, offer their condolences and a helping hand. Her freezer had been filled with comfort food and her kitchen benchtop had been crammed full of baked goods. An entire community had put aside the trouble her husband had caused them to comfort her in her loss. And in that moment, they'd chosen to forget the bastard of a man Thom had been to remember what he'd left behind.

The police SUV rumbled up the driveway, leaving a trail of dust behind it. Bridey hugged her mug tighter as the vehicle pulled to a halt and Cole Delaney climbed out. He slapped a broad-brimmed hat on his head, the hot March sun burning down on the land. For such a large man, he moved with a loping grace, an easy confidence that exuded strength and solidarity. So different from his predecessor who, she'd overheard Mrs Lee say, had grown overweight, sloppy, and tired of his job in Moonie River.

'Morning, Bridey.' Cole stopped at the base of the stairs, hands on his hips.

'Morning.'

'The clean-up crew are about ten minutes behind me. Did you want to take the boys out for a while?'

She shook her head. 'That won't be necessary. It's time for their lessons so we'll be inside for an hour or two.' A part of her wanted to watch as the shed was cleared of the mess Thom had left behind. As if that would bring closure, make the surreal real.

'Lessons?'

'I home-school the children.' Could that change now that Thom was gone? Would attending school in Moonie River with all the other children be better for her boys? Give them a chance at a normal life. Or would it make things worse? All these opportunities she'd never had to consider before.

'You're doing a great job. They're smart kids.' Cole smiled, an action that tipped his well-shaped lips up at the corners and carved dimpled grooves into his cheeks.

Bridey would bet that there'd be a few locals in Moonie River swooning over their new sergeant-in-charge. 'Can I get you a cup of tea or coffee? I have cake. Lots of it.'

Maybe he didn't want to eat before he faced the potting shed. She shivered. She'd only seen a glimpse of the mess yesterday and, judging by the flies buzzing around, it wouldn't be a pleasant scene.

'A strong coffee would be great, thank you.'

'Come inside.'

Bridey stood, brushed down her denim skirt and led the way into the kitchen where the boys were gathered at the table, drawing and colouring pictures. They looked up at Cole before looking down again, a habit they'd formed knowing not to look at their father too long for fear of being yelled at.

'Morning, boys.' Cole's voice was quiet as he went down on his haunches at the table, bringing himself level with them. 'Can I see what you're drawing?'

Alex lifted his head to look at Bridey. 'Sergeant Delany is a policeman and it's all right to answer his questions,' she reassured him, placing her hands on his skinny shoulders.

On the piece of paper in front of her son, red and black colours dominated the crude drawing of a stick man lying down in a field. Her heart ached at her son's depiction of his father's death. Alex pushed it across the table towards Cole, who eased himself into a chair to look at it. The twins passed on their pictures too. Theirs were a little more colourful, the fields interspersed with blue, yellow, and green, and birds in flight over the trees.

For a brief second, Cole's gaze met hers, deep concern reflected in his striking blue eyes. Her heart stuttered against her ribs knowing he'd had the same thought she had that Alex would be the one the most troubled by his father's death. Something she'd have to put before anything else on her list of things to attend to. Even the farm.

An overwhelming weight settled on her shoulders. She turned away to put the kettle on to boil. So many things she had to deal with now. Too many things still a mystery for her to unravel and a husband to bury. She'd spent the morning reading through the pamphlet Cole had given her. Once the coroner had released his findings, she could arrange for a funeral. Perhaps, after that, reality would truly sink in.

Bridey made the coffee, listening to the calming baritone of Cole's voice as he drew the boys out of their shell and into conversation. A stab of guilt hit her chest as she pushed aside the thought that conversation wasn't something Thom had encouraged with his boys. She pressed a hand to her stomach and the tiny baby bump growing beneath her clothes. What kind of a life would her baby have? What kind of a life might they all have had if Thom had been more like Cole?

'Everything okay, Bridey?'

She glanced over her shoulder at Cole and caught the speculation in his gaze. 'Everything's fine.' Turning, she placed his coffee on the table in front of him. 'Would you like some cake to go with that?'

'No, thank you. Just the coffee, thanks.' Tyres

scrunched on the gravel outside and he scraped back the chair to stand. 'I think that's the team arriving. Mind if I take this with me?'

'Of course. No problem.'

'Thank you. See you later, boys.' He nodded at them as they looked up at him wide-eyed, not used to being included in conversations.

The twins gave him a hesitant wave while Alex gave a stiff nod before pulling his drawing back in front of him and adding angry stabs of dots to it with a purple crayon. Bridey placed her hand over his to still the movement, avoiding looking in Cole's direction, her heart in her throat. Where had her beautiful, gentle, caring boy gone? She cursed Thom for making her boy even more vulnerable.

Chapter Five

An unseasonal rain shower fell in Moonie River on the day Thomas McCaffrey was laid to rest. Cole closed the manila folder on the coroner's report and dropped the file into the top drawer of his desk. Across the road in the small cemetery, a handful of people circled the open grave as they waited to farewell a man who hadn't topped the popularity charts in the community. Doc, the Lees, Jimmy from the bottle shop, and a man who stood way back in the line of trees away from the activity.

Cole reached for his hat and rainproof jacket and made his way across the street. He nodded to Doc as the hearse arrived, followed by the car carrying McCaffrey's widow and children. As the young family climbed out of the vehicle, he wondered if there'd ever been a time when the McCaffrey children had smiled or laughed. Shoulders stiff, features set, Alex took his brothers' hands. Behind him, Bridey set her hands on his narrow shoulders and gently nudged them forward until they came to a standstill at the edge of the grave, then she gathered them close.

Rain drizzled around them. Bridey released her hold on the children to raise a large burgundy umbrella imprinted with the funeral parlour's logo over their heads. Her hand trembled, the umbrella dipping in her hold.

Cole moved closer. 'Let me hold that for you.'

She nodded, a slow, uncertain movement of her head that dislodged a stray curl from her drawn-back hair. He found his fingers itching to touch it, to tuck it away behind her ear and tell her everything would be fine. That soon it would all be over, and she could start living again. That the baby she carried would be fine, and the boys would be free to live for perhaps the first time in their young lives, without fearing the anger and punishment of their father's notorious temper.

Hands free, she rubbed them over the twins' heads, before settling her fingers on Alex's shoulders again. Doc moved in on her other side and placed his arm around her shoulders as the coffin came to rest in front of them. The celebrant opened the ceremony, kept it short, before inviting the mourners to place their final tributes. Bridey and the boys stepped out from the protection of the umbrella to place cuttings of rosemary on the coffin. A symbol of peace. Cole wondered how long it would be before peace came to Thom's widow and sons.

She stood with her boys, head bent, dashing away her tears as they mingled with the rain, then she turned back to the protection of the umbrella. A woman amidst a town full of people, yet so isolated and alone. He wanted to reach out, hold her, absorb her vulnerability, and replace it with strength, but that felt too personal when he was still a stranger.

The coffin lowered into the grave in silence. No hymns or music to send off the man who'd been troubled enough to take his own life. He found himself feeling sorry for Thom. If Cole had come to the community sooner, could he have made a difference in the man's life? Had his predecessor known how bad things were out at Mindaleny Ridge? For Thom and Bridey? Beside him, she whimpered and dabbed at her cheeks with a tissue as people drifted away, the hearse rolled out empty, and only the car that would take the family home remained.

Mrs Lee stepped up to place a hand on Bridey's arm. 'The CWA have arranged a tea in the town hall, my dear. We'd love for you and the children to come. We weren't sure if you wanted anything after, but the people would like to offer their support and condolences.'

Bridey's breath shuddered out. 'That's kind, thank you. I wasn't expecting anyone to attend.'

'We were always here, my dear. And we always will be.' She patted Bridey's hand before turning her attention to Cole. 'Will you be joining us too, Cole?'

He thought about the pile of paperwork on his desk, then caught the look on Alex's upturned face and remembered his conversation with the boy on the day Thom had died. Maybe the best time to get to know everyone was now. His paperwork would still be there tonight, but the people of his town might not be. 'I'll come over for a while.'

'Good, good. See you there then.' Mrs Lee wandered off as Larry, the funeral director came over.

'I'll take you and the boys to the town hall, Bridey, and give you a ride home after.'

'Thank you, Larry.'

Cole found himself reaching for her elbow. 'I'll walk you and the boys to the car.'

She leaned in a little as if her strength was running out and she needed to draw on his. 'Thank you.'

The rain slowed to a drizzle as they walked the short distance in silence, Alex and the twins a step ahead. Cole had to adjust his stride, so he didn't trip over them. Larry opened the doors and ushered the family inside, Bridey checking the safety harnesses on the boys' booster seats in the back before claiming the front seat.

'I'd offer you a lift to the hall, Sergeant, but there's no room, sorry,' Larry apologised, closing the doors on the car.

Cole handed him the umbrella. 'That's okay. A walk will clear my head, and I've got my rainproof jacket. I'll be fine.'

The distance to the town hall would give him time to think, to ponder on why the niggle of his sixth sense wouldn't settle. He'd relied on those niggles back in Perth and ignoring them had cost him dearly before. If he'd listened to his gut, maybe, just maybe Carrie and their baby would be alive today.

The sun broke through the clouds, the rain stopped, and Main Street drifted by as he walked. Mrs Lee's general store that doubled as a newsagent and a post office, Top Knot Hair and Nails, the coffee shop chalkboard that invited passersby in for a cuppa and a browse of their bookstore. He made a mental note to do just that. A book he could lose himself in might stop him over-thinking things at night when he was alone without his job to distract him.

The cenotaph outside the town hall loomed large in the rose garden that circled it. Blue wrens flitted from one branch to another as a gardener trimmed hedges into submission with admirable precision. On the wooden bench near the fountain, a man sat with his hat in his hands, twirling it around as he contemplated the steps leading up to the town hall doors.

Cole walked past and dipped his head in greeting. He took the stairs two at a time. At the doors, he took off his jacket and shook the excess rain from it before hanging it up on a peg inside the entrance hall, placing his hat above it. Inside, the hall was abuzz with chatter, the sound of rattling teacups, and the clink of forks on plates. More people had come for the tea than had attended the funeral service.

The McCaffrey boys sat on three chairs placed along the wall, solemn looks on their faces as they watched a group of children gathered in a corner where they whispered amongst themselves. The outsiders. Cole spotted Bridey, her smile strained, her fingers gripping her tea cup and saucer as a young woman he recognised as the local schoolteacher chatted brightly to her. He understood how she'd be feeling right now. He'd been in that black hole. All he'd wanted to do was hide from the well-meaning conversations, but duty had called for him to stand his ground until it was over.

Cole did the rounds of the room. Stopping to chat to those he knew, introducing himself to those he didn't. He held conversations over the possible fallout from the impending ban on live sheep exports, poor harvests, and rising crime rates until Mrs Lee appeared with a plate and a mug of coffee.

'Strong and hot, Sarge. Help yourself to some food.'

'Bless you, Mrs Lee.'

'Bridey could use some rescuing from Janet. That girl will be nagging Bridey to put her boys in school. She means well, but our Janet is passionate about education which often makes common sense and propriety go out the window. There's a time and place for everything, and now is not the time. Be a good lad, will you, and butt in?' She gave him a conspiratorial wink.

Cole smiled. 'Of course, Mrs Lee.'

He made his way across the room, stopping for a quick word with the boys. 'Did you want something to eat or drink?' Cole eyed their empty hands. 'I can get you something from the table.'

'No, thank you,' Alex mumbled, head down.

'I'll be over there talking to your mum. If you need anything, come over and ask me. You don't need to be afraid. I won't be angry with you asking for help.'

Not entirely reassured by their synchronised nods, he decided to keep an eye on them as he came to stand at Bridey's side. Doc sent him a relieved look and a nod from a few feet away where he was engaged in a conversation with a frail-looking woman dressed in a lavender pantsuit.

'Excuse me, Janet. Do you mind if I steal Bridey away for a moment?'

Janet shot a quick look between him and Bridey. 'Of course, Sarge. Nothing serious, I hope?'

Curiosity sparked in her eyes and Cole realised that no matter what, by nightfall it would be all over town that the police had wanted a private word with the widow. It had taken him all of two minutes after his arrival in Moonie River to find that the grapevines in small towns had a mind of their own and rarely relied on facts.

'Nothing wrong at all. Excuse us?' With a light hand on her elbow, he led Bridey away to a quiet corner of the room close to where her boys sat.

'Thank you.' Exhaustion cut lines of strain into her face and the dark circles under her eyes paid homage to lack of sleep.

'You're welcome.' He pulled a couple of chairs closer. 'Sit down for a bit. Can I get you another cup of tea or something to eat?'

She shook her head and sat. 'No, thank you.'

'Should I ask Larry to take you home?'

'Thank you, but Mrs Lee has been kind enough to arrange all this, so I owe it to her to stay a while. I'm grateful for everything she's done.'

'She has a very kind heart.' Cole grinned as he sat down. 'Although I wouldn't want to get on the wrong side of her.'

Bridey answered his grin with a wavering smile. 'No, me neither. I'd say she has a low tolerance for nonsense.'

Her cup rattled against the saucer. Cole reached for it and placed it on a table beside them. Her hands turned to worrying the material of her long black skirt.

He stilled the movement with a hand on her arm. 'Bridey, if I can help you in any way, I'm here. You just have to ask.'

Her back straightened and her jaw set with determination. 'I appreciate your offer, and I'll keep it in mind, along with all the offers I wasn't expecting. Today is goodbye. Not only to Thom, but to life as we knew it. My boys deserve a fresh start. And I'm determined to give them that. I just need to work out how.'

Cole removed his hand and smiled. 'Promise me you'll at least get a solid night's sleep first?'

Sleep. That would be the last thing that she'd want to do. Every time she closed her eyes, the scene in the potting shed would replay in her head. The same way it had for him after Carrie's funeral. There'd be little escape for Bridey McCaffrey in the days to come.

Chapter Six

Bridey tied a knot in the black garbage bag filled with shredded paper. God only knew why Thom had kept some of the stuff tossed into what was meant to be a filing cabinet. Days of sorting through his office had uncovered little useful information. But then, he hadn't needed sowing and harvesting schedules or records of what was planted on their fifty-acre property. He hadn't planted a successful crop in as long as they'd been married. Guilt and regret warred with the rise of relief in her belly. No point wishing things had turned out a different way. Thom was gone.

Outside the office attached to the sorting shed, the boys played a game of tag. Soon she'd have to decide whether to send them to school or continue with homeschooling. How would they cope in a classroom full of strangers? Was it fair to send them to the local school when all the other kids were a term ahead already? Could she run a farm she knew little about and be mum and teacher too? So many questions rolled around her mind, keeping her awake during the long hours of the night.

She yawned as she yanked open another drawer, filled to overflowing with farm magazines this time. The boys had taken to sneaking into bed with her at night. She welcomed the sound of their breathing and the shuffle of their restlessness in the silence of the house. And their presence.

How many nights had she woken in the pitch dark, some distant fear gripping at her throat that Thom would walk back into the room? She'd lie as stiff as a corpse waiting for the sting of his hand, or the cruel grip of his fingers, or the smell of whiskey on his breath.

Shaking off the thought, she grabbed a handful of the magazines out of the drawer. A scoff slipped from her throat as she looked at the dates on the covers. They'd been lying around for a long time. Possibly before Thom's parents had come to the farm.

Bridey pushed open the window further and called out, 'Boys! Would you like to come and help me in here?'

'Yes, Mum.'

The chorus of voices made her smile. Slowly, her boys were changing. Growing in confidence in their new-found freedom. Less afraid of their own shadows, yet still erring on the side of caution in their exploration of the farm. So far, she hadn't had to remind them that the potting shed was out of bounds. Another thing she'd have to deal with if she was to plant seedlings any time soon.

But it had been less than three weeks since Thom's death and going into the shed filled her with dread. Were there stains on the walls, on the floor, reminders of that day? How could she not relive that moment she'd seen him lying on the cold, hard floor in a pool of his own blood. The sight of it haunted her dreams at night, the gunshot played on repeat in her head.

Three pairs of boots thudded up the stairs into the office and her boys gathered around.

'What can we do, Mum?' Alex leaned across the desk, his brothers mimicking his move.

She stacked piles of magazines side by side. 'How about you sort these out into date order for me? Month and year.'

Shaun reached for the one on top, his fingers tracing out the shape of a John Deere tractor. 'Can I drive a tractor one day?'

She ruffled his hair. 'Of course you can. When you're a bit older and taller.'

His smile lit up his face and her heart. They'd been laughing more, playing more, eating better thanks to the generosity of the neighbours and her stocked freezer. Bridey tallied the remainder of her grocery allowance in her head. When the supply was exhausted, she'd have to dip into her secret stash of funds. The pamphlet Cole had given her had said to contact the bank to inform them of his passing. Her meeting to sort out Thom's accounts wasn't until Friday, and she'd have to make her allowance stretch until she knew if she had a budget to work with from his estate.

Bridey sighed as she lifted the last pile of magazines from the drawer. A search of the office had failed to turn up anything that looked like bookkeeping. She'd found a mess of unpaid bills in the overflowing bottom drawer of the desk, some stamped overdue. They still needed to be sorted through. He'd shut her out from so much and she'd been afraid enough of his temper to let him.

She squeezed her eyes shut against the memory of how soon Thom had shown his violent side. She'd arrived on the farm, her heart and head full of dreams of a new life as a young bride. Thom had seemed so nice the day the New Lord had bound her to him. She'd hoped – prayed – that life with him would be different to the care homes, away from the church. It had taken less than a week for those dreams to be trampled under the weight of Thom's boot.

The phone rang on the desk as she pulled open the last drawer to find a pile of official letters from the tax office. Lifting the top one off the pile, she reached for the phone.

'Mindaleny Ridge, Bridey speaking.'

'Thom?' Desperation bled from the woman's voice.

Bridey's heart stuttered, unease a twisted knot under her rib cage. 'Who is this, please?'

'Thom. He must come.' The accented words were weak and whispered, the sound hollow like an echo in a tin can.

'Come where? Where are you calling from?'

'Thom knows. He must come.'

Fear weighed on Bridey's chest. 'Thom isn't here. Please tell me where you are.'

'Thom must help.'

'He can't help you. Not anymore. But I can. Where are you?'

A strangled sob filtered down the line. 'No more food. No more water. Too hot.'

'Are you on the farm? Can you describe your surroundings to me?'

'Too dark. Too small. Thom ... he breaks the lights.'

Bridey's throat closed. She'd known that terror too. The dark. Not knowing which direction he'd come at her from. Oh, dear God, what had Thom done to this woman? Did he have her imprisoned somewhere on the farm? Who was she? 'I'm going to get help for you. What is your name?'

'Kirana.'

'Is it only you in the dark?'

'Five. And children. The baby ... very sick.'

The fear gripping Bridey's chest turned to terror as all too familiar memories battered her mind. Babies, young children — young girls – afraid, lost and confused as they arrived at the care home she'd grown up in. 'Kirana, you have to help me find you. Do you live on the farm?'

'Yes.'

'Where do you go when you want to sleep?'

'*Pengiriman barang.*' The foreign words faded into silence.

'Kirana, are you there? Please, answer me. Kirana?' Bridey held the receiver in her hand, giving it a frustrated shake. Three pairs of eyes looked at her from across the desk, her fear mirrored on her sons' faces. As she reset the line to dial the police station, desperation overrode the questions that flooded her mind. What had Thom done?

∾

Cole drove out to Mindaleny Ridge, his mind racing through the information Bridey had given him. The urgency in her voice had him grabbing his keys and hat before she'd finished giving him directions to the farm office at the packing shed. He hoped with all his heart that her call didn't mean what he thought it did. People smuggling wasn't an unusual occurrence. Thousands of unlawful non-citizens had been spread out over the country, smuggled into remote areas, their rights abused while they searched for a new and better life. But having it happen in his town, on his watch ... he'd prefer to be wrong.

The gravel crunched under the tyres of the SUV as he pulled to a stop outside the packing shed. The rustic demountable office out the front sported an ancient air conditioner he doubted had worked in years. Framed by the dusty window, Bridey paged through paperwork, sorting it into different piles. He'd told her to stay in the office and not try to find the woman alone. God only knew what lay in wait when they found Kirana.

Bridey's hair was covered by a bandana-like scarf, a plain loose blouse hung from her shoulders, most likely tucked into a denim skirt he knew would cover her knees and fall almost to her ankles. His research into the McCaffrey family had turned up extraordinarily little, except for the information he'd garnered from the town grapevine. They'd kept to themselves for the most part, but Thomas had found trouble in town a few times, mostly before he'd married Bridey.

Cole ignored the misstep of his heart and climbed out of the SUV. Her husband appeared to have left behind a bigger mess than any of them could ever have imagined.

Bridey looked up as he slammed the car door and approached the building. The bruises on her face had faded since the funeral. Spots of colour tinged her cheeks. She pushed open the door to let him in. 'Thank you for coming out here so quickly, Sergeant Delaney.'

'No problem. Do you have any idea where Kirana might be?'

Bridey shook her head. 'I didn't even know Thom had farm hands on the property. With the farm so run down and little or no produce in the crops, I understood that Thom was doing everything himself.'

'Are there staff quarters anywhere on the property where these people might be staying?'

'No. There are a few derelict buildings scattered around but I've never been allowed inside them.' Bridey stepped forward and reached out as if to place a hand on his arm before withdrawing it again. 'She sounded so desperate. No food or water. In the dark. She mentioned children too.' Concern filled her eyes.

Cole reached for her hand. It lay tense, cold and small in his. 'I promise I'll do everything I can to find them.'

'Thank you.' Her hand slipped out from his and she moved away.

'I'll get a search and rescue team together.'

'Kirana said something, foreign words ... *pen giri ba run*? I'm not sure if that's right. I don't know what that means. I should have written it down. She sounded so weak. She whispered the words before the line went dead.'

Cole frowned. *'Pengiriman barang?'*

'Yes! That sounds like what she said.'

'Indonesian. Roughly translated, it means delivery of goods.' He shrugged when she looked surprised. 'I've spent some time in Bali. Is there another warehouse or shed on the property?'

'Only the packing shed behind the office. The only rooms inside that shed are a toilet and a cold room.' Bridey shuddered as horror dawned. 'Unless they're locked in the cold room ... Oh God, please don't tell me he could be that cruel?'

Covering her face with her hands, she turned away from him, but not before he caught a glimpse of the terror on her pale face. Bridey McCaffrey knew exactly the cruelty her husband had been capable of. 'Why don't you take the boys up to the house and I'll take a look?'

Bridey shook her head, tendrils escaping from the scarf as it loosened. She dragged the scarf off her head and twisted it through her fingers. 'No. We'll go together. It's my farm now and if anything has happened to those women and children, then they're my responsibility. The boys will be fine here in the office. Alex, Shaun, Garrett; please keep sorting through those magazines. Stay here and don't go anywhere until we come back.'

'Yes, Mum.'

'Thank you. We'll be right next door, so you don't have to be afraid.'

Cole watched as the boys settled on the floor with the pile of farming magazines and got on with the task they'd been assigned. He couldn't help but wonder what their life would have been like if they'd been raised by a loving, caring father.

Bridey led the way, running toward the back of the packing shed. She stopped short at the door, her hand hovering over the heavy handle, her reluctance to open it clear. He didn't want to think about the horror she'd be imagining would lie behind that closed door. The last door she'd opened had changed her life forever. If what

Cole was expecting to find held any merit, Bridey's life was about to take yet another unexpected turn.

He stepped up beside her. 'Let me open it, Bridey. Step aside for a minute.'

With a nod, she stepped aside, her hands covering her mouth, her eyes filled with anguish. Cole took a deep breath and pulled back the handle to swing open the heavy door. Stale, dank air greeted him. Empty. The cold room hadn't been used in a long time.

The terror on Bridey's face when he turned his head to look at her tore at his heart. 'We'll find them.' He placed his hands on her arms to try and reassure her, dropping them when she flinched away. 'Sorry.' Cole jammed his hands into his pockets. He should have realised she'd still be skittish, still be expecting the harder grip she'd experienced under her husband's hands.

'What if we don't find them?'

'I'll call Search and Rescue. They'll be on their way here in no time. I promise you that we will search every inch of the farm. If you can think of anywhere they might be being kept, you need to tell me.'

Frustration replaced her terror. 'I wish I knew. This area was always out of bounds for us. Thom didn't share farm business unless he was angry about something.' Her face told Cole that she'd felt the brunt of that anger. She rubbed her arms. 'I didn't dare ask questions.'

Closing the door again, he shot the bolt through the latch and secured it with the padlock hanging over the bar across the door. He didn't want the boys wandering into an unsafe space with their newfound freedom to explore the farm.

Placing his hands on his hips, he turned around to survey the sorting shed. Long trestle tables ran in lines down the middle of it, empty except for a thick layer of dust and sand. Whatever Thomas McCaffrey had been farming, it wasn't vegetables or anything that needed sorting or packing. Where had his income come from?

An old generator stood silent in one corner. An ancient conveyor ran the length of the far wall, rusted out from disuse and lack of maintenance.

His gaze came back to Bridey's stricken face. 'Bridey, what exactly did Thom farm?'

She dropped her hands from her face. 'Clearly not enough to require the use of the packing shed or cold room.' Bridey spread her hands to encompass the abandoned shed. 'There are a couple of old fruit trees that grow wild near the house, but nothing ever got picked from them, and he'd been working on an old strawberry patch that grew nothing.'

Cole ran a frustrated hand through his hair. 'You didn't know anything about his business?'

She shook her head. 'No. The children and I weren't allowed down here. A woman's place is in the home. Thom never discussed the farm with me. That's men's business. I received my housekeeping allowance and was told not to ask questions.'

'Give me a moment to make the call, and then we'll try to work this out.' Cole pulled out his phone and dialled, waiting for an answer before delivering instructions. Hanging up, he placed his hand under her elbow, guiding her back in the direction of the office. 'The search and rescue team will be on their way soon. When they arrive, I'll need you to take the children back to the house and wait for us.'

Bridey stopped walking. 'I want to come with you.'

'The children need you more right now.' Cole turned to face her. 'You can help by collecting as many blankets and towels as you can in case we need them. We don't always know how long these searches will take, so the search and rescue team usually have someone who volunteers as a cook. Gus is that person. He's the chef and manager at the Moonie River pub. He'll bring supplies and he'll need help preparing food for the team and for the people we rescue, depending on their condition.'

'Will he need to use the kitchen?'

Cole didn't miss the tremor of uncertainty in her voice. 'He can set up a camp kitchen if you're not comfortable with him in the house, but Gus is a lamb. I can vouch for that. It's your choice either way.'

She studied his face for a long moment, her gaze searching so deep he felt the impact all the way to his toes. 'He can use the kitchen.'

'Thank you, he'll appreciate that. Do you have a map of the farm anywhere?'

'On the wall in the office. It's old though. Most likely from before Thom's parents bought the place. There's not much on it except the location of the dams and a few markers for the crop fields.'

'It will gives us the boundaries and an indication of the layout at least.' Cole dragged a hand through his hair as he ran through protocol in his head. 'We'll need to use the office as a base. Do we have your permission to do that?'

'Of course. I'll round up the boys and we'll get out of your way.' Bridey took a step towards the office then hesitated. 'Please find these people, Cole. I don't want to believe that Thom hurt them in any way, but I know ... what he was capable of.'

She walked into the office leaving Cole to fight the rising anger in his chest and cursing the fact that Thomas McCaffrey had taken his own life before being brought to justice for his crimes against his wife.

Cole damped down on the fire in his belly. God only knew what they would find out there, if anything, and he needed to be prepared. If they were looking for illegals, he'd need to involve border security, but right now his priority was to reach them while they were all still alive.

Chapter Seven

B
ridey ushered the boys out of the office and onto the pathway to the house. While they'd waited for Search and Rescue to arrive, she'd answered as many of Cole's questions as she could, telling him the little she knew about the property that lay beyond the homestead, realising how isolated she'd been from all of it.

She stilled the flutter of frustration in her belly at once again being designated to the kitchen when she really wanted to be out there to help with the search. But Cole was right. Her boys needed her reassurance. Leaving them in the care of strangers when they weren't used to people around them wouldn't do them any good right now. Her inexperience might hamper rather than help the search and rescue efforts.

'What's happening, Mum? Why are all these

people here? Why is the police officer here again?' Alex tugged on her arm.

'Are we in trouble, Mum?' Garrett pulled on her skirt, uncertainty in his eyes.

'Did we do something naughty?' Shaun asked, tears welling in his eyes before he sucked on his thumb. 'Will that man come take us away like our dad said he would if we were naughty?'

Bridey hadn't seen him suck his thumb since the last time Thom had threatened to send them away with the New Lord. How could she prepare her boys for yet another shock? How many more of Thom's secrets would the farm give up? 'We're not in trouble, boys, and no, we didn't do anything naughty. No one will come to take any of us away. There are people lost out on the farm who need our help. Sergeant Delaney is going to find them. Those people arriving in cars are the search and rescue team who are here to help him.'

'Why are they lost on our farm?' Alex crossed his arms, his mouth set in a grim and angry line. 'Why does everything bad always happen on this stupid farm?'

For a terrifying moment, Bridey saw too much of Thom in her eldest son's features. 'We don't know the answer as to why they're missing yet, Alex, but we will when Sergeant Delaney finds them. Right now, we need to help in every way we can.'

'I don't want to help! Why can't we just leave this stupid place? Then bad things will stop happening.' Alex kicked hard at a stone in his path. It ricocheted off the side of the demountable office with a loud ping, snagging Cole's attention.

Bridey sighed. The new police sergeant was far more observant than his predecessor, and more caring too. She offered him a brief smile, relieved when he gave her the thumbs up and returned to his conversation with the head of the search and rescue team.

She turned back to her son. How many times since Thom's death had she not thought the very same thing about leaving the farm? With a fourth baby on the way, she had no idea how they would manage, but she had to try. Leaving meant nowhere to go. Staying brought with it a whole different challenge. Rock, hard place.

'Why don't we talk about this up at the house, Alex?'

'I don't want to talk about it. I want to go!' He took off along the path at a run.

Bridey let him go, confident he'd head straight for the house. It had been ingrained into him for too long that straying in any direction would only get him in trouble.

The twins clutched at her hands, their brother's outburst unsettling them. She gave their fingers a comforting squeeze as she looked at them. 'Shall we go home and get some juice and sandwiches?'

They nodded as they started along the path. The combination of exercise and fresh air would tire them out and they'd be ready for a nap after their snack which would give her time to talk to Alex alone.

Ahead on the path, Alex had slowed from a run to a fast walk, indecision and insecurity already kicking in. By the time the house came into view, he'd stopped after every few steps to pick up sticks and stones to toss as far as he could throw them with an angry arm.

Bridey looked past him, her heart hitching. Outside the house stood an unfamiliar SUV. Beside it, a mountain of a man leaned his arms on the hood, scanning the phone in his hands. He turned his head to look at them as they approached. Alex stopped dead in his tracks, turned around, and ran back to Bridey.

She lay a reassuring hand on his shoulder as she studied the man's white shirt with a mandarin collar and black and white checkered pants, a Royal Australian Navy cap on his head.

Relief washed through her. 'Boys, I think this is the cook Sergeant Delaney told us about. He's going to help us prepare food for the missing people and for the rescue team.'

The man pushed away from the vehicle using the bull bar for leverage as they approached.

'G'day, you must be Bridey. I'm Gus.' He held out a hand the size of a grizzly bear's paw for her to shake, breaking into a broad, kind smile that lit up his face.

Her hand disappeared in his for a brief second before he released it. 'I am. These are my boys; Alex, Garret, and Shaun.'

Gus bent down and held up a hand for a high-five, confusion stealing his smile when they shrank bank. 'So ... no high-five then.' He straightened his back and folded arms as thick as tree trunks, covered in tattoos. 'Tough crowd.'

'We don't receive visitors out here. They're not used to strangers,' Bridey explained, fairly sure her boys wouldn't know what a high-five was, but a raised hand didn't mean a greeting.

Gus nodded. 'Always necessary to be cautious around strangers.' He bent down again. 'See this, boys?' He pointed to the badge on his cap. 'Royal Australian Navy. To Serve and Provide, that was the motto of my ship, and I'm here to provide for my crew. Who wants chocolate brownies?'

'We're not allowed to have chocolate. Only on special occasions.' Alex turned to face Gus from the safety of Bridey's protection.

Gus scratched his head then looked at Bridey. 'Mmm, I'm not sure ... Is this a special occasion, Mum?'

Bridey smiled, her gut instinct rating Gus as

harmless as a teddy bear. 'I think we can call this a special occasion.'

'Good. Good.' Gus rubbed his hands together. 'I'm gonna need some big strong muscles to help me take some stuff inside. Does anyone here have big, strong muscles?'

Garrett put up his hand, the movement hesitant.

Gus made a show of measuring Garrett's height before giving him the thumbs up. 'Sweet. You look like you can handle the soup pot.' He opened the back door of the SUV and hauled out a stock pot almost as big as Garrett. 'Try that for size.' He gave Bridey a wink. 'Don't worry, Mum, it's aluminium. Light as a feather.'

Garrett lifted the pot to test its weight. 'Look at me. I'm strong. I've got muscles.'

Shaun nudged his brother aside. 'I bet I got muscles too! What can I carry?'

Gus pretended to think, squinting up at the sky as he tapped a finger against his chin. 'Mmm ... Oh, wait, I know!' He turned back to the vehicle and pulled out a cardboard box full of cooking utensils. 'Try that. No knives in there, Mum, so they're perfectly safe.'

Alex unfolded his arms. 'I'm bigger and stronger than both of them.'

Gus nodded. 'Yes, you are indeed. You must be the man of the house. I guess that means you can handle that box over on the other side with the veggies in it. We're going to make a pot of soup.'

'But it's summer. Soup is for winter,' Alex argued.

'Soup is for whenever we need it.' Gus hauled a cooler out of the back of the vehicle, picking it up like it weighed nothing at all. 'And it's exactly what these people will need. Delicious and nutritious. Mum, have a look in the drawer at the back there. There's a black roll-up under the false floor. I'm going to trust you with my knives. Not many people have that privilege. A chef's knives are sacred. Like a knight's sword. So, nobody touches my knives except me or your mum, Got it, boys?'

'Got it!' They all answered at once as they walked into the house carrying their loads.

'You're comfortable around kids.' Bridey retrieved the rolled-up knife kit from a drawer set-up at the back of the SUV. Gus appeared to be prepared for a pop-up kitchen anywhere, any time.

The man made a scoffing sound. 'Kids are easy. Try rounding up a shipload of hard-boiled Navy crew and try to get them to eat soup.'

Bridey laughed, surprising herself. How long had it been since she'd been enough at ease to laugh? Too long. Then she remembered the reason Gus was preparing to cook up a storm. 'I hope they find those people soon.'

Gus gave her a confident wink. 'If anyone can find them, it's Cole.'

'You sound so sure.'

Gus's grin widened and pride shone from his eyes. 'Of course, I am. He's my son.'

~

An hour later, briefed and coordinated, the search and rescue team fanned out across the planned route. No corner of the farm or the marshland beyond it would be left unreached.

Cole checked his phone as it buzzed and smiled. He shook his head at the gif of Popeye showing off his muscles. *Big Gus has it under control,* the message boasted.

With Gus at the farmhouse, he wouldn't have to worry about Bridey and the boys. His dad had a unique way of putting people at ease. Which had made him the perfect cook and manager for the only pub in town. There weren't too many places a retired Navy cook would find comfortable, but the galley-style kitchen at the Moonie River Pub and Grill had felt like home to Gus from his first visit.

Cole turned his attention back to the search. With a little luck, Gus would settle Alex down too. He was trying hard not to get too involved, to remain a distant third party, but he'd found his thoughts returning to Bridey and her children far too often lately.

Ed Lee approached him, the patch on his bright orange jacket identifying him as the coordinator of the search. 'Hey, Sarge. The team in the far north corner near the Marsh Road boundary have reported something unusual they want you to look at.' Ed spread the map from the office wall over the hood of Cole's SUV. 'If you cut through the service road here and here, and then across this field here, you'll arrive out back a lot quicker.'

'Got it.' Cole opened the door of his vehicle.

'Be careful. The team has said the service roads are in pretty bad repair. The field you'll cut across hasn't been tended to either so there'll be all kinds of ditches and hazards too.'

'Thanks for the heads up, Ed. Tell the team not to touch anything until I get there.' In his heart, he hoped they'd found something significant even though his head told him not to get his hopes up.

Cole followed Ed's directions, driving as fast as he could, pushing the SUV to its limits while navigating around the uneven surfaces, trying not to get bogged.

The state of the farm around him had his heart sinking. No way in hell could Bridey ever make a living for her family out of the mess her late husband had created. Not without major funding and a lot of help.

Up ahead, the rescue team came into view, their orange suits bright against the arid field and the contrast of the greener marshland beyond. Cole could only imagine what it must have looked like back when the farm was producing well. The only hint that the fields had once grown crops was the sprinklers rising like skeletons from the dust.

Under a line of gum trees stood a row of rusty shipping containers, the flat tops covered in leaves and gum nuts, shredded bark piling up around them.

Adrenalin spiked in Cole's blood as he rolled the vehicle to a stop. Thick, heavy chains, looped through stays and secured with heavy duty padlocks, linked six shipping containers together and effectively sealed the doors shut. A bank of solar panels on the roof of one indicated power to the containers.

He opened the door and climbed out of his vehicle, damping down on the spark of hope that they'd found the missing women and children. The containers could hold anything from farm machinery to fertiliser.

'What have we got,' he asked as he approached the team leader.

Harriet pointed to a spot near the roof of the first container. 'We found holes drilled into the container near the top. Almost like ventilation holes to create airflow. When we arrived, we thought we heard tapping noises from inside, but it turned out to be popping noises from expansion as the air heated up.'

'Let's get these chains off.' Cole assessed the thickness of the chains and padlocks. 'I don't think a bolt cutter is going to work.'

Harriet shook her head. 'Nope. The firies are on their way with the oxy cutter. I've told them to come in off Marsh Road. They're about five minutes away. Before they track all over the road though, we found something else you need to see.'

Cole followed Harriet to the boundary fence that backed onto Marsh Road. 'Fence has been cut.'

Harriet nodded. 'Yup. Marsh Road is an emergency fire exit. Pretty much a dirt service road. There shouldn't be any traffic on it, but judging by the tyre tracks, it was being used regularly.'

Cole hauled out his phone to take photos of the tracks. 'Looks like a vehicle or vehicles were driving in and out through the gap in the fence.'

'Yup. A lot.' She pointed to the deep grooves cut by fat wheels.

'Trucks?'

'Nope. More like SUVs. Trucks would get bogged using that road and the ground is like quicksand on this side of it. No truckie worth his salt would risk it. Too much downtime if he gets bogged. Time equals money when you're a truckie.'

'Thanks, Harriet. Good work. Looks like the firies are here with that oxy cutter.'

Cole pointed down the road to where the Bushfire Service four-wheel-drive made its way up the road with a trail of dust in its wake. He waited impatiently as they unpacked and set about cutting off the chains, pleased that the area they worked in backed onto marshland and not where the search might draw a crowd.

The moment the chains fell to the ground, the crew began wrangling doors open.

Beside him, Harriet blew out a long whistle. 'Looks like Thommy-Boy was farming all right, just not vegetables. Guess that explains the cut fence and vehicle tracks, not to mention the need for those solar panels on top of the container. He would have had a nice little business going here.'

'No wonder he didn't have time for the farm,' Cole agreed.

'Sarge!' A volunteer firefighter beckoned him over. 'We're going to need help over here.'

Cole's heart pounded against his ribs as he hurried towards the container furthest from him. The first thing that hit him was the smell of vomit, stale sweat, decomposition, and excretion. The second was the sight of a group of women and young girls huddled together in the furthest corner of the container, terror in their eyes.

Harriet dry-retched beside him. 'How in God's name are they still alive?'

The five bodies laid out near the door spoke for themselves. 'Move these first,' he instructed before calling out, 'Kirana?'

'*Iya?*'

Switching to his limited Indonesian, he explained who he was. 'We've come to help you.'

'Where is Mr Thom?' Kirana's question was weak, her strength clearly waning.

'He's dead.' Cole figured there was no point in lying to the woman.

She offered up what sounded like a prayer of thanks and held out the bundle in her arms. 'Please. Help the children first.'

Cole stepped into the container, his gaze taking in the squalor. An old fan rattled away in a corner, providing some relief in the stifling, stale air. Dirty mattresses and sheets lay scattered across the floor. Empty food cans littered one corner, and most heartbreaking of all, the 40-litre plastic container with no water left in it. They'd survived on meagre rations. How long had it been since they'd seen fresh food and water?

Questions churned through his mind, but now was

not the time to ask them. He leaned down to take the bundle from Kirana. A newborn baby looked up at him, still crusty with dried blood from its birth. His stomach churned, bile filling his throat as his thoughts turned to another baby, delivered moments after Carrie's death, stillborn.

Cole's voice cracked as he handed the bundle to Harriet. 'Get the paramedics out here. Now.'

'Already on their way, Sarge.'

One by one, Kirana pushed the children forward. He counted eight girls, all of varying age between four and twelve. Cole and two members of the rescue team carried out three women, all too weak to walk, all too skinny to be healthy. What the hell kind of a monster had Thom McCaffrey been?

Last came Kirana, her blood-stained clothes and legs proof that she'd given birth not too long ago. Cole placed her on the gurney, saying a silent prayer that she'd hold on.

'*Terima kasih,*' she whispered, her voice too weak to contain fear, only relief.

'No need to thank us, Kirana. You'll be safe now. These people will take you and the others to the hospital. I will come and talk to you about what happened here once you've been seen to by the doctor and nurses.'

He got out of the way so that Cath could attend her

patient, a drip already set up for rehydration. A few steps away, Harriet helped Doc assess the children, all eight holding glucose lollipops and sipping on electrolyte drinks, stiff with fear. He'd hate to imagine what they'd already been through, locked up and living in a metal box. Calls would have to be made to the Federal Police and Immigration, one to the drug squad in Perth, but first he had another crime scene to process.

Chapter Eight

Bridey's hands stilled on kneading bread dough as the door opened and Cole walked in. It had been over an hour and a half since they'd heard the ambulance sirens blaring, and the rescue team had filed in for refreshments before leaving the farm.

They'd offered up no information on what they'd found, but the expressions on their faces had said enough. The news would not be good.

Gus blew out a long whistle. 'Looks like someone needs a strong coffee.' He poured a mug of black coffee from the pot on the stove and handed it to Cole.

Cole grimaced as he took a sip. 'You sure this is coffee? Tastes like tar.'

'It'll put hair on your chin, son.' Gus slapped him on the shoulder. 'Drink up.'

Cole wrapped his hands around the mug. 'Bridey, can we talk outside?'

Her heart sank as she turned to the boys. 'Stay here with Gus. I'll be back in a minute.'

She followed Cole through the door, out onto the back verandah. The potting shed windows reflected the last rays of the sun, taunting her from the bottom of the garden. What had Thom done?

Cole tossed the remnants of his coffee into the garden bed at the foot of the verandah. 'We found them.' He dragged his hand over his face as if to erase what he'd seen from his eyes.

Bridey nodded, too afraid of the answers to ask the questions that ran through her mind.

'Have you ever been down the back of the farm? The area that borders the marshland off Marsh Road.' Cole turned to look at her.

'Never. There are parts of this farm I've never seen.' His mystified look had her elaborating. 'Like I told you before, my place was in the house, taking care of the home and the children. It was Thom's job to mind the fields. The running of the farm was never any of my business, and I never asked. Today was the first time I'd ever been in the office.'

'It sounds like living in a prison.'

The one time she'd mentioned feeling that way soon after they'd married, the punishment had been severe enough to never ask again. 'It was just ... the way.'

'Whose way?'

'The church's way.'

'I heard the McCaffreys left the church.' Cole leaned a hip against the verandah railing and studied her.

'I don't know if that's true or not. They'd left the farm before I came home with Thom as his bride.' Bridey shivered. The New Lord had made sure all the girls in the care houses knew their place. 'The rules were all we knew, so we continued to live by them.'

'I'm finding it hard to believe that a man with such God-fearing beliefs could hold nine women and eight children prisoner in a locked shipping container.'

'What?' Horror seeped into her chest.

'Five women are dead, Bridey. Kirana is hanging on by sheer willpower. The eight children are now nine. They'd spread their rations out, fed and watered the children first at a cost to adult lives.'

'Nine children?'

'Yes, nine. Kirana gave birth sometime in the last day or so. They were locked in a shipping container with little air, minimal food and their water had just run out. One more day, and they'd all be dead. Did you know about the shipping containers lining the back fence on Marsh Road?'

The anger in his voice had Bridey placing a protective hand over her stomach. She sank down on the top of the steps leading down from the verandah.

The sun glinting on the shed windows caught her eye again. She shook her head, numb with disbelief. But then ... hadn't she fallen victim to Thom's cruelty herself? How could she forget that time before the boys were born when he'd locked her inside their bedroom wardrobe for two days without food or water for disobeying him?

'Bridey? Did you know about the shipping containers?'

'No. I did not know.' Shock overrode the disgust rising in her throat. 'How could he do that?'

Cole sat down beside her on the step. 'Did you notice any significant changes in Thom's behaviour in the last few months?'

Had she? She'd grown so used to Thom's temper and punishment. Bridey cast her mind back. 'He'd become more ... erratic, angrier, stronger. Paranoid almost.' She drew a deep breath and let it out slowly.

'Have you ever known him to take drugs?'

Bridey shook her head. 'Not even a headache tablet. He only ever drank whiskey.'

'So, you knew nothing about the drug lab he'd built out on the Marsh Road border?'

Nausea curdled her stomach. 'Thom was making drugs? I don't understand. What kind of drugs?'

Cole avoided answering as he tapped out a rhythm on the empty porcelain mug with his fingertip. 'Did you ever see lights at night through those trees on the ridge? Like vehicles driving in and out at all odd hours?'

'No. The farmhouse has block-out curtains. They get closed at night and aren't opened again until sunrise. It's so quiet outside after dark, I would have heard if someone drove in close to the house, but over the ridge? No.'

Cole nodded. 'You wouldn't have heard anyone coming in from the Marsh Road end, right?'

Bridey frowned, the questions leaving an unsettled feeling under her ribs. 'No. I can't see over the ridge from the house. And the trees are thick up there. Was someone coming onto the property?'

'Yes.'

'Do you think they'll come back?' She wanted her boys safe. If someone came looking for Thom or the people Cole had rescued, or even the drugs Cole had mentioned. It was bad enough that she had to have a plan for their safety when the New Lord found out Thom was gone.

'With all the activity on the farm in the next few days, they'd have to be pretty desperate to show up.

The drug squad and forensics team will be here from Perth in the morning to process the scene. If you remember anything else, Bridey, please tell me.'

Numb, Bridey struggled against the fog of overwhelm. Thom had sure lifted the lid on his Pandora's box from the grave. One thing was certain, she'd have little sleep tonight knowing a whole operation she'd never known existed had run on the farm. More proof of the horrific things Thom had been capable of. 'I don't understand why he had those women and children locked up.'

'I've got a pretty good idea, but I'll have to prove it.'

'Will they be okay?' She could only imagine the horror Kirana, the other women and the children had been through. God knows, she'd experienced her own horrors at Thom's hands, but she'd never believed him capable of something like this.

'I hope so. I think we found the survivors just in time.'

'What will happen to them now?'

'Once they're well enough and released from hospital, they'll be placed in a detention centre until they can be processed through Immigration. There's a strong chance they'll be sent home.'

Bridey twisted her hands into her skirt and chewed on her lip. 'Can I see her? Kirana?'

'I'm not sure that's a great idea.' Their shoulders touched as Cole shifted.

'Please? I know what he put them through.'

His expression softened. 'I'll check with Doc, but I'll have to be present in the room with you. We'll have a lot of questions to ask you, Bridey. Even if you might not know the answers.'

'I understand. All I can give you is the truth. Thank you.'

They sat in silence for a moment as Bridey processed the events of the day and prayed that the farm wouldn't turn up any more of Thom's unwanted surprises.

'Bridey?'

She looked down at her hands in her lap. 'Yes?'

'Why didn't you take the children and leave him?'

'I tried once. He found me and nearly killed me. If he'd succeeded, where would that leave my children?' She leaned a little closer to his warmth as the memory chilled her skin.

'Why don't you leave now?'

She looked up at his face. His eyes didn't hold the madness that Thom's had, his facial expressions free of cruelty despite the hardness of his features that spoke of experiences better left untold.

'Where would I go? Mindaleny Ridge is the only real home I've had. If I leave here the only place I know to go back to is the church compound. That's not the life I want for my children, so I have to find a way to make this our safe place.'

He hesitated a moment, as if he wanted to ask more questions. Instead, he smiled as he stood, and she liked the way his eyes crinkled up at the corners, the grooves that softened his cheeks, and the sincerity that slipped into his words. 'Then I'll do my best to clean up this mess as fast as I can for you so you can have just that. I'll be in touch to let you know what the next steps are in terms of the investigation.'

'Thank you.'

As Bridey watched him climb into his SUV and drive away, she stilled the churn of her stomach with her hand. Cole Delaney wasn't the kind of man to stop asking questions until he had the answers, and the can of worms he would open doing so could spell even more trouble ahead.

~

Gus wiped the bar counter around Cole's paperwork. 'So ... Bridey McCaffrey ...'

Cole looked up from filling out his report. 'What about her?' He'd stayed to help Gus clear up and repack his cooking utensils into his SUV, then stayed a while to make sure she and the boys were settled before coming back into town.

'You two looked pretty cosy sitting on the step.' Gus wiggled his eyebrows. 'She's a peach.'

'A *peach*? Really, Dad? What century are we in?' Cole laughed. 'She's a new widow with three young children and another one on the way. She's also a witness in a case I'm working on. That's the only thing cosy about our relationship.'

'Hmm ... you can't haul the burden of Carrie's coffin around on your shoulders forever, son. At some point, you gotta let her and the baby go.'

Cole dropped the pen down on his paperwork and leaned his elbows on the bar counter. 'Says the man who never remarried after Mum died.'

'We're not talking about me. We're talking about you. Besides, I was a Navy man. No time for commitments or another wife.'

Cole scoffed at that, took a sip of his soft drink, and called it for what it was. 'Bullshit. I was ten, that was twenty-four years ago and here we are in a pub in rural Western Australia about as far away from the sea as you can get. You had plenty of time to change your mind.'

Gus whipped the drying cloth off his shoulder and whacked Cole hard on the arm with it. 'I gave it all up to be with my son. That's you, Cranky Pants.'

Cole grinned. 'And I appreciate that more than you'll ever know.' His dad had given up his ship and crew to take up a position as a cook in the mess hall at the RAN base on Garden Island so he could raise his son after Cole's mum passed away from breast cancer.

'I was lost without your mum. She handled everything. I had no idea how to write out a cheque to pay the bills, or about your nut allergy or your dislike for Vegemite. What kind of Aussie doesn't like Vegemite, anyway?'

'This kind.' Cole picked up the pen and tapped it against his chest before filling out another line in his report. 'Is there a point to all this reminiscing, Big Gus?'

Gus leaned forward, folding his mountainous arms on the counter. 'Bridey is like a goldfish in a bowl, swimming in circles with nowhere to go, surrounded by sharks. Whatever is going on up at that farm of hers needs to be sorted quick smart. She reminds me of me when your mum died, floundering in the dark, trying to find a sandbank so I could get my feet back under me.'

'Stop mixing your metaphors. I'm working on it, Dad.'

'I know you are. When I looked in the fridge today, she had little left to feed those kids with.' Gus shook his head. 'I don't like to speak ill of the dead but, by God, that man's lucky I didn't get my hands on him first.'

'Line up and take a number,' Cole agreed. 'I'm guessing you filled the fridge for her?'

Gus nodded. 'Hid some in the freezer too. It's only soup, bread, and the left-over vegetables, but it will feed them for a bit. I'm worried about her all alone so far out of town.'

Cole sighed and gave up trying to fill out the report because clearly Gus had something on his mind he needed to offload. 'Dad, you know I can't discuss the details of this case with you, but rest assured, from my experience on the squad in Perth, she's safe for now. Whoever holds an interest in those containers will play it cool while there's such a large police presence in the area. They won't risk getting caught coming back while police tape seals off those containers.'

Gus nodded. 'I know. But still ...'

Cole leaned back on the chair to study his father's face. At fifty-nine, Gus Delaney was still a good-looking guy with twinkling blue eyes and a cheeky smile. He'd set a few hearts aflutter on arrival in the small north-west town of Moonie River. At six foot five, weighing in at 110kg of pure muscle and Navy tattoos, he was pretty hard to miss.

'I'll call her before turning in tonight. Just to put your mind at ease.'

Gus grinned. 'Thanks, kid.' He turned to wipe out

the schooner glasses ready for service. 'You know who the eldest boy reminds me of?'

'Alex? Who?'

'You.' Gus shook his head. 'You were also so protective over your mum when she was sick. The only difference is, if we don't catch Alex in time, he could end up like his father. He's seen too much, felt more than a boy his age should. I'm afraid the trauma he's experienced will turn to anger and resentment. You've seen first-hand how the cycle continues with the children if the only thing they know is violence.'

'I know.' Feet on the bar's footrest, Cole rocked his chair back onto two legs.

Gus eyed him like he was two. 'Stop that. You'll fall flat on your arse, boy, or break the chair. One of the two.'

Settling the chair back down on four legs, Cole rubbed a thumb across his brow. 'Hey, Dad, do you remember that time in New South Wales when they busted a cult up in the Blue Mountains?'

'Messy business that. Goes back a while. They had a commune where they fostered children and pretty much brainwashed them. Created their own tribe. The kids the cops freed from it were pretty messed up.'

'Do you remember the name of the pastor involved?'

Gus shrugged. 'I could look it up. They had a

program on telly about it not too long ago. Why do you ask?'

'Just something I'm looking into.'

'To do with the McCaffreys?'

'You know I can't discuss a case with you, Dad.'

Gus scoffed. 'Righto. Not hard to work out though. Other than the more serious container load of women and children, the only other cases you have on your plate are Mrs Lee versus The Goat, and the two numpties who started a brawl outside the pub last Friday night.'

'Mrs Lee won that battle which is why Chewy is now my new lawnmower. As for the two numpties ... I reckon you've got that under control.' Cole grinned. Both were now gainfully employed as clean-up crew at the pub. 'Does the name Clifford Camden ring any bells?'

Gus thought for a moment. 'Nope. Who is he?'

'A person of interest.'

A shot in the dark, but the similarities between the set-up Bridey grew up in and the cult in the Blue Mountains was too coincidental to ignore. He'd learned not to ignore his gut instinct.

'Do you think there may be a connection to the people in the container, son?'

Cole shrugged. 'I wouldn't rule it out, but that case is in the hands of the AFP and Immigration, so outside my jurisdiction.' He gathered up his paperwork and stuffed it inside his backpack. 'I'm going to head off and see what I can dig up on Camden.'

Restlessness gnawed at him, an unsettling feeling in his gut as a thought fluttered just out of reach. The sense of urgency grew as he unlocked the door of his house.

Chapter Nine

Bridey stirred, unsure what had woken her. A halo of light from the night-light showed the twins asleep beside her, but she couldn't see Alex.

Pushing the covers aside, she swung her legs over the edge of the bed and pressed her feet into her slippers. Perhaps he'd gone to the toilet. If only they had a bathroom inside, the children wouldn't have to traipse out to the old dunny on the back verandah.

Pulling on a light cardigan, she made her way through the house. 'Alex?' she called softly, careful not to wake the twins. No response.

As she pushed open the door to the mudroom, an orange glow caught her eye almost at the same time as the stench of burning plastic flooded her sense of smell.

'No! Alex!' Panic burned inside her like the flames

'Yes, Mum,' they agreed, expressions sullen. Turning on their torches, they went to look under the back verandah. Swinging her attention between wetting down the shed and keeping an eye on the boys, she prayed help would arrive quickly as she kept calling out Alex's name.

'He's not here, Mummy.'

The faint sound of sirens in the distance reached her ears, as for the third time in as many months emergency services descended on Mindaleny Ridge. But she didn't have time to think about what the townsfolk thought of that. Dropping the hose and letting the water run, she turned away to search for Alex.

As the flashing blue and red lights of the fire engines became visible against the black velvet sky, she spotted Alex wedged between the rainwater tank and a pile of firewood, hands clutched to his chest.

Relief washed over her in a wave that made her a little dizzy. 'Baby, you're safe.'

His bottom lipped trembled in the flickering light of the flames. An explosion from inside the shed and the sound of shattering glass made him huddle further away from her.

As the shed creaked under the flames, she squeezed the twins into the gap with Alex, hoping that the water tank would provide some protection from the heat.

The shed was far enough away from the house, but if the fire spread into the dry grass around them, they'd have a problem. Bridey cast a look over her shoulder just as the iron roof buckled and caved, sending sparks showering into the air.

On the dirt driveway that curved around from the front of the house, Cole's police Landcruiser rode ahead of the fire crew. He skidded to a stop in the mud created by the water running from the hose. 'Bridey!' he called, slamming the car door.

'Over here! By the water tank.'

His boots thundered against the ground before the light touch of his hand rested on her shoulder. 'Is anyone hurt?'

'I don't think so.' She took his hand as he extended it to help her up.

'Let's get you all back to the house. It's safe now that the firies are here.' He picked up the twins and balanced them on his hips. 'Come on, Alex. Take your mum's hand.'

Alex shook his head and cowered into the darkness.

'Alex, come along, sweetheart. You can't stay hiding out here. You'll feel better if we all go inside.' Bridey reached in to take his arm, but he tugged against her hold, whimpering. 'There's nothing to be afraid of. It's only the shed.' How had the damn thing caught alight anyway?

'I hate it,' Alex shouted.

'I know you do, Alex.' For such a valid reason too. 'But you need to come out now.'

'I don't want to.' He shook off her hold, his arms clutched against his chest.

Bridey shone the torch into the gap so she could see his face. Tears streaked his dirty face. 'Please, Alex. Let me get you safe inside so the firefighters can do their job. We don't want to be in the way.'

'Am I in trouble?'

Bridey frowned. 'No. Why would you be?'

Slowly Alex turned his body towards her and held out his hands. Angry red burns had begun to blister on his palm and fingers. A new kind of fear rushed through Bridey.

'Oh, dear God, Alex, what have you done?' she whispered, stumbling back a step.

Beside her, Cole let the twins wriggle to the ground. 'Take Shaun and Garrett. I'll bring Alex.' When she hesitated, he reassured her, 'He'll be fine with me.'

She took the twins' hands and waited as Cole coaxed Alex out from behind the water tank in a gentle, soothing voice. How different he and Thom were. If it were Thom, he'd have dragged Alex out without a care for the boy's state of mind.

'You're not in trouble and I won't hurt you, Alex. But we need to see to your burns. They're going to hurt really badly if we don't get some cold water on them right away.'

'I'm scared.'

'Did you start the fire, Alex?'

'No!' Indignation took the edge off his fear.

'Then you have nothing to be afraid of. Come on out, let's get you cleaned up and fix your hands.'

'But the man ... he'll come back. He said he would.'

Ice-cold terror laced through Bridey's nerve ends. 'What man, Alex?' A man with a love for fire and punishment. Had he come for them already?

'The man with the mask.'

Memories of a man in a mask flickered in and out of her memories like the flames claiming the shed. A fire. A bonfire. Children dressed in robes that all looked alike. He couldn't have found out about Thom. Not yet.

Cole's soothing voice reached in to her memories. 'It's okay, Alex. You're safe now. He's gone. Come on, son. You'll be warmer and more comfortable inside with your mum and the twins. Come to me now.' He held out his arms, his words of encouragement kind and quiet as he talked Alex out of his hidey hole.

Alex emerged, shaking. Cole picked him up as he began to cry; harsh, uncontrollable, heart-wrenching tears. Her boy's arms circled Cole's neck as he clung on and cried. Cole rubbed Alex's back in comforting, soothing circles as surprise mixed with relief in his expression at Alex's unexpected show of trust.

'Whatever happened to the shed, we can fix it, Alex. All that matters right now is that you're all right.' Cole patted Alex's back, stilling the shivers that shook him. Turning his attention to Bridey, Cole said, 'Let's get these burns cooled down. Have you got some petroleum jelly to put on them?'

Bridey nodded. 'I have aloe vera and bandages.' God knew, she'd had to use them enough in the past to treat her own burns. She moved ahead with the twin realisation gnawing at her insides. The trouble th plagued Mindaleny Ridge wasn't over yet, and dream of flying under the New Lord's radar had ' trampled under his feet tonight. She'd need an plan.

~

Cole entered the kitchen after talking to the relief allowing his shoulders to sag.

Bridey sat at the table, her head in her

didn't stir at the sound of his boots against the hardwood floor.

'Are the boys asleep?' He touched her shoulder lightly.

'Yes.' The word came out strangled as she folded her hands to press them to her lips. The soft light of the dawn sun filtering in through the window caught the sparkle of tears in her eyes. Bridey let out a shuddering breath. 'The man Alex said he saw out there ... he told ᵉe the man chased and caught him, tried to push him ᵢ the ring of fire around the shed. He burnt his ₛ in the flames trying to get away.'

ˡe dragged a hand through his hair. What kind
ᵉr were they dealing with here? 'Jesus ...
he was hiding behind the water tank?'
ᵗ ᵈded. 'I believe him, Cole. My kids don't
ᵉr consequences for lying ... in the past ...
ᵉⁿ ᵖe my children will never see again.'
ᵗʰᵉʳ ᵤu more about the man he saw?'
ᵥore gloves, a black hoodie, and a
ₓ has an excellent memory and

ᵣₑ ᶜʰⁱᵉᶠ, ₘ what I've seen. Do you
ₛ sketch of the man? Or
ₐₙds. She ᵥ one?' Even a masked
ₒ who they would be

'I'll ask him when he wakes up.' She lifted her gaze to his. 'I'm scared, Cole. What if this man comes back?'

'Do you have any idea who it might have been, Bridey? Is there any chance Alex's description reminds you of someone?'

Her eyes darted from his as she dropped her gaze and her clenched hands to the table. 'No.'

The sudden tension in her shoulders told a different story, but he'd need patience to earn her trust. 'We'll find answers for you, Bridey. We'll have to ask Alex to answer a few questions about what he saw. We have officers on the force trained to interview children. Would you consent to that?'

'I think he'd prefer to talk to you. He trusts you.'

'Okay. Did he tell you anything else?'

Bridey shook her head. 'No. That's all I could get out of him. He's terrified, Cole, and I don't know what to do.'

'Of course he is. We can get help for him, look into counselling.' Her kids had seen enough violence in their short lifetime. Mindaleny Ridge appeared to attract and thrive on it. He'd advise her to move, but he knew from experience how hard it would be to give up the only home she knew just to find closure on the past.

'I'll think about it.' She pressed the heel of her hand to her eyes, stress and exhaustion taking its toll.

Cole clamped down on the impulse to run a soothing hand over her hair, loose down her back, tangled from the events of the night. 'The fire is out but the shed is history.' He couldn't help but think that was a good thing. No more silent monument to the man who'd died inside it or the mess he'd left behind. Although it didn't answer the question of who'd set it on fire and why. 'Once the fire chief has finished with the investigation, we'll get the debris cleared away.'

Bridey nodded and whispered, 'Thank you.'

'If it helps ease your mind, we know Alex didn't set the fire. We found an empty 20-litre jerry can discarded away from the shed. Still with some fresh fuel left in it. No way a boy Alex's size would be able to lug a metal jerry full of fuel around, pour it out, and then toss it that far away from the shed.'

'In his heart, I think he wanted to see that shed burn.' Bridey's chair scraped against the floor as she stood. She hooked a stray strand of hair behind her ear, her hand a little shaky as she tried to hold onto control.

He drew her hand down and pressed it between his palms. 'Bridey, I'm going to ask you one more time ... Is there anyone who comes to mind who might have had a problem with Thom? Any idea who he might have been involved with? Why was he making drugs and holding women and children prisoner in a container? If you know or suspect anything or anyone, please, you need to tell me.'

'So, you do think it could be linked to the people you found in the containers?' Concern furrowed her forehead as she looked up at him.

'I don't want to speculate, I'd rather find hard evidence, but I won't rule it out. I can't rule out that he won't come back. Maybe not now, but before we have enough evidence to find who did this. I'm worried about you and the children out here alone with everything that's happened.'

Sad green eyes searched his face. 'I am too, but what choice do I have?'

Cole held her gaze. 'Why don't I make arrangements for you and the children to stay in town? You'll be safe there.'

Bridey shook her head. 'I don't have money for board, and don't know anyone well enough to stay with them long term. I don't want to have to answer well-meaning questions. All these years we've lived almost reclusive from the townspeople. I can't take advantage of their kindness any more than I have already.' She withdrew her hand from his but didn't move away.

'Let me help you, Bridey.'

A spark of anger replaced the glitter of tears in her eyes. 'You can help by ending this. Find out who is behind keeping those women and children captive in the containers, who did these unspeakable things to them.'

Cole brought his face closer to hers. 'What if the person who did those things to them is already dead?'

'He sure as hell didn't come back to life to set fire to the shed he shot himself in.' Her eyes warred with his, full of defiance. 'All I can do is give you the description Alex gave. It's all I have. It's all I can give right now.' The last word came out on a strangled hitch as if she wanted to cry again but wouldn't give in to the temptation.

Cole frowned at her choice of words. 'I will find answers, I promise you that.' He drew her into his arms and held her until the stiffness left her spine and she sagged against him, her cheek to his chest. 'I won't let anyone hurt you or the kids.' Even if he had to stand guard on the property himself. He'd let criminals hurt Carrie and the baby, a mistake he wouldn't make again. 'You have to trust me to do my job, Bridey.' Just as he had to trust himself.

She pulled back to look at him. 'I know you'll do everything you can.'

He held her gaze, softer now than it had been before, the fight extinguished from her eyes and replaced by trust instead. All he could do was pray that he didn't fail her the way he'd failed Carrie.

Tucking her head back under his chin, he held her

a little tighter, absorbing her strength and faith as much as she sapped his. He had to find answers fast. For her. For the kids. And for the women and children who had been held captive in a box for God knew how long.

Big Gus stuck his head in through the open door of the mudroom and called, 'Hey, big fella. You gotta come and see this. Chief Aslan found something interesting.'

'I'll be right there, Dad.' He hadn't seen his father arrive but wasn't surprised to find him back on the farm. Gus went wherever he was needed most.

'Take all the time you want,' he said with a smug grin over Bridey's head.

Cole shook his head. Now Gus had completely the wrong idea about why Bridey was in his arms. For a man so disinterested in his own love-life, he sure as hell spent a lot of time meddling in Cole's.

He set Bridey away from him with gentle hands. 'I'll go and see what they've found.'

She nodded and straightened her cardigan that smelled of smoke from the fire. 'I'll be right out as soon as I've checked on the boys.'

Cole picked up his hat from where he'd put it down on the table when they'd first come into the house after finding Alex. 'I'll see you out there.' He watched her walk in the direction of the bedrooms, his emotions a knot in his chest. The only other woman

123

who'd felt so right in his arms was his wife. He didn't deserve that privilege again.

Slamming his hat onto his head, he stalked out the mudroom door and jogged down the steps. 'What have we got?' he called as he approached the smouldering remains of the shed.

'It's too hot yet to inspect it, but it looks like a trapdoor in the floor.' The chief brushed at an area in the centre of the smouldering mess with a spade. 'We found it while we were shifting the metal to cool the debris underneath. Lucky we got here when we did. If the ammonium-nitrate in the shed got hot enough to cause an explosion, whatever is down there would have just been a massive hole in the ground. We'll know more once it cools down enough to get closer to it.'

Bridey's hand touched his arm as she leaned around him to see. 'What is it?'

Cole glanced down at her. 'I was hoping you could answer that. What's under the trapdoor?'

Confusion crossed her face. 'What trapdoor?'

'You didn't know it was there?'

She shook her head. 'Why would there be a trapdoor in the potting shed? That shed was there already when I came to the farm. It was another one of the no-go zones. Thom said it was because the fertiliser was stored there, and it would be safer if we didn't go in and interfere with anything.'

'Or because he was hiding something.' Cole placed his hands on his hips and studied the door, the parts of it not blackened and twisted by the fire shining through the ash in rusty red.

The chief straightened his back and rubbed at a spot on his side. 'There was something over the top of it. Like a table or a shelf or something. We moved what was left to check under it for heat, and that's when we saw the trapdoor.'

'Good work, guys.' He patted the chief's shoulder. 'We'll wait for the heat to cool down and find out what's under there.'

Dread leeched up Cole's spine. After their discovery in the containers, all he could hope for was that the trapdoor didn't conceal any more nasty surprises.

Chapter Ten

B ridey sat on a tatty, upholstered cushioned base in a row of worn seats in the main banking hall. It seemed as if the big city bank had forgotten all about their Moonie River branch. The decor hadn't seen an update in a long while.

Beside her, the boys fidgeted and swung their legs back and forth, too short for their feet to touch the ground. How long would the bank manager make them wait? She twisted the strap of her handbag between her fingers, turning her mind to what was left of the potting shed. She shuddered at the thought of what new horror lay beneath the trapdoor. The fire chief had said they'd be back in a few days to remove what was left.

She'd been so used to not asking questions to

protect the children from the violence Thom could inflict that she'd turned a blind eye to far too much of what was happening on the farm. Not that she'd have been able to stop anything Thom did.

'Bridey McCaffrey?'

She looked up from the worn blue pattern on the carpet into the face of the man who held their financial future in his manicured hands. In his fashionable city suit, with groomed black hair, he was the opposite of what she'd expect to find in a relaxed and aging country bank. But then she'd never had to set foot inside a bank before. That had been Thom's business.

'Yes.'

'Pleased to meet you, Bridey. My name is Dean, and I'm the new bank manager. Mr Brinkley retired last week but he has passed on your query to me.'

Bridey's sinking spirits took another dive. She hadn't been expecting great news either way, but the grave expression on the bank manager's face had her wondering if it was even worse than she'd already gathered from all the outstanding bills she'd found.

'We have a lot to talk about.' Dean's polite smile didn't quite reach his cold blue eyes. 'Please, follow me into my office and we can go through the details.'

Dread weighting her feet, Bridey stood to walk with him, the children following behind her. His office was cold and impersonal. She wondered briefly if Mr Brinkley had been any different. Would he have shown compassion for a widow and her three young children?

Dean's desk was as empty as his eyes. This was his job, not his end goal. He was young, too ambitious for a small town like Moonie River. He slid into the chair behind the desk. Bridey could smell the new leather in the room. He pushed aside a small pile of dog-eared manila folders and logged on to a shiny new computer.

'Mr Brinkley was a little behind the times. He preferred the old ways to new technology.'

'I'm a little old school myself.'

Surprise raised his eyebrows. 'You don't like technology?'

'I've never had it, so I don't miss it. My husband didn't believe in computers or mobile phones.' Except for the one Kirana had used to call for help while locked up in the container. Bridey shivered. How had she got that? Had Thom given it to her? Or someone else?

'I guess that explains the absence of a bank account in his name then.' Dean hit a few buttons on the keyboard and peered at the screen. 'We don't have any McCaffreys listed on our records.'

'That's impossible. This is the only bank in town. He should have had an account for the farm at least. Isn't it in one of those folders?' Bridey frowned, her heart sinking further into the pit of her stomach. She'd seen bank statements when clearing out the office, but then Kirana's call had come through and she hadn't returned to the office to continue sorting through things.

'Nope. And the house doesn't belong to him either.' Dean sat back, a smirk on his face that added to Bridey's growing frustration.

'It might be in his parents' names. I don't know how to reach them.'

'I have a copy of the title deeds. It doesn't belong to his parents. Mindaleny Ridge is a deceased estate that passed into state hands when no beneficiaries came forward to claim it.'

'But it's our home ...' Her words caught in the constriction in her throat. She blinked against the burn of tears.

'A home you are considered to be squatting in, unfortunately.' Leather squeaked as he leaned back to consider her thoughtfully. 'I'm afraid it's my duty to report the matter to police.'

Shock numbed Bridey's mind. 'We have nowhere to go.'

Dean leaned forward, his stern expression softening a little. 'Bridey, we couldn't find a will filed or even a life insurance policy for your husband.'

Bridey covered her face with her hands, willing the

panic that coiled in her chest to subside. Even from the grave, Thom still kept throwing his punches. Anger warred with the sadness and terror that churned inside her. All she had left now was the children, and they had to be her priority.

'Please, help me. I have the boys to take care of and another baby on the way. Please don't report us until I've had a chance to find somewhere else to stay.' How she would do that with no money aside from what was left of her housekeeping allowance, she had no clue.

'What about friends? Family? Can they help out?'

Bridey shook her head. 'I have no one.' She could feel his gaze travel over her, taking in her blouse, the red scarf on her head as he reached an assumption.

'What about your church?'

The terror that the Children of the New Lord church would be her only option raised bile in her throat. 'If we're squatting, how come no one has reported us before? I've lived on the farm for over seven years now, and Thom lived there with his parents before that. Everyone in town knows we live there and would have known who lived there before us.'

Clutching at straws as reality crept in, Bridey's thoughts turned to the barren farm. It explained so much. The abandoned machinery, the sorting shed that had stood silent in all the time she'd lived there.

Thom's lack of skill when it came to farming. His half-hearted attempts at planting the strawberry field.

'I don't know the answers. Abandoned properties bring all kinds of trouble to small towns. It's possible everyone was simply happy that it wasn't standing empty.' Dean shrugged. 'Look, I'm no lawyer, but given your circumstances, I'll make a suggestion. You might consider applying for adverse possession if the family have lived in the property for over ten years and can prove that you've made improvements in the time that you've lived there.'

Bridey's laugh bordered on hysterical. Did an arsonist on the property, a burned down shed, barren fields, an illegal drug laboratory and a people smuggling operation count as improvements? Probably not. It would only give the state more reason to evict them.

Dean reached out to push a business card toward her. 'This is the name of the closest law firm. Why don't you reach out to see if they can assist you? I'll hold off reporting this to the senior-sergeant-in-charge for a week or so. Perhaps you could raise this matter with him yourself?'

Bridey took the card, a useless piece of paper when she didn't have money for food, let alone a lawyer to defend her for a property she'd never had the right to own. Dead inside, she gathered up her bag and the boys, thanked the bank manager, and walked out. A week ... If nothing else, it gave her a little more time to find a path out of the hell Thom had left behind.

～

Cole waited for Bridey and the children to get out of the car. He'd stalled the search for as long as he could, waiting with the search warrant in his hand. He hated to be the one to add to the mountain of problems her husband had left behind.

He'd spent every night since the fire at Mindaleny Ridge patrolling the area around the farm, making sure Bridey and her children were safe. And, on the occasions he'd popped in to check on them, he hadn't missed the fact that she had a shotgun placed within easy reach for herself but high up out of the reach of the children. The dark circles under her eyes testified to the fact that she was getting as little sleep as he was.

Apprehension clung to her expression as she approached him. He hated that she had every reason to associate him with more bad news.

'Bridey. Hello, boys.'

'Sergeant.'

The inevitable caution that coloured her greeting made him feel like a traitor. He wished more than ever that this was a case he could solve quickly and erase from the whiteboard.

'How did it go at the bank?'

'As well as can be expected.' Her shrug and the way she avoided looking him in the eye spoke volumes about the outcome of her meeting with the new bank manager. Her shoulders sagged, the strain of the last few weeks etched into her being and exacting its toll.

Cole shot a glance at Constable Nick O'Hare waiting for his signal to go ahead and open up the trapdoor. 'I'm sorry to be the one to add more to your troubles.' There'd be gossip for the dinner tables around Moonie River tonight for sure. He held out the piece of paper to her. 'It's a warrant to search under the trapdoor.'

Bridey stared at the paper as if she expected it to burst into flames the way the shed had. 'You didn't need one, Sergeant.'

She'd stopped calling him by his name, building a fresh brick wall between them. 'Protocol. Did you want to be present when we open it up?'

Bridey took the piece of paper and unfolded it. 'Yes. I need to know all the secrets Thom had hidden away. There've been enough nasty surprises. I'd like to think that all you'll find down there is cobwebs and some old farming tools.'

'I hope that's all we'll find.' He looked down at

Alex who stared back at him with serious eyes. 'How are your hands?'

Alex shrugged. 'They sting a bit. Doc put bandages on.' He held out his hands to show Cole. 'Mum has to put stuff on them two times a day.'

'They'll be better in no time at all then.' Cole reached out to ruffle Alex's hair.

'Alex, take your brothers inside, please. I'll be there in a little while.' Bridey herded them up the back stairs into the house before walking beside Cole to where the trapdoor beckoned.

Their hands brushed, and Cole held hers briefly before letting go again. 'It will be fine, Bridey.'

'I hope so.' She stopped short of the edge of the trapdoor.

Cole gave Nick the go ahead and they began to pry open the metal warped by the heat of the fire. The door squeaked on rusty hinges before clanging backward onto the ground, sending up a puff of dust and ash left over from the fire.

'We have stairs, Sarge. More a makeshift ladder, really.' Nick shone his torch into the black hole. 'Looks like a sea container someone buried at some point. Can't see much from this angle, so I'll go in.' He removed his gloves from his belt and put them on.

Cole watched Nick disappear into the hole, the

light from his torch fading as he descended. Beside him, Bridey stood silent with her arms crossed, shoulders tense, and he wondered how much more she could take.

From inside the container, Nick's voice echoed out. 'Sarge, you need to get down here. I've found something.'

Cole read the warning in his tone and glanced at Bridey. 'Go inside and wait with the children. I'll come and find you when we're done.'

She nodded, her face pale, resignation in her eyes that she was about to be hit by yet another blow. As she walked away, Cole lifted his phone from his pocket and dialled Doc's number.

'Sarge? Is everything all right?' Doc's voice filled with apprehension.

'Hey, Doc. If you're not tied up at the surgery, I might need you out at Mindaleny Ridge. Bridey's had a few shocks today and I'm a little concerned about her. With the baby on the way and everything that's happened, I'm not sure how she's holding up.'

'Sure thing. I'd planned to come out and check on her anyway. I'm on my way.'

'Thanks, Doc.'

Cole hung up, put on his gloves, and made his way down the ladder into the container. Nick had found a switch to the single, dull globe that dangled from the roof, throwing a glow into the shadows of a six-metre-long shipping container.

'What have we got?' His eyes adjusted to the light.

'Over in the back corner.' Nick led the way, his torch aimed at a pile of rags.

Cole added his torch light. 'Bones.'

'Judging by the clothing, a male and female.' Nick pointed to cavities in the skulls. 'Blunt force trauma?'

'Possibly.' Cole picked up a ragged leather wallet lying in the dirt and flipped it open. 'So ... it looks like Mr and Mrs McCaffrey didn't take off in their caravan after all.' Dropping the wallet into the evidence bag Nick held out, he sighed. 'We'll have to get Forensics back down here. It looks like we may have a murder scene on our hands.'

'Poor Bridey. This will be another shock for her.' Nick shook his head.

'Unless she knew about it.' He hated to think that she may be involved.

'I doubt it, Sarge. Bridey came to town a while after the McCaffreys supposedly left. They'd gone before I arrived at the station, and I was posted here before Bridey came to live at Mindaleny.'

'Damn it.' Cole removed his glove to drag his hand down his face. 'Anything else down here?'

'A heap of boxes and junk that may or may not

have something in them that might serve as evidence. We'd have to go through it all.'

'Right. Let's seal the place up and get the forensics team back down here. I'll go and break the news to Bridey.' He turned away from the remains and walked towards the ladder.

'Sarge, what if the person who started the fire comes back? This might be exactly what they were trying to destroy.'

'We'll take turns on watch until Forensics is done.' What he really wanted was to pack Bridey and the kids up and move them somewhere safe, away from the horrors they'd endured. 'Would you mind making the call to Perth and arrange for the team to get out here ASAP?'

'Sure thing, Sarge. Poor Bridey. You'd think she'd endured enough.' Nick stamped the dust and ash from his boots.

'You'd think. All I can say, mate, is that it's a good thing Thomas McCaffrey is already dead because I sure as hell would have great satisfaction in throwing his arse in jail and tossing away the key.'

Nick agreed. 'I'm with you there. I was unlucky enough to have a few run-ins with the bloke. Why Bridey stayed with him is a total mystery to me.'

'That's the sad fact of victims of domestic violence, Nick. Leaving is often the hardest thing to do.'

Cole placed his boot on the bottom rung of the ladder and gripped the sides to haul himself up it. Could he convince her to leave Mindaleny Ridge after this latest find? Would that be the final catalyst after all she'd endured? But if she left town, he'd never see them again. He didn't quite know what to do with that thought. As he climbed the ladder towards daylight, he was torn between convincing her to leave and begging her to stay.

Chapter Eleven

Bridey watched from the kitchen window as Cole approached the house, her stomach sinking at the serious look on his face. What else had Thom kept hidden? How much more would they uncover?

She thought of the upper levels of the house and wondered what was waiting to be uncovered up there. Please, God, no more surprises. The stairs had been boarded up ever since she'd arrived. Thom had made it perfectly clear that the space was off limits and that she was to keep to the bottom floor. How often had she had it drummed into her that it cost money to run a place this size?

Cole climbed the stairs, and Bridey opened the back door to let him in. 'How bad is it?'

'Bad enough for me to have to ask you some questions, I'm sorry.'

Bridey studied his face, her hands over her growing baby bump. She thought of Kirana and the girls they'd found in the containers, the loss of lives Thom had caused, the harm he'd done, the secrets he'd kept. She'd lain awake every night since Thom's death mulling over the secrets she'd been forced to keep, the lies she'd been told, the things she'd been made to do in the name of the Children of the New Lord. Doubts warred with logic now that she could see things more clearly, and Thom wasn't there to convince her otherwise.

'Come and sit down then. I'll make some tea.'

'Doc's on his way over. I asked him to come. I'm worried about you and the baby.'

Bridey nodded. 'Thank you. I appreciate that.' She turned to put the kettle on to boil.

Beside her, Cole folded his arms and leaned back against the kitchen bench. 'I'll need you to tell me everything, Bridey. Including whatever you know about the church.'

'No more secrets.' She wanted to ask him what they'd found under the trap door but a part of her didn't want to know. She'd find out soon enough. 'I'll just check on the boys while the kettle boils.'

Cole laid a gentle hand on her arm. 'I really am

sorry, Bridey. I'll help in any way I can to make this easier for you and the boys.'

'I appreciate that, Sergeant.' She drew in a deep breath and blew it out slowly.

All her life, she'd kept things secret, bottled up inside, the Pandora's Box now full to overflowing as Thom's hands continued to reach for her throat beyond the grave. She desperately wanted to spill the overflow, accept Cole's offer of help as the real threat of homelessness reared its head. Could she trust this man with her secrets and the safety of her boys? He was the law, and the law wasn't on her side. Bridey turned to look at Cole. His mouth and jaw were pulled tight, but his eyes were soft with empathy. Her throat jammed on words, her eyes burned with the threat of tears as she stood at the crossroads of her life, forced to choose a path. One led to an unholy hell, the other led to the unknown.

'We have to leave Mindaleny Ridge.'

'Why? The property should pass on to you as the next of kin.'

She shook her head. 'Thom didn't own the property and neither did his parents. According to the bank manager, the house and land is part of an abandoned deceased estate. He's advised me to apply for adverse possession. He is obligated to inform you that we're living here illegally, so I'm doing it for him.' Her heart ached with the knowledge that her options had narrowed right down. The walls of secrecy crumbled. 'I don't know what to do. I have nowhere to go. I don't want to return to the Children of the New Lord compound, but I may not have a choice. They're the only family I know. I need to feed the boys. And the baby when it comes. I haven't even paid the funeral director for Thom's funeral yet.'

Cole frowned. 'There are alternatives. Did the bank manager tell you about some of the social support options you can apply for?'

Bridey shook her head. 'No, but even if he had, I wouldn't even know where to start. I didn't realise until now how closed off I am from the real world. Thom handled everything related to finances. I cooked and cleaned and raised the children. When I started going through Thom's office, all I found was overdue bills.'

Outside, a car pulled up. 'Doc's here.' Cole turned towards the kitchen bench. 'I'll make the tea while you go and check on the boys. Once I've wrapped things up here, we can talk about a few things I can do to help, like look into the laws around adverse possession. I'll take you into town to the welfare office so we can get the ball rolling on some assistance for you.'

'You'd do that for me?' Her eyes searched his face, so far above hers. His size didn't threaten her the way

Thom's had. She felt safe in his presence. Maybe because he represented good rather than evil.

'For you, for the boys, and for the baby.' A shadow crossed his face, and in that moment, she recognised a sadness in him.

'You've lost someone too.'

Cole nodded. 'My wife and baby.'

'I'm sorry.' She covered his hand with hers where he'd braced himself against the kitchen bench.

'Thank you.' Cole turned his head to look at her. 'It takes a while, Bridey, but time heals. Memories remain.' He reached out to run his thumb across her cheek softly, her hand slipping from his. 'You're young. You have the children. This is your second chance to live the life you want to, where you want to, and make the best of it. I will help you in a way I couldn't help Carrie because I was too late.'

She placed a hand over his heart, feeling the steady beat as she closed her eyes, the seriousness in his too much to handle. 'Then we'll help each other.'

'I like the sound of that.'

Doc's knock at the door had them stepping apart. 'I'll be back as soon as I've checked on the boys.'

As Cole turned to greet Doc, Bridey walked out of the kitchen to the lounge room where the boys played together, her fist pressed to the heaviness in her heart and confusion in her mind. She'd never felt that sizzle and spark with Thom, that connection that bounced between them like a lightning bolt. She and Cole shared a loss, a common connection. His went deeper than the relief she'd felt once the shock had passed.

Her challenge now was what the future held for her family. She couldn't change what Thom had done or the years that had passed, but she could make a difference to their future and that would mean getting in touch with the world outside of Mindaleny Ridge. Starting today, whatever the secrets about to spew out from the cellar.

Satisfied that the boys were settled playing their game, she returned to the kitchen. Life had dealt so many blows already, what was one more?

'Bridey! How are you feeling, my dear?' Doc's cheerful voice was a balm to her soul. In all the turmoil since she'd arrived on the farm outside Moonie River, he'd been her rock-solid port in a storm. But even he didn't know everything.

'I'm managing, Doc.' She turned to Cole. 'Let's get this out of the way.'

He nodded and pulled out a chair for her to sit then placed her cup of tea in front of her. 'Are you comfortable with Doc being present to hear all this?'

'Yes. I'd prefer it. I'm sure you'll have questions he can back up the answers for.' She wrapped her hands around the mug, absorbing the comfort of its warmth.

Cole sat opposite her and placed his phone on the table between them. 'Do you mind if I record the conversation? Much easier than trying to take notes.'

Bridey shook her head. 'I have no problem with that, Sergeant.' She'd allowed him to slip past her defences earlier, but this was police business, and she had to put him back in that box.

'Starting the recording now.' He pressed the red dot to start his voice memo. 'Bridey, have you ever met your husband's family?'

'No. Thom was an only child, and his parents left the farm before we got married.'

'Did you have any contact with them after you were married? A phone call, a letter, an email?'

'No. Thom said they were travelling around Australia and not contactable. The family don't believe in using mobile phones or computers.'

'The family?'

'The church family. The Children of our New Lord.'

'And you were a member of this church?'

'Yes.'

'Yet you never met your husband's family.'

'It's not that kind of church.' Bridey swallowed the bile that rose in her throat.

Cole frowned. 'What do you mean?'

'It's not a church like the one in town where the

people gather together and sing and be happy. It's a community for lost children. The New Lord runs care homes for orphans and runaways. He recruits handlers to take care of them. We were taught how to take care of a home, serve and obey a man, and when we were ready, the New Lord would arrange a marriage with a suitable husband. Some had more than one wife.'

An oath slipped out, as Cole closed his eyes and pinched the bridge of his nose. 'How old were the girls when they were given in marriage?'

'It depended on how fast they learned. Some learned faster than others. Some were defiant and needed more time and punishment.'

'Punishment?'

'If a girl was defiant, their handler would call in the New Lord. He would deliver their punishment according to their misdeed. Beatings, solitary confinement ...'

Bridey covered her mouth as the memories flooded back in and nausea threatened. She couldn't bring herself to voice the awful things that had happened in confinement when the New Lord came to deliver his punishment. It had been enough for most girls never to resist their lot again.

Cole's voice fell into the silence, his words full of understanding. 'We can stop now and finish this later if you need to.'

Bridey dropped her hand from her mouth, picked up her cup and took a sip of tea. All the questions about Thom's parents. Had they disobeyed the New Lord? She'd seen the consequences of handlers defying his rule too. 'I need to know what you found down there, Sergeant.' Even when every nerve in her system already suspected what they'd found. In what way had Thomas's parents displeased the New Lord?

Cole leaned forward, his gaze holding hers. 'Bones. Most likely the remains of Thom's parents.'

Bridey pushed her chair back, rose from the table, and ran for the bathroom.

~

Cole turned off the recording as Doc followed Bridey to check on her, his mind spinning.

What kind of a sick individual was this church leader? Had he known about the murders? Was that perhaps the motive for setting fire to the shed? And why leave the bodies in a secret cellar? Why not bury them or dump them somewhere? Or had Thomas McCaffrey kept their remains as trophies?

He had more questions than answers, but at least he had a lead. The problem was, following that lead might put Bridey and her children in more danger, especially once the story leaked about finding the remains. There'd be no way of keeping that quiet in a small town where people already speculated about the McCaffreys and Mindaleny Ridge. Add to that the fact that they'd been squatting on abandoned land. Another mystery for him to solve. How had they got away with it in a community where everyone knew everyone else's business?

A knock at the door diverted his attention to Nick who stood in the doorway.

'Sarge, I think you need to see this.'

Cole rubbed his forehead where an ache had begun to form. 'What have you found?'

'Whoever set fire to the shed had reason to. If young Alex hadn't interrupted them, they would have destroyed evidence.'

'Evidence of what?'

Nick shrugged. 'Evidence that maybe Thomas McCaffrey was involved in people smuggling. Might be a motive for why there are two bodies down there. Maybe Mum and Dad McCaffrey stumbled onto what their son was involved in and ended up down there with it.'

Cole pushed up from the table and put his phone in his pocket. 'We can't afford to speculate. And it doesn't explain why someone else wanted the shed burned down to destroy the evidence post mortem. But if there is something down there that is worth destroying, it means the firebug might not be done yet. If he's gone for the shed, he could come back for the house. God knows what else we're going to uncover.'

As he followed Nick back down the ladder into the depths of the buried container, Cole dreaded to think what else the house might be hiding. He walked to where Nick had gathered boxes under the dim light.

'I found these going through the boxes and bagging things I thought might be evidence.' He lifted up a pile of small books in his gloved hand.

'Passports?'

'And birth certificates. From all over the world. Some of them match the girls we found in the containers over the ridge.'

Cole swore as he peered into the box. 'Which begs the question of where the rest of these people are.'

'It sure hints at people smuggling. Confiscate their ID, maybe create new ones for them?'

'They may not have needed new identities. Not if they all end up living like Bridey did. No modern technology, no need for a passport because they don't travel anywhere, and little or no contact with the outside world. No welfare registration because they don't exist in the system.' Was Bridey's face on one of those passports? The sick feeling grew in his gut. What kind of monsters were the people behind this? Could one man wield this much power working alone? 'I'm not liking the direction this investigation is taking. When Forensics hit town again and word gets out, the farm will attract a lot of attention. And if the media gets hold of it ...'

'It'll bring hordes of stickybeaks to Bridey's door.'

'Exactly.' The dull ache transformed into a steady thump in his head. It was that kind of attention that had gotten his own family killed. 'We managed to fly under the radar when we found the girls because that news hasn't leaked yet. This find will only bring more focus on what's been happening at Mindaleny Ridge, and someone out there is bound to talk to the press.'

'Should I load all these boxes up and take them to the station to sort out there? In case someone decides to come poking around in here.'

'Yep, let's load them up. When you get back to the station, give Detective Senior Sergeant Mark Johnson at the Organised Crimes Unit a call. Let him know we're dealing with more than just a simple case of people smuggling and murder. And tell him I don't want anyone on this case but him and his team.'

'Will do, Sarge.'

'I'll help you load these up and go check on Bridey. We're going to have to step up security for her. Once the press starts to connect the dots, it's going to be mayhem. Nick, has anyone ever mentioned the name Pastor Camden to you?'

'Pastor Camden?' Nick's hands stilled on repacking the passports into the boxes.

'You know him?'

'Not personally. He was in Mrs Lee's shop one day when I was there. This was years ago. Not long after the McCaffrey's bought Mindaleny Ridge. Not my idea of what a pastor should look like, but then I'm not much of a churchgoer.' Nick shrugged. 'I just thought he looked ... cold. There was something about him that made my skin crawl.'

'Mrs Lee said the same thing. She thought he was a bit creepy.'

'It's a while ago, and I didn't think anything of it at the time, but he asked for directions to Mindaleny Ridge. Mrs Lee was reluctant to tell him, but our resident sticky beaker was in the shop, and old Mrs Wilkins is always happy to share information. Especially after she's had her tipple of the homemade sherry at the bingo hall. That stuff could rival truth serum any day.'

'Did he say why he was looking for them?'

'He said they were part of his flock, and he wanted to check up on them to see if they were settling in all right.'

'A plausible enough reason.' Not one that flew with what they'd uncovered in the last few weeks.

'Unless they moved to get away from him and his church? It could also be why they're not alive to talk.'

'All things we're going to have to prove.' Cole rubbed at the ache behind his eyes. 'Let's get rolling on the paperwork and entering all this as evidence. I'm going to need a strong coffee and some painkillers.' The last thing he needed was a damn headache.

Cole lugged boxes up the ladder with Nick close behind until the last carton was loaded and the tailgate of the SUV was closed.

'You go ahead and get started, mate. I'll catch a lift back with Doc.'

'Sure, no worries, Sarge.'

Cole stood for a moment as Nick drove away. He looked around at the farm, the trees that hid the secrets beyond the ridge, the ground where the shed had once stood. Slamming the door shut on the grave in the container, he locked it up and re-tied the police tape. So much for quiet country policing.

As he turned towards the house, he spotted Doc coming down the stairs. 'How's Bridey doing?'

Doc shook his head. 'Not great. Her blood pressure is up which is understandable. She's resting now. I'm worried, Cole. All this stress isn't good for her or the baby. The poor girl can't take much more.'

Cole hooked his thumbs into the loops on his belt. 'I'm aware of that, Doc.'

'I don't like it that she is so isolated out here and alone.'

'I'm not happy about it either. I'm going to organise a rotating watch until Forensics have been. I want to make sure no one interferes with the evidence. Please keep the find between us. I don't want the press or anyone else jumping fences for an interview or a sticky beak.'

'Not a word, I promise.' Doc shuffled his feet in the dust, his eyes focused on something over Cole's shoulder. 'I can't say too much. Patient confidentiality and all that. But Bridey isn't responsible for any of what happened here.' His gaze returned to search Cole's. 'If you'd seen that girl on the few occasions Thom allowed her to receive medical treatment, you'd understand.'

'I saw the bruises.'

'It was far worse than that sometimes. I, for one, am not sorry Thomas McCaffrey is dead.'

'I think there's a queue of people who feel the same, Doc.'

'Keep her safe. The girl doesn't need any more violence in her life, and neither do those children.'

'I'll do the absolute best I can.'

'I know you will.' Doc sighed. 'Need a lift into town? I see your ride has left.'

'Thanks. Can I check on Bridey first? I just want to let her know I'll be back to take first watch.'

Doc patted his shoulder and moved around him to the car. 'You do that. I'll be here waiting when you're ready.'

Cole made his way up the stairs, hoping he could keep that promise.

Chapter Twelve

Bridey rose from the bed, unable to rest as Doc had ordered her to. The children were too quiet. They'd spent their whole existence being quiet, tiptoeing around Thom and his moods. She'd rest more comfortably hearing them now. There'd been far too much silence and too many secrets on the farm.

With a sigh, she slipped her feet into her shoes. Lying down gave her too much time to think. Had Thom really murdered his parents and just left them to decay in an underground cellar? She hated to think about the pain they may have endured.

Questions swam in her head as she walked to the kitchen. She didn't doubt for a minute that Thom was capable of murder. Enduring her punishments, she'd often wondered if this might be the last time she'd draw a breath. The only thing that had stopped her from giving up was the thought of what would happen to the children. And his last threat had been that if she tried to run away again, he'd kill the children first and make her regret it for the rest of her life. The pain of that alone might have killed her. There'd been many a time when she'd wondered if death for them all was the only way out. So, yes, Thom had been perfectly capable of murdering his parents.

The boys sat building blocks at the table. She'd heard Doc explain to them that she needed to rest for a while, listened to their quiet agreement. And Cole was coming back. They'd be safe tonight.

Alex looked up from the ship he was building. 'Are you okay, Mum?'

She ruffled his hair. 'I'm fine, baby.'

'I'm not a baby.' His bottom lip quivered.

'Of course, you're not. You're the man of the house now. But you'll always be my baby, Alex. Now, I think we still have some of Gus's soup in the freezer. How about I bake some fresh bread, and we can have that for dinner tonight?' She'd never given them a choice before, she realised. She'd never had the means to.

'I like soup and bread.' Shaun stopped sorting the blocks into colours.

'I like bread and soup.' Garrett grinned up at her.

Bridey laughed and kissed the top of their heads.

This is what had kept her alive. 'What about you, Alex?'

Alex shrugged.

'How about you choose what's for dinner tomorrow night? There is still plenty of food in the freezer to choose from.'

Alex nodded. 'I like Mrs Lee's curry chicken.'

'Then we'll have that tomorrow,' Bridey agreed.

She took the food out of the freezer and placed it in the sink to defrost. 'Do you boys want to play outside for a while? I need to hang out the washing.'

'Can we pick wildflowers?' Garrett scrambled off his chair, eyes alight.

'Can we dig in the garden?' If Thom had been more interested in his children, he would have recognised that Shaun would be the farmer. Not that it mattered now because the farm didn't belong to them.

Alex said nothing. He walked into the laundry and came back with the peg basket. 'The laundry basket was too heavy. One day I'll be able to carry it for you.'

Bridey hugged him close. 'Thank you, Alex.'

Dear God, how she wished for a normal life for her children. A happy life, a place with no violence, murder, or fires. Which brought her back to who'd started the fire in the shed if it wasn't Alex. If it was the New Lord, would he come back to finish what he'd started? Had he known about the McCaffreys' deaths?

Was he involved in the capture of those women and children too? It would explain how the Children of the New Lord had come to be. Why so many orphans and unwanted children had come to live at the compound. And it all raised so many questions around everything she'd been raised to think was normal.

The afternoon sun warmed her back as she hung out the washing. The boys played in a barren vegetable patch, digging in the soil with some old plastic pots Thom had dumped around the side of the house. She could dream that she'd get their finances sorted and find a new place to stay. She could look for some toys for them to play with, a ball they could bounce outside. Freedom. Choices. Picnics on the grass. All the things they could have and do now that Thom was gone, except for the one threat that remained.

For now, she had some measure of protection in Cole, but when the investigations wrapped up, she'd be alone again. And that was the one thing that kept her from telling Cole that she knew who may have set the potting shed alight and who would have every reason to destroy evidence in order to keep his sacred church a secret, as he had done many times before. She dared not tell. Not when he'd already tried to harm Alex.

The sound of a car engine had her shoulders tensing up. Too early to be Cole. Old instincts made her want to gather up the boys and hide, but as the vehicle drew closer, she recognised it as Gus's SUV. Releasing her breath, she continued to hang the last few items in the basket. The boys liked Gus. As he climbed out the vehicle, the twins spotted him.

'It's Gus!' Shaun shot up out of the garden patch, covered in soil and rushed over to wrap his arms around Gus's leg.

'Hey there, little guy.' Gus smiled down at him as Garrett attached himself to his other leg. He reached down to ruffle their hair. 'Looking a little grubby there, boys.'

Mortified at the soil now covering his jeans, Bridey tried to call the boys back. 'Gus, I'm so sorry! Look at the mess they've made of your pants.' Thom would have had a fit.

'Nah, it's all good, Bridey. A little dirt never harmed anyone.' He scooped Shaun up onto his back. 'Hang tight, little fella, while I pick your brother up.'

The boys' laughter filled the air, the sweetest sound to Bridey's ears. At her side, Alex stood watching. She placed her hand on his skinny shoulders. 'They're safe with Gus.'

He shrugged. 'I know.'

Gus walked over and eased the twins to the ground. 'Hi, Alex.'

'Hi.' His grip on her skirt released.

'What brings you out here?' Bridey smiled up at Gus.

'Mrs Lee has sent me on a mission. She was cleaning out the storeroom at the shop and she found some things the boys might like.'

'That's very kind of her.' Mrs Lee had always been kind to them. Maybe one day she could repay some of that kindness in some way. Venture beyond the gates of the farm without the need to rush home in fear of punishment.

'She's a sweetheart. She also sent your mail. I'll go and grab the box of stuff from the car in a minute.'

'Do you have time for a cuppa?' Bridey ushered the boys inside.

'I was hoping you'd offer.' Gus grinned. 'I brought a cake just in case. Baked this morning. Chocolate, of course.'

'How can we say no to that?' Bridey laughed.

'Are we allowed cake, Mum?' Alex tugged on her arm.

'Of course you are. You boys have been so good at helping me today, I think a treat is well deserved.' Her reward was Alex's smile. He hadn't used it in a long time. 'Come along, let's put the kettle on.'

Gus fetched in a cardboard box and placed it on the kitchen floor. He scooped a pile of mail off the top, handed it to Bridey, and removed the container with the cake in it before turning to the boys. 'Get in there, boys. Remember to share though.'

The boys gathered around the box, staring at the pile of toys inside, hesitant to touch anything. They looked at Bridey, waiting for her permission.

'Go ahead. Once you've sorted through it, you can all sit down and write a thank you note to Mrs Lee and ask Gus nicely if he'll deliver it for you.'

'It will be my pleasure.'

Bridey poured the tea and placed a cup in front of Gus. 'Would you like to stay for dinner? We're having soup and I'm just about to bake a loaf of bread.'

'Thank you, I'd like that.' He looked down as Garrett patted his arm. 'What have you got there, young man?'

'I found a ball. A big orange one.'

'Ah, that's a basketball. Pretty cool, huh? How about when I'm done with my cake and tea, we go outside, and I'll show you a few tricks with the ball?'

Shaun looked up from the box. 'Can I come?'

'Of course you can! Basketball needs a team. If we had four people, we could play two-a-side. What about it, Alex?'

'I don't know how.'

'I didn't know how either until I started practising. How about you give it a try? If you don't like it, that's perfectly acceptable, but you won't know if you don't try.' Gus's gentle coaxing won Alex over.

'Fine, I'll try.'

'Great! Now come over and eat your cake first, then we'll go play ball while your mum bakes the bread.'

The boys scoffed down the cake and drank all their juice with an appetite that had been missing for a long time. Bridey smiled as Gus herded them out the door. Maybe things would be okay after all. Maybe the New Lord would leave them be now.

~

Cole entered the station, pleased that he'd stopped off to see his dad first. At least he could get some work done knowing that Gus was out at Mindaleny Ridge, keeping an eye on things.

The station was quiet now the investigation team had returned to Perth. The next wave would be the immigration officers once the captives were well enough to talk, and the forensics team back again for round two.

There'd be more questions to ask, more decisions to be made about charges to be laid, and a long list of suspects to be followed up before Bridey was free of that nightmare.

'Anything exciting happen while I was out?' Cole tossed his hat on his desk and raised an eyebrow at Constable Sam Mayne.

Sam had been at the station almost as long as Nick had. Cole counted his lucky stars that he had two officers for back up. Most of the small-town stations he'd applied to had none. But they did have a larger area to cover. The recent intake of officers from overseas had also boosted their numbers in the much-needed rural areas.

'The Donnelly girl got caught shoplifting again.'

Sunshine Donnelly was anything but a ray of sunshine. Cole had found that out the hard way when he'd tried to talk to the little hellion the last time she'd lifted stuff from Mrs Lee's store. 'What did she take this time?'

'Deodorant, lip balm, soap and a roast chicken.'

Staples. Things she needed to have some semblance of a normal life. Cole sighed. 'Did you talk to her?'

Sam shook her head. 'Didn't have to. One of the CWA ladies offered to pay for the goods and took her over to the bowling club to use the shower.'

'I'll go have a chat to her mum.'

Sam scoffed. 'Good luck finding her sober, and in any shape to care. Sunshine's dad took off and left them. Elle's been in a downward slide since then. Not that she cared much for Sunshine before that even. If it wasn't for Mrs Lee and the CWA, the kid would probably have run away by now.'

He didn't get it. Why did people have kids if they had no intention of caring for them? And then there were those who had all the love to give and no children to give it to. He'd looked so forward to being a dad.

'What about you, Nick? Find anything interesting in those boxes.'

'Dunno about interesting, Sarge. I'd call it downright disturbing that there are so many.' He turned to point to the organised evidence bags lined up on the desk behind him. 'Passports. All different countries, some Australian. I've sorted them into the countries they've come from.'

'Nice work. We can start running checks against the missing persons lists. Did you call Mark?'

'Yep. He's on the case already.'

'Good work. I need to organise a rotating watch at Mindaleny Ridge until forensics have processed the remains. I'll take first watch tonight. Sam, can you please do 6am to midday? Nick, if you can do midday to 6pm, I'll take night watch again.' He picked up his hat. 'Would you mind getting started on those missing persons matches? I'm going to pay Mrs Donnelly a visit.'

'Good luck with that, Sarge.' Nick grinned.

'Thanks.' He hadn't met Elle Donnelly yet, but if her daughter was an example to go by, maybe it was time to file a report with social services.

Located off the main street a block from the station and close to the bottle store, the Donnelly house painted a picture of neglect that had started long before Sunshine's dad left.

Cole knocked at the door. 'Mrs Donnelly?'

'What?' The shout came from the front lounge room.

'It's Sergeant Delany. Can I come in please? I need to talk to you about Sunshine.'

'Fuck me. What's the little troll done now?' Elle ripped the door open.

The stench of alcohol and cigarettes had Cole taking a step back.

'She was caught stealing.'

'So what? Who cares? Throw her in jail for all I care. Her bloody father shoulda taken her with him.'

'I'm sure you don't mean that, Elle.' Cole looked over her matted blonde head into the gloomy depths of the messy house. The stale smell of slow decay drifted out.

'I fucking do.' The fight left Elle's lungs in a long, smelly breath. 'I can't do this anymore. I can't.' She collapsed at his feet in a mess of old pyjamas that hung from her skinny frame and hair that hadn't seen shampoo or a brush in who knew how long.

Taking a deep breath, Cole hauled her up and sat her on the tattered old armchair on the front verandah. 'We're going to get you some help, Elle.'

'Don't need it.'

'I think you do.'

'Fuck you.' Her response had less blister in it than before.

'Mind your language.' Cole moved away to the edge of the verandah and hit call on Doc's number in his phone and waited.

'Bridey again?' The concern in Doc's voice came across clearly.

'Elle Donnelly. We need to get social services involved.'

'That bad, huh? I'll give them a call, but it might take a while to get someone down here.'

'No one local?'

Doc laughed, the sound bitter. 'The department cut costs. It's wait for someone to get here from the Perth office or wait until the mobile service bus comes around next month.'

'They don't make it easy do they, Doc? Where can I get help for these people until social services get here?'

'We've all tried to help Elle at some point, Sarge.

She chases everyone away. With a broom. All we can do is make sure Sunshine gets food and the odd shower.'

Cole squeezed the bridge of his nose between his thumb and forefinger. So much for a quiet small town.

'If you happen to spot Sunshine anywhere around, can you take her to the station? I'm taking Elle in to get her sobered up.'

'I'm not goin' anywhere with you.' Elle's grumble had no fight left in it.

'Since you're in no state to hold a broom, let alone chase me off with one, I'd say you have no choice.'

Doc chuckled from the other end of the phone. 'Good luck with that, Sarge.'

'Thanks, Doc.' Cole hung up and hauled Elle out of the chair. 'Come on, Elle, up you get. I'm taking you down to the station.'

'For what?' She tried to shake him off but the combination of too much alcohol and too little food had made her weak.

Cole couldn't help wondering, if he'd left it any longer, if he'd have had another body on his hands. 'I don't know yet. Maybe I can arrest you for stinking the place up? Or how about we go with neglecting a minor?'

Elle had the sense to look ashamed. In that moment he saw the real Elle, the woman who'd lost

everything, all hope of coming out on the other side a
survivor.

'This is your chance to turn things around, Elle.
Don't waste it. Come on, a walk in the fresh air will
help clear your head.'

'Not doin' the walk of shame.' She tried to tug
away. 'People will talk.'

'A bit late for that, don't you think?' Cole raised an
eyebrow at her.

'Go f...'

'Don't you dare tell me to go fuck myself because
then I'd have to add abuse of a police officer to the
charges. Let's go. Quietly. The less fuss you make, the
easier this will be.' He walked her off the verandah and
down the front path, through the gate. 'I'm trying to
help you here.'

'Don't need your effing help. Or theirs,' Elle
grumbled as they walked toward the station, turning a
few heads along the way.

Pushing open the door, he guided her inside. 'I'm
going to suggest you accept our help, whether you want
it or not.'

Sam looked up from logging the evidence from the
boxes, confusion on her face. 'Sarge?'

'Elle will be our guest for the night. Nick, lock the
boxes away for now. I need you to go and find
Sunshine. Pick up a change of clothes from the Op

Shop for both of them. I'll give you some cash. Sam, can you help Elle get cleaned up? She can sleep it off in room one. Sunshine can have room two, so we know she'll be okay tonight. And this means a change of plans with the Mindaleny watch. I'll take the 6am shift as well if you can you stay with these two tonight?'

'Sure can, Sarge.' She smiled as she took Elle's arm. 'Come along, Elle. You'll feel better after a shower.'

'Don't give my constable any trouble, Elle,' Cole warned. 'This is your one and only chance.'

Nick came back from locking away the evidence boxes. 'Should I pick up some food for them too, Sarge?'

Cole shook his head. 'I'll get Gus to bring something over for the Donnellys and for Sam. Thanks, Nick.' He picked up his car keys. 'I've got to get over to Mindaleny Ridge so Gus can come back and get ready for pub service tonight. Give me a call if there's any trouble.'

As Cole climbed into the police SUV, he realised that there'd been nothing but trouble since he'd arrived in Moonie River. And he was fairly sure peace wouldn't come for a while yet.

Chapter Thirteen

Bridey smiled. Gus had been entertaining the children with the toys from the box Mrs Lee had sent. Even Alex had joined in. She pressed a hand to her heart. This was what life should be like. A house filled with laughter, happy children playing out in the dirt and sunshine.

She'd had so much time, lying awake at night, thinking about her own childhood. How different would life have been if she'd had real parents? What if everything she'd learned in church was wrong? How could a God who had preached kindness and tolerance support the violent punishment she'd endured even for minor wrongs? It certainly wasn't what she wanted for her children.

Cole's police SUV rattled over the cattle grate into the yard. After seeing no one at the farm, except for Ed delivering the mail on occasion, she was getting used to seeing him. Even if the circumstances weren't pleasant. What would happen to the McCaffreys after their remains were removed? She couldn't help but think they at least deserved a decent burial.

Cole climbed out, removed his hat, and tossed it onto the front seat. Bridey's heart fluttered. Was it wrong for her to notice that he was an attractive man? And a kind man.

He stopped for a chat with Gus, admired the tractor Shaun showed him, dug a small trench with the digger Garrett gave him before turning to Alex. Whatever he said to Alex made her boy smile a little and her heart did another flutter. Was it wrong to wish Thom had been more like Cole? That their whole life hadn't been about hellfire and punishment, but about love and nurturing instead?

Cole entered the kitchen after knocking on the door. 'Hi, Bridey.'

'Hi.' She looked up at him as he came to stand beside her. 'You look tired.'

'It's been a helluva day. Have you met the Donnellys?'

Bridey shook her head. 'I only know Doc and Mr and Mrs Lee. And the bank manager now. Who are the Donnellys?'

'A single mum and her daughter who live in town.

171

They've gone through a rough patch too, and things got a bit too real for Elle today. Which reminds me ... I haven't forgotten about taking you down to register for welfare. The Moonie River Community Resources Centre runs the agency but they're only open on a Tuesday and Friday.'

'You sound like you're busy. I can go on my own. I need to learn to do these things now.' She turned to put the kettle on. 'Let me make you a coffee. You look like you could do with one.'

Cole grinned as he pulled out a chair and sat. 'I think that's the best word I've heard all day. Coffee. Strong and black, thank you.' He caught her hand in his as she stepped in behind him to the kitchen bench where the kettle stood. 'I'm here to help you, Bridey. Whenever you need help.'

The warmth of his hand on hers was reassuring, his touch gentle as his thumb absently stroked the back of her hand. The movement started a funny feeling inside her. Not fear, or annoyance or even awkwardness. It felt ... right ... and oh so wrong at the same time. So different yet so exciting.

She turned her head to look at him. 'Thank you.' The words came out on a whisper.

Their eyes met and held. Mesmerised by the heat in his gaze, she couldn't look away. Here was something she'd never felt before. Need. An almost overwhelming need she didn't understand. Thom had never made her feel this way. But then, she'd never felt safe in his arms or in his presence. Not in the way Cole made her feel safe, cared for.

'Bridey, I hate to do this, and I know it's painful, but I need to ask you more questions about Thom.'

'I know.' Bridey tugged her hand away and turned to make his coffee. Placing it in front of him, she took a seat at the table. 'I'm ready.'

Cole wrapped his hands around the mug. 'Can you tell me more about what happened in the lead up to Thom's death?'

She picked at a knot in the wooden table top. 'Thom was always angry about something, but in the last couple of years he grew worse. He'd disappear for hours, sometimes late at night. I didn't know what he was doing. He wouldn't tell me, and I dared not ask.' What was marriage like outside of The Children of the New Lord rules? Did man and wife discuss business together over dinner? She had no idea what normal was in the homes of outsiders.

'Did he ever mention the container set up on the other side of the ridge where we found Kirana and the girls?'

Bridey shook her head. 'No. Thom talked, I

listened.' She wouldn't have dared try to engage in conversation. Thom ordered. She obeyed. 'I had no idea that the other side of the ridge was even part of his land, and I don't recall him ever mentioning it.'

'How would you describe Thom's typical behaviour?'

'Angry. Drunk. Cruel ... Thom had the same approach to punishment that the New Lord has. If he thought I was being disrespectful or disobedient, he'd force me to stay in the house. He'd lock all the doors and windows so we couldn't leave. He'd tell me it was for my own good, that I needed to learn to listen to him. And if he thought I hadn't learned my lesson ...' Bridey broke off, the memories of broken bones and bruises too hard to think about. 'He'd beat me.'

Cole swore under his breath. 'This New Lord ... can you give me a name?'

She hesitated. Could she speak his name and risk his wrath if the outsiders went looking for and found him?

'Are you afraid of him, Bridey?'

On this she could be honest. 'Yes.'

'Okay, we'll come back to him later. How was Thom towards the children in those last days?'

'Thom didn't care about the children. If he thought they were misbehaving, it would be my fault, and I would take the punishment. The boys knew to find somewhere safe to wait things out. They'd hide under Alex's bed until I came to find them, and it was safe to come out.'

'Did you notice any significant changes in his mental state recently?'

Bridey took a deep breath and let it out slowly. Her fingers ached. She hadn't realised she'd entwined them so tight.

Cole reached for her hand, his touch warm on her icy skin. 'Let me know if you need to stop.'

'I need to do this. I need to move on.' She released another breath. 'Thom's spiral into the bottom of the whiskey bottle had us all walking on egg shells. We never knew what might trigger him. It might have been something as simple as a speck of dust on the furniture or the fact that I hadn't got around to vacuuming the carpets yet. I tried to help him. Begged him to stop. All that did was earn me more bruises.'

'And you tried to leave him?'

Bridey nodded. 'One day, when I was given permission to go into town to get supplies, I kept driving. It hit me that I had nowhere to go. No knowledge of where to go for help. How would I feed my children? Where would we sleep? How would we survive? I stopped on the side of the road just outside of town, trying to figure it out, and Thom found us ...'

'What happened then?'

'He brought us home, threatened that if I left again, he would send the children to Pastor Camden. I didn't want that life for them either, so I stayed but Thom got worse. For the children's sake, I had to be the obedient wife he wanted and tried hard not to have questions answered with his fists.'

This time the oath that slipped from Cole's lips was the harshest she'd heard from him. Bridey pushed back her chair and stood by the kitchen window, watching the children laugh and play with Gus.

Cole stepped in beside her, his warmth comforting, the arm he laid around her shoulder kind and gentle. 'I'm sorry, Bridey. No one deserves to be treated that way.' He turned her into his arms and held her, his hold loose, giving her the option to move.

She lay her head against his heart and listened to the steady beat, gathered strength from the sound. The ordeal wasn't over yet, but one day it would be, and she had to hold onto that.

Gus stomped into the kitchen. 'Oh ... am I interrupting something?'

Bridey eased out of Cole's hold and turned away, her cheeks hot.

Cole dropped his arms to his side and cleared his throat. 'Ready to go, Dad?'

Gus chuckled. 'Yes. I've still got some prepping to

do for dinner service. I didn't want to leave the boys alone outside in case they wander off.'

'I'll go and keep them company.' Cole pushed his chair back under the table and placed his coffee mug in the sink.

'Great idea. See you later, Bridey. Yell out if you need anything. I'm just a phone call away.'

She turned to smile at him. 'Thank you. And please tell Mrs Lee thank you for the toys.'

'Sure thing.'

As Gus and Cole left the kitchen, Bridey lifted her hands to her warm cheeks, confused by how she felt about Cole and what it might mean.

~

A cool breeze blew across the land, a hint that autumn was on its way. Cole looked up at the dark sky from where he sat on an old, worn sofa on the back verandah overlooking the crime scene. The stars were brighter out here in the country without the interference of city lights. Inside, Bridey settled the boys in for the night and an eerie silence fell across the farm. It was strange not to hear a television or even a radio playing.

Bridey came outside, a flask in her hand and a blanket and pillow under her arms. 'It's warmer inside.'

'I know, but if I stay inside and something happens out here, I might not see it.'

Bridey handed Cole the blanket and the flask. 'These should keep you warm. It gets cold out here at night. Autumn is coming.'

'Thanks.' He patted the seat beside him. 'Sit for a while.'

She sat and curled up in the corner, her arms tucked around her to ward off the chill. Cole draped the warm blanket over them both. She smiled her thanks. Had there been happier times for her and her husband when they had shared this couch under the stars? Cole doubted it. People seldom transitioned into being bullies. The monster was usually cultivated early in life and fed until it grew out of control.

'How do you stand the silence?' Cole slid down in the seat, stretched his legs out and rested his head on the back of the sofa.

'I don't understand.' Bridey looked at him, her face illuminated by the soft glow of the verandah light.

'No television, no radio. What do you do to break the silence?'

She sat up, her fingers curling into the blanket. 'Sometimes silence can be a blessing. Silence means no trouble tonight.'

The relief in her voice had him reaching out to

place his hand over hers. 'You're safe now, Bridey. Safe and free.'

She looked down at his hand on hers. 'Not yet. So many bad things have happened here. I'm not free until I know what happened to the McCaffreys. Who brought Kirana and those girls here and what happens to them now? Who tried to burn down the shed? I won't ever be free until I know the answers and that person will never come back again.' Her sigh was shaky, as if tears shimmered below the surface, waiting to be released but she was too proud — or maybe too conditioned — to let them fall.

'I promise to find those answers for you.' Cole moved closer and drew her to him with a gentle arm around her shoulders. 'I promise to make sure no one ever harms you or the boys again.'

'That's a big promise, Cole.'

'It's one I plan to keep.' At first he'd thought his conviction had been born out of the guilt he'd felt for not being able to keep that promise to his wife and child. But the more he grew to know Bridey and her boys, the more different it felt this time. 'You mentioned Pastor Camden earlier. Is he the man you refer to as the New Lord?'

Bridey stiffened against him, raising her hand to cover her mouth. 'I shouldn't have said his name.'

'If you think he's the one responsible for the fire, I

179

need to know. I can't help you if I don't have a list of suspects to investigate.' If Camden was the one who'd set fire to the shed, it meant he'd known about what lay under it.

'You don't understand, Cole. Thom was cruel but the New Lord? His power and reach are a whole new level.' Bridey sighed. 'It saddens me to think that he might be the ultimate reason we have to leave. Mindaleny Ridge could be such a beautiful, happy place. I look out the window and imagine the fields alive with crops. It all makes sense now why the fields never flourished. And its history just got sadder. How could anyone leave all this abandoned the way it was?'

'It happens. No family or descendants to inherit the property so it falls into the State's possession. This far out of the metro area, the land is forgotten until maybe one day a developer comes along to snap it up or, like the bank manager suggested, someone applies for adverse possession. Do you really want to stay here, Bridey? After everything that's happened on Mindaleny Ridge?'

She hesitated as she looked around her at the landscape and up at the stars against the sky. 'The alternative would be unbearable. For me and the children. Here, I feel a shift happening. Thom is gone. I want to be a part of the kindness that's crossed onto the land since he passed. I have the beginnings of friendships ... Mr and Mrs Lee, Doc, Cath, the people who brought us all that food, Gus ... you.' She turned to face him, her gaze searching his. 'I want to be happy here, but I can't until I know I am free. Not just from Thom, but from the New Lord's reach too.'

Cole lifted his hand to brush her hair aside. The scarf that usually covered her head was gone tonight, maybe an indication of another step toward freedom for Bridey. 'Then I'll help you stay. I spoke to Dean at the bank. He got it wrong. The land hasn't passed to the state yet. It's still in the original owner's name with the land taxes being paid out of the estate. It's one of those abandoned properties that has fallen through the cracks because of its rural location. You meet all the criteria for squatter's rights for adverse possession. There will be some fees involved in the application, but we can work something out. There's time if you want to stay, Bridey. I'm not about to evict you any time soon, even if I would prefer you to be staying somewhere safer. And I'm fairly confident that all those friends you named before would be happy to provide letters of support to allow you and the children to stay.'

'You'd do all that for me?'

The wonder in her eyes had his heart skipping a beat. It beggared belief how a man like Thomas

McCaffrey could have been so cruel to such a beautiful soul. 'I promised to help you, and I will.'

'Thank you.' Her hand brushed over his cheek before she lowered it back onto her lap and settled back on the sofa, their arms touching.

They sat silent for a while, surrounded by the sounds of the night. Crickets chirped, frogs called, and an owlet-nightjar churred and yapped. Somewhere in the distance, he heard the distinct sound of someone doing a burnout and made a note to investigate it in the morning. Most likely bored youths making what they considered to be a bit of fun for themselves. Always fun until someone got hurt. Or worse. Beside him, he felt the tension seep from Bridey's shoulders as she relaxed into his warmth and the peacefulness of the night.

'Tell me about your wife. Were you happy together?'

Bridey's question surprised him. He thought about Carrie and the baby a lot, but he seldom spoke about them. Thinking about them was painful enough. Talking about them had been almost impossible. Yet, somehow, sitting here under the stars with a woman who had seen far too much pain of her own made it easier than it had been for a long time.

'Carrie and I met at the police academy. We were on the same training squad together. She was funny, beautiful, and smart, and we hit it off right away. Our squad was like our family. We always went out in a group and spent a lot of our free time together. I guess it was a natural progression from friendship to a relationship.'

Beside him, Bridey shifted. 'It sounds wonderful.' Sadness coloured her words blue.

'It was.'

'What happened to her?'

Cole took a deep breath, waiting for the pain and guilt to hit, but all he felt was the peace around him. 'Carrie went on to be a detective and I joined a special task force that investigated and took action against underworld crime. The case we were working on involved some really nasty individuals who we were looking forward to taking off the streets. Our raid on their clubhouse cost them millions of dollars in seized drugs and hot money. The ringleader got off the charges on a technicality, although we suspected he'd bribed or maybe even extorted the judge.'

Beside him, Bridey sat silent. He looked down to find her watching him, and then found himself needing to hold that steady gaze for the strength to tell what came next.

'Carrie was off on parental leave. The baby was due in four weeks. I was wrapping up on an undercover assignment and planned to spend those last weeks preparing the nursery and getting ready for the next step in our lives.'

He took a deep breath and released it, his throat growing tight with sadness.

'I got home, relieved to be off duty for a while, looking forward to seeing Carrie. There was broken glass everywhere, the furniture had been trashed. I couldn't find Carrie downstairs, so I went upstairs. I found her. On the bed. They'd stabbed her. Fifteen times.'

Cole looked away from the horror on Bridey's face as he swallowed the pain and rubbed at his chest with his fist. His gaze fell on the police tape where they'd found the McCaffreys. Too much death. Too much violence. When would it end?

Bridey's hand was warm on his cold, damp skin as she reached up to turn his face to hers. 'I'm so sorry, Cole. Carrie didn't deserve that.'

'They took not just one but two lives that day.'

Her hand dropped away from his face, and he missed the warmth and comfort of it. 'Why are people so cruel to each other?'

'Power is the devil's sharpest tool, Bridey, and some people prefer to use that power to harm rather than heal. All we can do is keep trying to get the bad guys off the streets, and sometimes that feels like a losing battle against a flawed justice system.'

'Is that why you came to Moonie River? To get away from the crime?'

'I had this idea in my head that country policing would be quieter. I thought it would be all about arresting goats for chewing petunias, and half-hearted drunken brawls outside the pub.'

She pulled the blanket up higher. 'I guess that didn't work out so well for you.'

'No, it didn't go exactly to plan. But here, I can make a difference. I can help people change their lives without the influence of the big city crime gangs, and judges who interpret the law too broadly or deliver sentences that are too light, without a care for the victims.'

They sat in silence for a while, a sense of peace and healing in the cool night air.

Bridey's voice was soft and sleepy beside him. 'I'd like to give the McCaffreys a proper burial to lay them to rest. Can you help me with that?'

'Yes, I can help you do that for them. As soon as their remains are released back to you, we can arrange it.'

'Thank you, Cole. Maybe peace and happiness can come to Mindaleny Ridge. Maybe all the darkness can disappear. That is my wish. I wish to make my home beautiful and happy, with no fear hiding in the dark.'

'Then that is what we'll aim for.'

He snuggled down under the blanket next to her, knowing he wouldn't sleep because he was here to make sure Bridey's fears were extinguished and that she and her family were safe. Her head came to rest on his shoulder. He reached for her hand under the blanket and entwined his fingers with hers as her breath softened in sleep. For the first time since Carrie's death, he felt real peace.

Chapter Fourteen

Bridey awoke to the sound of birds chirping and Cole speaking into his phone. The sun had only just broken dawn. She sat up and brushed her hair out of her eyes as she caught snippets of Cole's conversation.

'Tell her to calm down, Sam. I'll be there as soon as I can ... No, she can wait until I get there.' He hung up, shaking his head.

'Trouble?' Bridey folded the blanket and placed it on top of the pillow she'd slept on.

'Elle's kicking up a stink at the station. I'll have to go sort it out. Nick's tied up with an overnight complaint and Sam is pulling her hair out trying to keep Elle and Sunshine under control.' He dragged a hand through his hair. 'I'll be back as soon as I can.'

'We'll be fine, Cole. I doubt anyone will try to mess with anything in the daylight.'

'Most likely not but you never know ...'

'Go. If I see or hear anything suspicious, I'll call you.'

'We need to get you a mobile phone.'

'I would have no idea how to use one. I have the phone in the house and the one in the farm office. That's where I'll be today trying to make some sense of the mess Thom left things in. I can see the house and the shed from there.'

'Just ... be careful, Bridey. Any sign of something out of place, call me right away and I'll come back. Even if I have to bring Elle and Sunshine with me.'

'I promise, I'll call you.'

He stared at her for a moment, his reluctance to leave evident. His hand moved from her arm to cup her cheek, the touch soft and warm. 'I don't want anything to happen to you or the boys.'

Bridey covered his hand with hers. He leaned down and kissed her forehead before stepping back, his arm dropping back to his side.

'Sorry. That was overstepping the mark.'

Face hot, Bridey pressed her hands to her cheeks. 'No ... it was ... nice.'

Cole laughed, the sound strangled and awkward. 'Nice?'

She stepped closer. 'No one has ever kissed me like that before.'

Confusion creased his forehead. 'Not even Thom?'

She shook her head, her movements hesitant as she raised her hands to hold his face. His skin was warm, overnight beard growth bristly against her palms. 'Will you kiss me again?'

'I'm not sure that's a good idea, Bridey.'

'Why not? Is it wrong?'

'It's right in too many ways to count, but it will mean taking a step in a direction I'm not sure either of us should take right now.'

'What is it like to kiss someone you like?'

Affection had been banned in the homes she grew up in. There was only discipline. No one had ever told her she was doing a good job the way she praised the boys when they did something well. Thom had forbidden any affection in the house, so she'd saved her natural instinct to show love for her children for when he wasn't around.

Cole placed his hands on his hips and looked over her head. 'It's ... good. No ... it's great. It's warm and exciting and can lead to even better things. A kiss can make you feel loved and cared for, but there are different kinds of kisses. There are kisses of cherish and affection, like those between a parent and child or a greeting between friends. And then there is the way lovers kiss, like the whole world ceases to exist and they only see each other.' He brought his gaze back to hers. 'I don't want to kiss you like a friend, Bridey.'

A tingle of excitement surfaced in her belly. 'How do you want to kiss me?'

The gap closed between them, his hands encased her hips, and he held her against him. 'Like this ...'

His lips were warm on hers; soft, gentle ... cherishing. His arms closed around her in a way that made her feel safe, not trapped. And when his mouth coaxed her lips to open, she could taste a gentle, caring persuasiveness, almost an invitation, that made her lean in closer as heat curled up through her, creating a need she'd never felt before.

Cole eased out of the kiss, leaving her wanting more. He leaned his forehead against hers, his hold relaxing until his arms dropped away and his head lifted.

'Wow,' Bridey whispered, opening her eyes to find him watching her.

'Wow indeed.' He smiled. 'That's how you deserve to be kissed, Bridey.'

Bridey pressed her fingers to the tingle still on her lips, any words she might be able to string together sealed in behind the need to keep his kiss there.

'I'll be back as soon as I can.' He walked to his

SUV and climbed in, before driving away with a wave goodbye.

Speechless, Bridey watched until the dust settled behind him. Dazed by the depths of the feelings churning around inside her, she turned and walked into something hard and solid.

'Hello, Bridey.'

Terror chased her daydreams into nightmares as cruel hands gripped her arms. She looked up into the face of the devil himself.

'What do you think you're playing at?' Mean eyes, black as a snake's, glared down at her.

Bridey tried to wriggle out of his hold, but Clifford Camden tightened his grip. She looked past him at the house.

'Don't worry. The boys are fine. They're playing nice and quietly, just like I told them to.'

'How did you get here?' Cole's car had been the only one on the property. They were outside the whole night with Cole keeping watch. He would have heard another car. 'How long have you been here?'

'It doesn't matter how, only that I'm here now. It's the why that's more important. You need to keep your mouth shut, Bridey. I see how close you're getting to that cop. That's not the church way. You have a week to pack up your things and I'll be back to collect you and the boys. We need to find you another husband. The boys will go to the Grooming House.'

'No! You can't take my boys from me!' Panic and terror joined hands. The Grooming House was where the boys went to be taught how to control their wives. She'd worked so hard to create gentle, caring souls. She didn't want them to be like Thom. She wanted them to be like Cole and Gus and Ed Lee.

'That's the way it's going to be, Bridey. Thom isn't here to teach them anymore, so they will learn from myself and the House Fathers now.'

'No! Please, Pastor Camden, please don't take my boys. I want to stay here on the farm.'

'That's not how it works.' Camden's voice rose to a shout, spitting out the words. He shook her hard. 'You will obey! You know the consequences if you don't. This is not your home anymore and I won't have you telling these strangers the church's business! The McCaffreys had no right to want to leave the church. Thom knew that. He was making amends for it and then he went and killed himself, the useless, drunken bastard.'

Her spine ran cold with a shiver. 'What do you mean?'

Camden pushed Bridey away, causing her to stumble and fall backwards onto the ground.

'That's not your business. Did Thom not teach

you to not ask questions about things that don't concern you?' He stood over her, his size blocking out the sun, his face the angry mask of the devil. 'A week, Bridey. I give you a week. Pack your things.' He kicked her hard — the blows coming fast, one after the other — before stepping over her. 'And if you think of running, I want you to remember that you don't exist outside the church and the boundaries of this farm. No one does. You won't get far. I'll be watching.'

Bridey curled up in a ball, thoughts crowding her mind. It made sense now. The reason Thom had dragged her back to the farm when she'd tried to run. The girls in the container, the bodies in the cellar. Thom had been recruiting for the New Lord. She thought of what Cole had told her about his wife and their life together. How Mr and Mrs Lee lived. Gus and his work in the navy. Doc and Cath, helping people with care and concern. That was the real world outside the confines of the church. That was how life should be. That was the life she wanted for herself and the boys.

Pain stabbed at her lower back, cramps took hold in her abdomen and a warm, wet sensation covered her legs. Alone, curled up in the dust under the hot sun with her hand between her thighs, trying to stop her baby being born too early, Bridey cried.

~

Cole tossed his hat on his desk as Elle's foul mouth spurted out words that would make a sailor blush.

'Cut it out.' His yell shocked her into silence. 'I said this was your last chance to make things right, Elle, and by God, you will.'

Sunshine sat at the table with Sam, staring down at a bowl of oats but making no attempt to eat it. The little harridan he'd encountered stealing from Mrs Lee's shop had transformed into a miserable child who'd seen far too much squalor and lack of care.

Cole walked up to the cell bars. 'I want you to look at your daughter, Elle. Look hard. If you keep going like you are, that child will end up being just like you because you are the only role model she had. I can get social services to take her away, sure. But guess what her life could be like then. Would you like me to paint you a picture?'

'Fuck you.'

'You have a choice to make here. It's not going to be an easy road back, but you can do it if you try. You can clean yourself up with our help and start again, or you can continue to spiral in the mess.'

Elle threw herself down on the cot and covered her ears, so Cole opened the unlocked door and sat in the chair next to the cot, keeping his tone even. 'You can get your daughter thrown into a foster care system that can never replace her own mother or you can take a step in the right direction and care for her yourself.'

'She can go any time she likes and find herself a happy family.' The response held little conviction.

'Sure, she might be lucky to find a family that will care for her and love her, but she will spend the rest of her life wondering what happened to her real mother. She might even look you up one day. Where will she find you, Elle? Homeless and drunk in a gutter somewhere? Dead from an overdose? Or will she find you cleaned up, with a job and a home that you've made for yourself because you took back control and decided to make the changes?'

'He left me.' Elle sat up, arms folded and a sulk on her lip.

'So what? That says more about him than it does about you. He made his choice, now it's time for you to make yours. What's it going to be?'

Elle lifted her filthy pyjama top to wipe her face and wrinkled her nose. 'I stink.'

'Yes, you do. And you wouldn't stink if you'd cooperated with Constable Mayne last night and cleaned up. Why don't you go and do that now? I guarantee you'll feel a whole lot better after. And when you're done, we can talk about the next step.'

'Okay.'

Cole narrowed his eyes. Her agreement had come way too easily. 'I'm not playing games. I mean it. Every step backwards you take from here on, you'll be spending a night in that cell until you shape up.' Cole looked around him and made a note that the holding cells were way overdue for an upgrade.

Elle sat up on the edge of the cot. 'I need help.' Her shoulders sagged.

For the first time Cole saw tears of defeat in her eyes. 'Those better not be crocodile tears.'

Elle shook her head. 'The support service bus doesn't come until next month. I've got no money.'

'So, here's how it's going to go. First, you get cleaned up then I'm taking you to see Gus at the pub. He needs help in the kitchen. You'll get a meal included in your wages. You're not allowed to touch alcohol, and I'd recommend you start cutting down on smoking. You'll join Alcoholics Anonymous down at the CRC.'

Ambulance sirens wailed as Cath drove past the station in a hurry. Cole braced himself for another emergency.

'One step out of line and it's back in here, got it?'

'Yes. Arsehole,' she muttered.

Cole grinned. 'That's Sargeant Arsehole to you, thank you.'

A little smile appeared on Elle's cracked lips.

'Right, go get cleaned up. I'll see if I can round up some of the ladies from the CWA to give you a hand to get the house back into a liveable state. When they're done, I expect you to keep it that way.'

'Why are you doing this for me?'

Cole looked hard at her. 'I'm not doing it for you. I'm doing it for Sunshine. You should too. Make it work, Elle. You don't have to do it alone anymore.' He picked up the stack of folded clothes Nick had brought back from the Op Shop and handed them to her. 'Starting right now.'

Elle took the pile of clothes and headed for the shower block.

'Want me to watch her, Sarge?' Sam stood.

Cole shook his head. 'We have to trust she'll do the right thing.' He sat down next to Sunshine. 'We're going to get your mum some help, but I need you to help me with something. Can you do that?'

The girl nodded, swirling her spoon around in her bowl of oats.

'Great. First, you're going to need to eat your breakfast because you need to be strong to help your mum. No more stealing, no more running away, no more trouble. If you're hungry, you go and see Gus at the pub, and he'll give you food. If you need soap to wash or anything like that from the shop, you ask Mrs Lee to put it on a tab, and I'll make sure it gets sorted out when your mum's welfare payment comes through. If you're scared or worried about your mum, you come and find me or Sam or Nick, and we'll help you. Promise?'

'Promise.' Sunshine ate a spoonful of oats.

'I need you to pinkie swear.' Cole held up his pinkie finger. 'A pinkie swear can't be broken.'

Sunshine dropped the spoon in the bowl and hooked her finger around his. 'Pinkie swear.'

'Deal. Now finish your breakfast.' He stood and moved to where Sam leaned against the wall watching.

'Sarge, you just worked a miracle. Pete gave up trying to help the Donnellys. There was trouble in Paradise there long before Sunshine's dad took off.'

'Yeah? Well, I'm not Pete and I won't give up. I don't think it's going to be a fun rollercoaster ride, but I won't accept the alternative.'

'You're a good man, Sarge.'

'I'm just doing my job. We need to record this in a report for social services. Can I get you to do that for me while I go tell Gus I've just dropped him in it?'

Sam grinned. 'I can do that.'

'Great, thanks.'

Mrs Lee ran in past the front desk, ignoring Nick's shout. 'Cole! Doc says you have to come. It's Bridey.'

The words that followed fell over each other and came out garbled as she tried to get the message out.

'Slow down, Mrs Lee. What's happened to Bridey?' He placed his hands on her shoulders to try and calm her down.

'Doc wouldn't say. He just said to tell you to get out there fast. Cath just went out there with the ambulance.' Her eyes teared up. 'Please, Cole. Hasn't the girl been through enough?'

Cole let go of Mrs Lee and grabbed his hat and keys, his stomach churning. He should never have left her alone.

'Sam, fill Mrs Lee in on the situation with Elle and Sunshine. We're going to need your help, Mrs Lee.' Jamming his hat on his head, he walked past Nick at the desk. 'You're in charge, Nick. Make sure Elle follows through and behaves.'

'Sure thing, Sarge. You go. Don't worry about a thing here, Mrs Lee and I will take care of the situation here.'

As Cole sped out towards Mindaleny Ridge, visions of being too late haunted him. He'd been too late for Carrie, please God don't let him be too late for Bridey.

Chapter Fifteen

She was done being kicked and hurt. Excruciating pain cramped her abdomen in unrelenting waves, far worse than any of her previous miscarriages. With every breath she took against the cramps, her right side hurt. The twins lay in the dirt, cuddled up against her back.

Alex kneeled over her, stroking her hair, his tears falling on her face. 'Don't die, Mummy. Please don't die. We don't want to go with that man.'

'I won't let him take you away, baby.' She winced as another cramp hit. It hurt to breathe. 'I won't leave you.'

'I called the ambulance, Mummy. I remembered how you did it last time. They're coming to help.'

'Thank you, Alex. Well done.' How proud she was

of her boy, stepping up and taking responsibility even when he was too young to need to.

She closed her eyes against the pain and rising nausea. No matter what Pastor Camden threatened, he wouldn't take her or her children. He wasn't a lord or a saviour. He wouldn't turn them into the monster their father was. How was that normal? How was anything that had happened in her life normal? The pastor's words echoed in her head. He'd said so many things. She tried to remember what he'd said but the waves of pain kept coming and chasing the memory away.

In the distance, she heard the sirens approaching. 'We're safe now.'

After everything that had happened, she wanted to believe that. For her children's sake, she couldn't give up. As the ambulance wheels rattled over the grid, she lay there in the dirt, nursing an angel baby in her hands, promising herself that this would be the last time anyone kicked her while she was down.

Cath's calm voice floated down as she asked the boys to step aside. 'Go sit there on the steps for me, so I can take care of your mum. We're going to take good care of her, I promise.' A moment of silence hung in the air before Cath kneeled down beside her. 'Oh, sweetheart, I'm so sorry.' She stroked a soft hand over Bridey's hair. 'Let me take care of you.'

She disappeared from Bridey's view, returning a few seconds later with a tiny container. 'We're going to make your baby nice and comfy in here for you. Did you want to say goodbye? It helps ease the sadness a little.'

Bridey nodded. 'Thank you.' Cath's sweet kindness brought tears to her cheeks.

'Bruce, can you please take care of this baby angel for us?' She handed the container up to her colleague and returned to attend to Bridey. 'Are you hurting anywhere else, hon?'

Bridey placed a hand on her right side. 'Here. My ribs.'

'We'll give you some pain meds for your ribs and the cramps.' Cath opened her bag, pulled out a box, and extracted a green, whistle-shaped device, prepping it before handing it to Bridey. 'Here, hon, this is a pain inhaler. It works a little faster to ease the pain. Can you tell me what happened to make your ribs sore?'

Bridey grasped the inhaler. 'I fell.'

'I'm just going to have a little look to see if anything is broken. I'm going to lift up your shirt, okay?' Cath's cool fingers touched Bridey's heated skin, the pressure light. 'You've got a bruise developing there, hon, and maybe a couple of cracked ribs. We'll get you X-rayed at the hospital.' She called for Bruce to bring a backboard. 'We're going to lift you up onto the stretcher, but it might hurt a bit because we need to roll you onto the board. Can you take six to eight breaths in and out into the inhaler for me? Cover that little hole in the whistle when you breathe in, so you get a full dose, sweetheart.'

'My boys ...'

'Doc is just pulling in now. I asked him to come too. The boys will be fine.'

A car door slammed and, seconds later, Doc knelt beside her. 'Diagnosis, Cath?'

'Trauma to the right side, possible fractured ribs, and a spontaneous abortion.'

Doc rubbed a hand over Bridey's head. 'I'm so sorry, Bridey. We'll take good care of you. Don't worry about a thing. I'll make sure the boys are looked after.'

Tears slipped down Bridey's cheeks, the medication kicking in for the physical pain, allowing the mental pain to sneak in. She needed to warn him the boys were in danger, but the medication was making her drowsy, and the words wouldn't come out.

'Let's get you into the ambulance, hon.' Cath motioned for Bruce to put the backboard in place so they could roll Bridey onto it. 'You let me know if you have any difficulty breathing and I'll pop an oxygen mask on for you.'

She felt little pain as the cramps subsided and the drugs masked the pain in her side. Secured, they lifted her onto a stretcher, removed the backboard, strapped her in again, and wheeled her to the ambulance doors.

Another car raced down the gravel drive, another door slammed, and Cole's voice reached her ears.

'What happened, Doc?'

'Not sure yet, Sarge. We can save the questions for later when she's been seen to at the hospital.'

'The baby?'

'Too late.'

Bridey felt the warmth of Cole's hand on hers. 'I'm so sorry, Bridey. I shouldn't have left. I should've let Nick deal with things at the station.'

'Not your fault.' She curled her fingers around his. 'I want to see my baby.'

'I'll bring your baby to you, hon.' Cath reached out to take the container from Bruce.

Bridey rested the pain whistle at her side with one hand and clung to Cole's with the other. Cath raised the stretcher so Bridey could sit up a little. She placed the tiny surgical container in Bridey's hand.

Miniature toes and hands, almost perfectly formed, her angel baby slept for eternity on a bed of cotton swabs, not much bigger than a newborn mouse. Tears of regret and grief fell into the container. She turned her head into the pillow, felt Cole stroke her hair and press a kiss to her forehead.

As Cath removed the container and put a lid on it,

Bridey looked up at Cole. 'No one will ever hurt my children again.'

~

The image of the tiny embryo burned in Cole's mind as he stood beside Bridey. Guilt battered his heart and head. He'd promised to look after her and the children, just like he'd promised Carrie. Feeling Doc's hand on his shoulder, he lifted his gaze from Bridey's face.

'We need to get her to hospital, Cole.'

Cole nodded, his throat too tight for words. With one last stroke of Bridey's hair, he stepped back so Cath and Bruce could load her into the ambulance. The boys sat huddled together on the verandah steps, watching another parent being loaded into an ambulance, their faces pale. He walked over to where they sat and knelt in front of them in the dirt.

'Cath, Bruce and Doc will take good care of your mum, I promise.' He wanted to promise them she'd be fine, but how could he after all she'd been through?

'Will the man come back?'

'What man, Garrett?' Cole frowned.

'The man who kicked my mummy.'

'Shush, Garrett,' Alex shouted. 'We're not supposed to tell!'

Cole placed a hand on Alex's skinny shoulder.

'When someone says not to tell anyone about something bad that's happened, that's all the more reason to tell. Who was this man?'

'He said if we tell he'll take us away from our mum, so I'm not telling. You promised to look after my mum. I heard you promise! And now she's hurt.' Alex took the twins by the hands and pulled them up. 'I hate you!'

Together the boys ran down the stairs to Doc Hamilton. Cole stood and dusted off the knees of his pants. He'd have a hard time winning back the boys' trust now. If he wasn't committed to helping Elle and Sunshine out of the mess they were in too, he'd curse Elle for dragging him away and leaving Bridey vulnerable.

Cole lifted his hat and dragged a hand through his hair. He needed to stop doing that or he'd be bald before his time was up in Moonie River. Slapping his hat back on his head, he watched as Doc piled the boys into his car and the ambulance disappeared down the drive. When everyone had left, he turned around and climbed the stairs hoping to find something that would tell him the identity of the man who had been there.

Garrett had said the man kicked Bridey. The thought made his blood boil. He could have handled it if the miscarriage had happened naturally, but knowing someone had hurt her again and that it may have led to the miscarriage ... that was unacceptable. Until he had proof or Bridey's statement, all he had was assumptions, but he'd bet that the man who'd been here today was the same person who'd set fire to the shed.

His phone rang and he pulled it out of his pocket to check the number. With a sigh and a premonition of more trouble, he hit the call answer button. 'Matron, how are the patients doing?'

Matron Margaret Hind wasted no time or words. 'Sarge, a man came by and asked to see Kirana and the girls. He said they were his charges, and he'd come to take them. He had some official looking letter with him giving him permission to take them into his care.'

'What did you tell him?' Cole frowned.

'That until they're ready for release they're not going anywhere.'

'Did he give a name?'

'No. He just said he was a representative from a humanitarian organisation who'd been alerted by Immigration of the girls' circumstances.'

Alarm bells rang for Cole. Immigration hadn't cleared any paperwork for the girls to be moved to a detention centre or anywhere else yet. Even if an agency had been assigned to the girls under the Community Support Program, there was plenty of red tape to cut through before they could be released. And if he wasn't from an agency, how had he found out about the case? 'Can you describe this man for me?'

'Tall, late forties or early fifties, salt and pepper grey hair, reasonably good-looking with dead eyes. But I can do better than that. I've got security footage for you.'

Cole smiled at the matron's smug tone. 'Even better. Good job, Margaret. I'll swing by to pick it up and check on the girls' progress at the same time.'

He hung up and dialled Mark Johnson's number.

'Hey, Cole. What's up?'

'We need to put on extra security until we have some answers and Forensics have finished processing the remains out at Mindaleny Ridge.'

'Why's that?'

'Bridey McCaffrey was attacked this morning.'

Mark's curse echoed down the line. 'Is she okay?'

'I'm not sure yet. She's just left in an ambulance. Garrett told me a man kicked her, which explains why her ribs are bruised, possibly cracked. She lost the baby.' A sense of *deja vu* settled on Cole's shoulders. How had he let it happen again?

'It's not rocket science that all these incidents out at Mindaleny Ridge are connected. Someone has plenty to hide and it all comes back to why Thomas McCaffrey shot himself. We just have to find that link.'

'I think we have that link, we just need to prove it.

Right after the attack on Bridey, someone showed up at the hospital claiming he had permission to take the girls into his care.'

'Do we know who it is?'

'Not yet, but my guess is it's the same person who threatened to take the boys away from Bridey today. I'm picking up the security vision from the matron at the hospital and I'll ask Bridey a few questions while I'm there.'

'Great. Send it through to me when you have it. Does Moonie River have a security patrol?'

'Yes, lucky the population is big enough to warrant one.'

'Good. Book them in to cover the McCaffrey property. I'll raise a purchase order to cover the cost. Have you processed the evidence you found in the cellar?'

'Nick's almost done bagging them up. We'll send them down to Perth with Forensics when they're done here. He's running the IDs through the missing persons database to see if there's any matches.'

Mark's tone was grim. 'That will help, thanks. We're a little snowed under here. Nothing like a growing population to spike a growth in organised crime.'

'Too snowed under to run an investigation into a church called The Children of the New Lord?'

'I'm interested. Fill me in.'

'I knew you wouldn't be able to resist.' Mark Johnson had had his own run in with child exploitation in the hills surrounding Perth. 'According to Bridey, the church is like an orphanage or foster care program but with a setup that resembles more of a cult. Right down to arranged marriages.'

'You're shitting me. That's fucking modern slavery shit right there.'

'That's how Bridey met Thomas McCaffrey, and it wasn't all rose petals and learning to love each other.'

'I've read her file.' Mark's tone was grim. His own wife, Lily, was a survivor of domestic violence, and her late husband had been a bastard of note.

'So, what happens when the government tightens rules around adoption and foster care? Maybe your flock is wising up a little and starting to flee the coop?'

'You have to find your stock somewhere else. Hence the seized passports and bodies in shipping containers.' Mark heaved a loud sigh on the other end of the line. 'I wish you'd stayed on my task force, Cole. We always did make a good team.'

'That's why I wanted you on this case. There is one person who could be getting extremely nervous about the discoveries we're making out at Mindaleny. Any chance you could check on where he's been and what he's been up to in the last month or so?'

'Give me name.'

'Pastor Clifford Camden. I have a hunch that it's his face we'll see on that security vision. And if I can get Bridey to talk after what happened here today, her testimony might confirm it.'

'We'd still have a lot to prove though to make an arrest or even request a search warrant for his church.'

'I want a watertight case, Mark. If the bastard who did this to these women and children is still alive, I want his head on a chopping block and no room for him to wiggle past a lifelong prison sentence.'

'You don't think Thomas McCaffrey was working alone.'

'I think he was just the middle man, and his parents got in the way.'

'First step ... Get those girls out of that hospital. Is there somewhere they can all stay together until I can get an agency rep on their case?'

'Gus's place. No one will get past him.'

'Do it and I'll prod Immigration for a hurry up on their protection visas. I think my caseload just doubled.'

The resignation in Mark's voice made Cole smile. Everyone knew Senior Detective Mark Johnson lived and breathed for justice and loved his job with the same passion he loved his wife.

'Say hi to Lily for me.'

'I'll do better than that. Lily and TJ have expanded their teenage refuge operations, and now run an arm that helps keep victims of domestic violence safe in their homes. I'll have a chat to them to see if they can take on trafficking victim support as well. Depends on their case load, so I won't promise anything. I'll call you back as soon as I hear something. Let me know if you find anything else.' Mark hung up.

Blowing out a long breath, Cole climbed into his SUV. He needed to get to Bridey and the girls before anyone else did.

Chapter Sixteen

Bridey lay in the hospital bed, a drip in her arm, bruising to her ribs and an empty womb. Doc had left the children in Mrs Lee's care and promised she would bring them to Bridey after lunch once she'd had a chance to rest. She wanted to see them, reassure herself they were safe, and that Pastor Camden hadn't followed through on his threat to take them away.

'Miss Bridey?'

Bridey turned her head to look at the woman in the bed beside hers. 'Yes?'

'I am Kirana. You sent people to save us. Thank you.'

'Kirana.' Bridey's eyes stung with fresh tears. 'I'm so sorry. I didn't know!'

The woman slipped off the bed and tip-toed over to place her hand on Bridey's. 'Please. Don't worry.'

The young woman at her side was too thin than was healthy but exceptionally beautiful. A pink scar on her temple suggested a fresh injury. Bridey lifted her hand from under Kirana's to touch it. 'Did Thom do that?'

Kirana nodded. 'Better now.'

'Why did he hurt you?'

Kirana lowered her eyes. 'I did not obey.'

Bridey's throat closed around the tears. Bad enough Thom had punished her but being faced with him harming others — strangers — brought a new feeling of humiliation and disrespect for Pastor Camden's teachings on how women should be disciplined. This wasn't how life was meant to be.

'Don't cry.' Kirana reached for a tissue and wiped away Bridey's tears. 'The gods will punish him.'

'It should never have happened to you.'

'Or you.'

'How did it happen, Kirana? How did you end up locked up in that container on the farm?'

Kirana reached down to pull a plastic-covered hospital chair up to the bed. 'I come from a village on the Samosir Island in Indonesia. There I am a teacher.' She leaned forward to fold her arms on the bed. 'One day, these men, they come. They choose young women and children from the village and take us away.'

'Who were these men?'

'Men from our village.' Kirana raised her eyes to Bridey's face. 'They take us to another village. There is another man there who chooses the ones he wants. We walk to the sea and go on a fishing boat. We travel for a very long time. The sea is rough, storms are bad and the children, they're afraid. The women too.'

Bridey reached out to touch Kirana's arm. 'I am so sorry.'

Kirana nodded. 'We come to Australia. The man from the other village is there. The women and children are crying. They give us *obat tidur*_and we sleep. When we wake up, Mr Thom is there, and we make beds in the big box. It is hot in there, but we had the thing that makes a bit of wind. My people want to go home, but if they cry, Mr Thom beats them.'

Nausea threatened as Bridey could only imagine the horror Kirana and her people had lived through, and the pain of losing those who hadn't survived. 'Were you brought to work on the farm?'

Kirana shook her head. 'The other man will take us away again, but we don't know when, so we work making the *obat-obat* for Mr Thom.'

'Do you know the name of the man who came to the village to choose the women?'

'No. The village men say he was from a church. They say we will have a better life in Australia. Get married. Have houses to keep and men to make happy.'

Bridey thought back to the girls who had come to The Children of the New Lord. She'd never asked where they came from, and they'd never been told. Was the man who had taken Kirana from her village Pastor Camden? Was that how he collected girls for the church?

'I'm so sorry, Kirana. Your baby? How is your baby doing?'

Kirana nodded. 'The baby is weak but getting strong now. A girl.'

Bridey blocked out the thought of what the baby's future might have been if Thom had lived. Another horrible thought crossed her mind. 'Is Thom the father of your baby?'

Kirana shook her head. 'I make *hubungan* with a man from my village. The other women tell the village men I am bad so I must go away.'

Relief did little to ease the horror of Kirana's journey. 'Have you told Sergeant Delaney your story?'

'Only how we come on the boat. I am afraid.'

'You're safe now, Kirana. And so are the children. You need to tell Sergeant Delany everything. He will help you. I will help you too, I promise.'

'Please, Miss Bridey, don't let them send us back to our village. Life will be very bad for us.'

'How?' Bridey frowned. 'Would their parents not be happy to have their children back?'

'The girls will be given to men before they are ready because they are not clean anymore.'

'Did Thom ...?' Bridey couldn't finish the words.

Tears welled in Kirana's eyes. 'And the other man.'

The nightmare of her own upbringing reared its head as memories flooded in of girls coming back from the punishment room, crying and bloody. Sick to her stomach, Bridey wondered how she could have been so blind to what The Children of the New Lord had truly stood for. All the preaching about obedience and fearing the wrath of the New Lord ...

Bridey eased herself up on her elbows, ignoring the pain in her ribs. 'I promise you, Kirana, no one will ever hurt us again. I will fight every step of the way to help you make a new life here. And together, we will help stop these people from hurting others.'

'Thank you, Miss Bridey.'

'Just Bridey. I am your friend and your equal, Kirana. You have such a pretty name. What does it mean?'

Kirana's lips lifted in a wobbly smile. 'It means *beautiful sunbeam*.'

'Then we need to bring the sunshine back for you.

Can you forgive me for not knowing what my husband was doing?'

'In my village it is not the woman's need to know the man's business. I understand. We are not so different.'

'No, we're not.'

They sat in silence for a while, two women with a difficult past and an unknown future.

～

Cole stepped into the hospital ward to find Bridey and Kirana talking in quiet whispers, their hands firmly entwined. His hands itched to plug the USB in his pocket into his laptop so he could view the security video footage and confirm his suspicions. But right now, Bridey and her boys, the girls, and their safety were his priority.

He approached them slowly, taking in the exhaustion and pain on Bridey's face and the skittishness Kirana displayed as she watched him walk towards them.

'How are you doing, Bridey?' He stood with his hands on his hips, resisting the urge to catch the tear on her cheek with his finger. 'I'm really sorry about the baby.'

'Thank you. Reality hasn't quite sunk in yet. I keep

seeing the baby, so impossibly tiny yet so perfect, like an angel sleeping.' Her response caught on the release of fresh tears trickling down her cheeks.

He took a deep breath and let it out to ease the tightening grip of sadness on his throat. 'Are you well enough to be moved? We have a bit of an emergency on our hands.'

'As long as I can rest up, Doc says I don't have to stay in. This isn't the first miscarriage for me. I know what I need to do.'

'It angers me that you have been in this situation before and that you need to know what to do. It shouldn't have happened again. I'm sorry I let it happen.'

'It's not your fault.'

Cole took off his hat and spun the brim through his fingers. 'I've got to move you and the others out of here. Someone came in wanting to take them away, and it wasn't an immigration officer or the AFP.'

'Please don't let them take us.' Terror etched itself onto Kirana's face. 'It will be very bad.'

'I won't let anyone hurt you. Not again. Would you be willing to identify a man we have hospital security footage of, Kirana? We need to know if you have seen this man before.'

Kirana nodded. 'I will help.'

Cole looked at Bridey. 'Will you take a look too,

Bridey?' The flicker of her eyes told him she knew who it was on that video footage. 'The faster we wrap this up, the sooner you and the others can start a better, safer life. Help me do that.'

Bridey cast a glance at Kirana before settling her gaze back on Cole. 'Promise me we'll be safe.'

Her words slashed at his heart. Cole lowered his head. How could he look her in the eye and make a promise he'd failed to keep too many times already. 'You'll be safe with Gus. Head office has approved extra security for the farm and if you're all in one place here in town, it will be easier for Sam and Nick to keep an eye out for trouble.'

'Where are my boys now?'

The panic in her question ate at Cole's soul. The boys would never trust him again. 'Doc has taken them over to Gus. Everyone will be moved to the rooms above the pub until we can get the red tape sorted with Immigration.'

'No.'

The quiet determination in her voice had him looking up. 'Bridey ...'

Kirana stepped away as Bridey sat up on the edge of the bed, tiny enough for her feet not to touch the floor.

'I made a promise to Kirana that I would help them and fix the mess Thom made of their lives. I intend to keep that promise and I'm going to need your help, Cole, because I haven't lived enough in your world.'

'The authorities will take good care of the girls when the paperwork comes through. They will arrange counselling, financial support and temporary housing ...'

Bridey's smile was sad. 'It's not only about financial support and safe protection. I've had time to remember a lot of things lying here in this bed and on the ground waiting for help.' She ran her fingers over the sticky gauze tape that secured the drip in her veins. 'The one thing I remembered was the outside authorities visiting my care home and the lies they were told about how the girls got their bruises. It would go in a report to be buried in a file somewhere, never to be looked at again, and the harm would continue. I can't let that happen to Kirana and the others.'

'There's a process that needs to be followed, Bridey.' Frustration gave his voice an edge.

'You believe in processes and justice. I believe in care and nurture, more so now than ever before. You take care of the legalities, I'll take care of the reality.' She reached out to ring the bell that would bring a nurse to the ward. 'I'll take Kirana and the girls with me. There is a whole second floor to the farmhouse that is boarded up and not being used. If you want to get the authorities involved, you get them to help me make a home for these people.'

'And what about their safety? And yours and the boys? Aren't you leading the wolf to your door? Deliberately placing yourselves and these people in danger?' He bit the words out, a lot harsher than intended, as he strode towards the bed. He regretted his tone and action when he saw the flicker of fear in her eyes. It would take a long time for her to learn not to flinch at raised voices and aggressive moves.

She raised her eyes to his, her voice quiet determination. 'Then do your job, Sergeant Delaney. And if you can't do that, find me someone who can.'

Her words cut. Hard, deep slashes that burned his skin as if they were delivered with a real, hot knife. Words locked in his throat, but he forced them out, almost on a whisper. 'What if he comes for you again, Bridey?'

'I'll be ready for him, and he'll be staring down the barrel of my shotgun. He won't creep up on me again.' She reached for his hands where they clamped his hips and tugged them into her gentle hold. 'Help me, Cole. Help these people. Stop them from becoming a number in someone's case file. Tell me where to start.'

Matron bustled in. 'What's going on here? Why are you out of bed, Miss Kirana?' Her blustery tone fooled no one as she guided Kirana back to her bed and helped her up. 'Cole Delaney, are you upsetting my patients?' She eyed their clasped hands. 'What am I running here? A dating service?'

A smile teased Bridey's lips as she released his hands. 'What's it to be, Sergeant?'

'I'd prefer you to stay with Gus.' Cole rubbed his thumbs in a circle at his temples as he ran through the logistics in his mind. 'It's a long story that started in a car garage in the foothills of Perth, but I know someone who might help. I've reached out to them via Lily's husband and my ex-boss. First, I need to get security set up at the farm and get everyone settled.'

Bridey winced and held a hand to her ribs as she moved to climb off the bed. 'I want to get dressed and go see my children.'

Matron bustled over. 'You're not going anywhere until Doc signs you out, young lady. You get back in that bed and I'll bring you some more painkillers for those ribs.' She turned to Cole. 'You've got some phone calls to make, Sergeant. Off you go. And when you're done you can bring the kiddies back to see their mum, but these ladies need to rest now.'

Cole delivered her a mock salute. 'Yes, Ma'am.'

'Too bloody right. Off you go. I'll make sure everyone is looked after until you can make the necessary arrangements.'

As Matron hurried away to deliver orders to the

staff, Bridey pulled the sheet up over her legs. 'Help me stop what Pastor Camden is doing, Cole. I need to understand how Thom was involved and why his parents are dead so I can right these wrongs. I promised to tell you everything I know about the Children of the New Lord, but first I need be sure he won't come back to harm any of us again.'

'Then our end goal is the same.' All he had to do was bring all the threads together and tie them into a neat bow that would lock away a devil forever.

Chapter Seventeen

Despite drowsiness induced by the painkillers, Bridey couldn't sleep. Her mind spun with thoughts about the farm and everything that had happened out there.

She'd promised to help and provide a home for these women and children when she didn't have the means to keep that promise. With every solution she found, her mind presented another hurdle she didn't know how to jump over.

Cole had said he knew someone who could help, but did they have enough time for that? Clifford Camden would be hating the attention his church would receive if the police started asking questions. He'd always hammered home his strict rules on privacy and secrecy — physically as well as verbally — from his podium in the New Lord's Great Hall every night.

She remembered how the handlers had hung onto his every word, mesmerised by his passionate speeches and lessons. No one had questioned his authority or his beliefs, except maybe the McCaffreys who now lay dead in a cellar at the farm. Why had they left the compound? No one left unless they all left together to make a new home in a new place if the church attracted too much attention. A vague memory of one move teased the edges of her memory. She remembered boarding a church bus with the other children and travelling for days and nights at a time before settling somewhere else, away from towns and cities.

Why had Thom been allowed to take his bride away from the church? Had that been all part of a bigger plan to set up a new location? Why? The word echoed in her head, more questions than answers.

'Bridey?'

Bridey turned her head to find the bank manager at her bedside. 'Yes?'

'I'm sorry to trouble you, but I thought it best to come and see you in person as soon as possible.' A frown marred his forehead, and his lips were tight around his words. The cold, impersonal man who'd sat behind his desk and given her notice had been replaced by someone who looked like he was way out of his depth.

Bridey eased herself up on the pillows. 'How did you know I was here?'

A flush ran up his neck into his cheeks. 'Small town grapevines work faster than telephone lines and social media. I was in the newsagency when the call came through. Mrs Lee told me where to find you.' His smile brought warmth to his otherwise cold face. 'She threatened to run me out of town if I told anyone else though.'

'What phone call?' Bridey's stomach curled.

'I received a call from a man wanting to claim adverse possession of the property. He claims his son has been living there and managing the farm for over ten years, so I could only assume it was Mr McCaffrey senior.'

The curl tightened to a knot. Dead men didn't make phone calls, but the bank manager wouldn't know about the McCaffreys yet. 'Did he say his name?'

The bank manager shook his head. 'No, but he was insistent that I agree immediately. Bridey, everyone is aware of the police presence and hushed up activities at your farm, but as much as small town grapevines bear more gossip than truth at times, in this instance it remains stubbornly silent as to the reason. Not so much as a whiff of speculation, and that in itself is odd. No one knows about the farm ownership except you, me and my manager, and adverse possession hasn't been lodged by you yet, so there have been no public notices published. I tried to confirm his identity, but there was something odd about the call. When I said someone else had already expressed interest in claiming possession, he became angry and abusive, almost out of control. So, I put the phone down on him and came to talk to you.'

'Thank you. Did he say anything else?' A headache threatened behind her eyes. When would this nightmare end?

'His story didn't add up. First he said it was his son who lived there, then he changed his story to say that he was a friend of the family. But when he went off his tree at me, I figured real friends don't behave like that.'

'You did the right thing. Please give me a little more time, Dean. My late husband dealt with all the finances, and I need to work out how much the claim for the house will cost. I have no idea where to start. I don't want to lose my home. I have three children to raise.'

Dean pulled up a chair and sat. 'I'll buy you as much time as I can. It'll be a hard sell with head office, but I can approve a small low-interest rate loan to cover the costs like the land survey, evaluation, and application to the Registrar of Titles.' He pulled out a folded piece of paper from the top pocket of his business shirt. 'I've printed off some information on what you need to do, and the evidence you'll need to provide to support your claim.'

Bridey took the piece of paper, unfolded it, and scanned the contents. 'I don't know how I'll pay the loan back.'

'You could approach the welfare office and apply for a special benefit for income support. I'd say apply for the Farm Household Allowance but given the state of the farm, the current ownership, and the fact that it's not producing, I don't think you'd qualify. It's worth a shot though, once you have your claim on the property lodged.'

'Thank you, Dean. I appreciate your help.'

He pushed the chair back and stood. 'If you need anything else, please let me know.'

'I will, thank you.'

'What should I tell that man if he calls about the property again?'

Bridey placed her arm over her aching eyes to cut out the light that had suddenly become too bright. 'You can tell him he needs to talk to me. I believe I have something to say to him and it's all about where to go.'

Dean's chuckle retreated along with his footsteps. Bridey sighed. Her words felt a lot braver than she did. Closing her eyes, she rubbed at the pounding headache at her temples. At least she had a starting point now. With Cole's and Dean's help, she could make this work. As soon as her headache settled, she'd read the information Dean had given her. Then, when the welfare office opened on Tuesday, she could apply for the assistance he'd suggested.

Finally, she could see a way out, look forward to starting a free and happy life on the farm with her children, help Kirana and the others. She'd tell Cole about the phone call, watch the video footage from the hospital security cameras to identify the mystery visitor, and hopefully that would take care of Clifford Camden for good.

Her headache receded as she planned a small ceremony in her head for the McCaffreys. And a memorial stone for the baby who hadn't stood a chance against a monster. She grieved for her tiny baby, no bigger than a mouse, who would never grow up to be loved and adored by her older brothers. She liked to think that baby was a girl.

A gentle hand touched her shoulder. 'Bridey?'

She opened her eyes to see Cole beside her, his face drawn. Her calm evaporated like the morning mist.

~

Cole watched resignation transform Bridey's face as if she'd known more bad news was coming. Would there be a time in her life when she wasn't expecting the worst?

She lay against the pillows, beautiful but battered. Cole wished that, just once, he could bring good news so he could see her smile light up her face. With a sigh, he sat on the edge of the bed and took her hand in his.

'There is no way to sugarcoat this for you.'

Bridey closed her eyes, her lips drawn tight. 'Just tell me. Get it over with. Then bring me my children and take me home.'

The defeat in her voice broke his heart. She'd been so strong until now. Another blow, another strike. It had to be wearing her down.

'We've matched passports to the women we found at the farm but found nothing for the children. The federal police will take the unidentified passports and attempt to trace the women Nick has already matched to missing persons. There are a lot. It looks like this scheme has been running for years, but not always from Mindaleny Ridge.'

Bridey opened her eyes and eased herself up on the pillows. 'So, Thom's parents were involved?'

'It's possible, yes, but we'd have to prove it. The other theory is that they took the passports and planned to expose the operation.'

'And that may be why they're dead now.'

Cole nodded. 'Correct. Based on what you've told us about the church and their approach to marriage, we ran a few of those names through the records database. We came up empty. There is no record of Pastor Clifford Camden ever conducting a wedding ceremony or signing off on a marriage licence. We can find nothing on him.'

Bridey frowned. 'There is a lot of secrecy around the church. No one is allowed to talk to strangers about it. The places we lived were usually secluded and self-sufficient so there was no need to go into towns like I have to do here. No hospitals like this if we needed medical attention. We had our own nurses and doctors who treated us in the homes.'

'What if they couldn't be treated at home?'

'Then it was the way of the New Lord that they would be placed in eternal sleep.'

A sickening feeling formed in the pit of Cole's stomach. 'How were they placed in eternal sleep?'

'The doctor would give them an injection. After two days, we would go in, wrap them in sheets and the men from the Grooming House would take them away.'

'What happened to the bodies after they were taken away?'

'When there were enough, the men would build a bonfire around them. The New Lord would commit them to the underworld because they had failed to meet the standards set by him.'

'Failed in what way?'

'Any weakness, even illness, was considered a failure. They'd failed to make the New Lord happy, and their punishment was death.'

A string of oaths left Cole's lips, the sick feeling intensifying. 'Bridey, who was it that attacked you today?'

She hesitated. 'You don't understand, Cole. I too have displeased the New Lord, failed to make him happy. I've brought eyes on his church and his people. If I can't protect myself, my children, Kirana and her people, we're all destined for the underworld. He will come and he will take us all. You won't be able to stop him.'

'Then I am absolutely not happy about letting you go home.' The thought of Bridey and her children being harmed by this psychopathic pastor was one he refused to entertain. 'Bridey, we couldn't find any record of you anywhere either. No birth record, no marriage record, no welfare record, no passport, no driver's licence. How did you come to be at the church?'

'I don't remember. I must have been young, maybe a baby. I told you before that we weren't allowed to ask questions. When I got older I realised that the girls were all given new names when they arrived. The New Lord performed a naming ceremony for all new arrivals. He said it was a cleansing of the old world. I never questioned my own name because I don't remember being called anything else.'

'Did you have a surname?'

'No. Only the men had surnames, and they were gifted those by the New Lord too. When we married, we took on their surnames and signed a contract of subservience.'

'Do you have a copy of that contract?'

'No. The New Lord keeps it. For those who stay on the compound, the contract is reviewed to ensure obedience. I don't know why Thom and I were allowed to stay on the farm. Maybe the New Lord was going to build another compound there?'

'That would explain the influx of new people and why they were kept at the farm for as long as they were.'

Bridey's grip tightened around his fingers. 'That would have made me a handler. That's an awful thing to be because you're powerless to stop the bad things from happening.'

'It's also a motive for burning down the shed and

trying to get rid of evidence.' Cole ran a frustrated hand through his hair and wished he still believed that small town policing was all about arresting goats with a petunias fetish. He pulled his phone from his pocket with his free hand and checked his messages. 'Forensics have arrived at the farm. I've got to go. I'll get Nick to come get you and the girls and bring you out to the farm once Doc has discharged you all.'

'No!' Her nails dug into his skin, panic in her eyes. 'I trust no one but you.'

'I've failed to keep you safe twice already, Bridey. If you're worried about Nick, I'll make sure Sam is with him too. I've organised security for the farm. I've done everything I can to keep you all safe this time.'

'Cole, no. I want you and only you.'

If the circumstances were different, those words would be music to his ears. 'Bridey ...'

'You couldn't stop what happened. Security won't stop him coming back. It doesn't matter where we go or who is protecting us, he will come back. He will wait for his moment. I'd prefer he come for me where I'm expecting him, and I know my surroundings. You don't know this man like I do, Cole. I realise now he is not a god. He is the devil incarnate, and he will not rest until he has destroyed us all.'

Cole blew out a long breath. He knew how long it could take for the wheels of justice to turn. How long it could take for evidence to be reviewed and an arrest to be made, the reports and red tape that followed before a conviction by the court. And if he didn't get this one a hundred percent wrapped up, this psycho who thought he was God would walk free to continue his reign of terror.

'We've got to work out the logistics here on how I'm going to get you all out of here in one hit.'

If this Camden bloke had come for the girls, he could still be out there somewhere watching. Did Camden have the power to take them by force? Probably not if he'd tried producing a fake letter designed to release them into his care.

'When the New Lord moved us between compounds, he used a bus.' Bridey interrupted his thoughts. 'I've seen a school bus in town when I went to get supplies.'

'Good thinking. I'll arrange it.' He dialled the station and got Sam. 'Hey, Sam. Who drives the school bus?'

'Harriet's partner, Bernie. She's had the school bus contract for a while now. Why?'

'Can you contact her? I need to move five women, eleven children and a newborn out to Mindaleny Ridge.'

'Sure can, Sarge. Pick up from the hospital?'

'Yes. I need you on the bus with them. Can you please bring my laptop with you?'

'Yep. Anything else?'

Cole looked at Bridey, her face pale, exhaustion, and pain leaving dark bruises under her eyes. 'Can you please pick up a pre-paid SIM card from Mrs Lee and see if you can find an unclaimed mobile phone that works in Lost and Found? I'm going to need Bridey to have a phone on her at all times.'

'No problem, Sarge. I've got a couple of spares lying around at home. I keep meaning to send them away for recycling. Just as well I didn't. I'll bring one with me.'

'Thanks, Sam.' Cole hung up and dialled Gus. 'Hey, Big Fella. I need food to feed sixteen people delivered out to Mindaleny Ridge.'

'You don't ask for much, do you, son?' Gus laughed. 'Will soups and stews be enough to start?'

'Perfect. Keep a tab so you can claim it back once we've cut through the red tape.'

'I'm happy to help, son. Did you want me to bring the kiddies over to the hospital to see their mum or drop them at the farm with the food?'

Cole's gaze captured Bridey's. 'Their mum needs to see them. I think she'll rest easier knowing they're with her.' Her soft, thankful smile made his heart beat a little faster.

'I'll drop them over now and come back to cook up a storm. I might need to get some help in the kitchen.'

'Thanks, Dad.'

'You take good care of that girl, Cole.'

'I will.' He hung up before Gus got any ideas about talking romance.

Chapter Eighteen

The orange and white school bus bounced a little on the uneven road out to Mindaleny Ridge. Bridey winced as the movement jarred her bruised ribs. Above the noise of the engine, Kirana comforted her people in a language Bridey didn't understand. She could only imagine their fear of returning to the place where they'd been so badly mistreated. And their nightmare wasn't over yet.

Her life had changed so much since Thom's death. With her boys huddled close beside her on the seat at the rear of the bus, Bridey shifted to look out the back window, relieved to find Cole following behind them in the police SUV. With a strong police and security presence at the farm, they would have a chance to be safe for a while. The fear of what could happen when that security lapsed made her stomach turn. If the New Lord was the one who'd burned down the shed, what was to stop him from burning the house while they slept?

Doubt etched its way into her mind. Had she made a mistake insisting they come back to the farm? Would they have been safer staying at Gus's pub? She'd glimpsed inside it a few times, curious about what kind of place it was, when she'd gone inside the attached bottle store to buy Thom's whiskey. It had grown much busier since Gus had taken it over. She'd never understood why until now because she hadn't known much about the outside world except what she'd needed to know to stay alive. Now she understood that with so many people crowded into the pub, the New Lord could easily have come in unnoticed. He'd proven to be a master of disguise before. No, they'd be much safer here where she could see him coming.

Bridey turned her attention to the people occupying the seats in front of her. She was handler to four women and nine girls plus her own boys. But she would be a different kind of handler to the one who'd raised her, and she'd be damned if she'd allow the New Lord or anyone else to change that.

The bus rattled over the grid, bounced up the drive and stopped on the rutted driveway in front of the house. At the site of the old potting shed, men in white plastic suits worked around a table full of things they'd retrieved through the trapdoor. Bridey shuddered to think that perhaps among the things scattered across the table were the remains of two people who had once lived and breathed on the farm. She refused to let that be the fate of the people on the bus.

The constable stood up. 'I need everyone to stay in their seats, please. We'll get everyone off the bus, but I need you all to stay calm. Kirana, can you please explain that we first want to make sure the house is safe?'

Kirana nodded and relayed the message. It did nothing to stop the children from whimpering or alleviate the fear on the faces of the four women. Her own children huddled closer to her, confused and afraid of what might happen next. Bridey would give her soul for them to just be happy and free from the fear that dogged their lives.

She watched out the window as Cole and Sam mounted the stairs to the verandah and spoke to two men in uniform. The car out the front had writing on it that said they were from a security firm that Bridey recognised as local.

She reached out to Kirana. 'Tell everyone they don't need to worry. We're safe. Nothing bad can happen to them while these people are on the farm.' She didn't want to think about what might happen if they left before Cole could stop the New Lord from coming again.

Sam poked her head through the open door. 'Let's get everyone inside.'

Kirana passed on the instruction to the others, and everyone filed out to gather in the sunshine. Bridey led the way into the house, stopping in the kitchen to put the kettle on. As everyone piled in behind her, she was thankful that the farmhouse had a large kitchen. Where would she put all these people? She had no idea what the upper level of house held or if it was even liveable. Doubt crept in. Had she been too hasty and made a promise she couldn't keep?

'Hey.' Cole moved to stand beside her where she watched and waited for the kettle to boil. 'How's the ribs?'

'Tender. I have some liniment to apply. It will be better than taking painkillers that make me sleepy.'

'You still need to rest though.' With a gentle hand on her shoulder, Cole turned her to face him. 'Promise me you'll rest.'

She looked up at him, studied his face. Concern etched his features, his eyes serious and a frown drawing at his forehead. 'There is a lot to do. I need to find a place for these people to sleep tonight. There is a whole upper floor to the farmhouse that needs to be cleaned. It hasn't been used in years.

Thom boarded up the staircase so we couldn't go up there. I don't even know what I'll find up there. Have I made a mistake, Cole?' Doubt, pain, and exhaustion clouded in on her thoughts and the sting of tears burned behind her eyes. 'I don't even own this property.'

Cole's arms came around her and he drew her in against him, giving her room to move away if she wanted to. Instead, she sank into his warmth and strength, so different from anything she'd experienced before. He leaned against the counter to take her weight and rested his cheek on her hair.

'You're not alone anymore, Bridey. Gus, Sam, Nick, Mrs Lee ... me ... we're all here for you now.'

She rested her hands on his waist for balance, heat seeping through her cold hands, and lay her head against his heartbeat. The smell of his aftershave teased her nose. Cole's arms tightened around her, and she felt the touch of his lips on her hair.

'I'll need help taking down the panelling that blocks the staircase.'

'Consider it done. Gus and I will come and do that in the morning. It's Saturday so the station will be closed.'

She eased back a little in his arms to look at him, not ready to step away from the promise of his strength. 'Thank you. You're a kind man, Sergeant Delaney.'

'And you're a strong woman, Bridey McCaffrey.' He smiled at her.

'I don't even know if that's my real name.'

'Then I'll help you with that too. I'm not going to lie to you, there's a long and bumpy road ahead and God knows what else we'll uncover along the way, but if I promise you anything at all, it's that we will solve this case and we will make this man and whoever he's working with accountable for their actions.' Cole tipped up her chin with his forefinger. 'And then you will be free.'

For a long moment, Bridey stared at him. Free. It's what she'd tried to be, it's what she wanted to be. Free from the violence that had dogged her life, free to live in the world outside of restrictions that had imprisoned her. Free to find love, true love that nurtured and cherished in the way Cole held her now and promised to keep her and her family safe.

Cole's arms fell away, and he cupped her face in his warm hands. Slowly, his head descended to block her view, and the firmness of his lips pressed to hers in a gentle kiss that sealed every promise he'd made. Bridey's eyes fluttered closed as she lost herself in the sensation of his mouth on hers, the touch a commitment not a threat, everything she'd ever dreamed of feeling. Her hands found their way up his chest and settled over his heartbeat, the steady thud a comfort.

The exaggerated sound of someone clearing their throat penetrated the blissful fog in her mind. 'Sergeant Delaney, I hope you're not leading my witness.'

~

Cole took his time to lift his head. He smiled at Bridey and rubbed his thumbs across the flush on her cheeks. 'Wow.'

An embarrassed giggle slipped from her lips as she stepped aside, her hand shaking a little as she lifted cups from the cupboard above her head. Cole gave her free hand a little squeeze as he moved away and found everyone's eyes on them, including young Alex's glower. He'd been so wrapped up in Bridey that he'd forgotten anyone was in the room. He made a mental note to chat to Alex later. The boy was hurting more than he needed to and Cole had to make that right.

'I thought I'd doubled your caseload, and you were going to be too snowed under to make it down here.' Cole moved to shake Mark's hand.

'Well, I made an exception just for you. I hope you feel honoured by that?' Mark's grin lit up his face as his gaze slid past Cole's shoulder to Bridey and back again.

'I can see you have everything under control.' His eyebrows lifted in query.

'Just about. There's still the out-of-control goat to wrangle and a girl named Sunshine with sticky fingers to deal with.'

'Sounds like fun. Just as well I brought the cavalry then.'

Cole walked around him and pulled first Lily then TJ into a hug. 'Thanks for coming down.'

TJ glanced at the group of women and children huddled together in the corner. 'I see we have a bit of work to do?'

Cole nodded. 'We're going to have to find somewhere for everyone to sleep until we sort out the rooms upstairs. We'll get started on that tomorrow.'

'Good thing we called ahead and spoke to Gus then. I've got some inflatable mattresses and swags in the car, and Gus has kindly given us extra bedding.' Lily tugged on TJ's arm. 'Why don't you boys take your testosterone outside while we get to know everyone? Your constable can stay. What's your name, hon?'

'Sam.'

'Nice to meet you, Sam. I'm Lily and this is TJ. We run the Tiny Watts Foundation in Perth.'

Sam shook their hands. 'The place that started out as a teenage rehabilitation centre. I've heard about your work with street gangs. Good to see you branching out. I'll introduce you to Bridey and Kirana.'

Confident Sam had it under control, Cole led Mark outside onto the back verandah. They sat down on the lumpy sofa that overlooked where Forensics continued to rifle through and bag evidence.

'She's pretty.' Mark stretched his legs out in front of him and relaxed against the backrest of the sofa.

'Beautiful and been through too much.' Cole didn't feel nearly as chilled as Mark appeared to be, but he knew from experience that appearances could be deceiving. 'So, what really brings you down here because I know that TJ and Lily are more than capable of driving themselves wherever they need to go.'

Mark shrugged. 'That's why we came in separate cars. Not that there was much room in the car for me anyway with all the stuff they brought with them. I looked into that church you asked me about.'

'And?' Cole tried to still the unsettled gnaw at his instincts. He knew what might be coming but he needed proof and confirmation.

'Not much we could find. They're not a registered organisation, they don't own any property that we could trace back to the church, and the name you gave me was that of a dead man. The real Clifford Camden died from a suspicious overdose of gamma hydroxybutyric acid and ketamine downed with a bottle of whiskey.'

'What made the overdose suspicious other than the obvious uses of those drugs?'

'The neck of the bottle was lodged so deep in his throat, he drowned in the whiskey.'

'Fuck.'

'Exactly what I said.'

'So, who is this bloke claiming to be him? Bridey only refers to him as the New Lord.'

'She probably knows him as Camden too. The real Camden has been dead for years. His remains were found about twelve months ago on a deserted property, discovered by a couple of urban explorers who go around making video documentaries about abandoned houses and speculate on what happened there. The case had been put on the backburner as a bizarre suicide until you came along and dropped the name Camden. I've got another team of forensics back out at the property now. If we can lift some prints, we might be able to formally identify him but given the church's practice of stripping people of their identities, there's a good chance we may not find a match.'

'They're ghosts.' Cole pinched the bridge of his nose as another headache loomed. 'We haven't found any identification amongst the paperwork that came out of the container to match to Bridey to yet.'

Shattered

'We'll need some DNA from your girl to see if we can match her up with someone on the missing persons register. We have a lot of loose ends to tie up, my friend.'

'She's not my girl.'

Mark snorted. 'No? Looked like she was to me. Unless you go around kissing girls randomly ... in which case we may have a problem here and God help the nation. I've never seen you so soft and gooey-eyed.'

'Want to compare? You and Lily have been together for how long now and I still see your hard arse all gooey eyed over her.' Cole laughed.

'Well, I mean, look at her. She's beautiful inside and out. And I love her more every day.'

'Bridey has a long way to go, Mark. You've seen her file. I have to tread carefully. She has children who haven't had much of a fatherly influence and who are damaged themselves.'

'Kids are resilient, mate. I've seen it in the work that TJ and Lily do. A little love and care go a long way. It's time you moved on. You can't keep the candle burning for Carrie forever. She'd want you to move on.'

Cole realised he hadn't thought of Carrie and the baby for a while and guilt stabbed at his conscience. 'The question is, am I attracted to Bridey because she reminds me of Carrie? Do I have these feelings toward

249

her because I'm looking to make up for what I failed in before, and that was to keep my family safe?'

'You didn't fail to keep Carrie and the baby safe. The blame there lies with the arseholes who considered it their right to take lives. And those arseholes are now behind bars where they belong, getting the punishment they deserve.'

'You sound like Gus.' Cole sat forward and watched as Forensics placed bagged evidence into boxes. 'I need to settle this case. Until we have answers and a conviction, Bridey will never be free.'

'That's why I'm here. To speed things up a bit. I don't like what we've uncovered so far. I don't know if we'll solve the murder in that container down there because the killer might already be dead, but this New Lord business might prove to be a lot worse than we thought. And the bodies are stacking up the deeper we dig.'

Cole looked up as Bridey came out with a mug in each hand. 'Coffee? Two sugars for you, Mark.' She handed Mark a mug. 'Lily says to tell you to enjoy it because from tomorrow she's cutting you back to one. She says you're sweet enough.'

Mark chuckled and took the mug. 'Thanks. I guess I'll keep my stash of chocolate hidden then.'

Bridey handed Cole his mug, her eyes not meeting his and colour in her cheeks. 'Just the way you like it.'

'Thanks. Sit for a minute.' He shifted on the sofa to make space between him and Mark. 'I want to show you that video footage I got from the hospital.' He placed his mug on the floor, pulled out his phone, and opened the email he'd sent to Mark. Clicking on the attachment, he turned the phone on its side for a landscape view.

'I didn't know a phone could do that. The only one I've ever used is the one on the wall in the kitchen.'

The wonder in her voice had Cole remembering that Bridey had never owned a mobile phone. 'I've arranged with Sam that she get you one so you can contact me whenever you need to from wherever you are on the farm.'

'I won't know how to use it.'

Cole squeezed her hands where they lay entwined in her lap. 'I'll show you how.' Ignoring the amused sound Mark made, he pressed play on the video. 'Tell me if you know this man.'

Bridey concentrated on the screen as a man approached a nurse at the hospital reception desk, his profile clearly visible. He turned his head to look at the matron. Bridey shot up from the sofa, knocking the phone out of Cole's hand.

'It's him. The New Lord.' She stared at the phone as if expecting Clifford Camden to jump out of it like an evil genie from a bottle to come for her.

Mark retrieved the phone as Cole stood to comfort Bridey. 'I'm sorry, honey, but for the record, I need you to say his name.'

She stood, icy cold to his touch in the dwindling heat of the afternoon sun, stiff as a board. Then she looked into his eyes and held his gaze. 'Clifford Camden.'

The flyscreen door slammed behind her as Bridey hurried inside, looking terrified that if, just by saying the name, it would conjure up the devil himself.

Chapter Nineteen

Her hands still shaking and her mind whirling, Bridey sat at the kitchen table with her three boys and tried to explain the presence of all the strangers in their house. This was something she'd been used to at their age, but not what her boys had been exposed to.

Missing pieces of her childhood memories began falling into place with a scarily adult, new world view. Girls arriving at the Grooming House, confused, and upset, crying to go home. Girl babies brought in, some newborn and screaming. The sorting process before the new arrivals were distributed to their handlers, and the ones who had remained in her home. None of them the orphans they were portrayed to be, she realised now, but rather stolen children from all parts of the world. She understood too how the new handlers came to be, but the mystery of how the New Lord had recruited their husbands still remained.

The face in the pictures on Cole's phone ... It only confirmed in her mind what she already knew in her heart. The New Lord was an evil, murderous being and Thom had been working with him all along to increase his following, maybe even create a new settlement right here at Mindaleny Ridge. Now the fruits of their efforts gathered in her front lounge, already damaged and afraid, and she was their handler. But a different kind of handler than she might have been if Thom was still alive.

TJ stepped into the kitchen. 'Am I interrupting?'

Bridey shook her head. 'Come in and sit down. I was just explaining to the boys that we'd have some guests for a while.'

TJ pulled out a chair and sat. 'Is it okay to talk in front of the children?'

'Yes. This is their home too, and life will be quite different now, so they need to understand why we need to look after these people.'

'As I explained earlier, Lily and I run the Tiny Watts Foundation. We started out rescuing homeless and disadvantaged children in Perth, but we've recently been awarded a tender to be part of the government's Victim Support Program and work with police to protect victims of domestic violence and human trafficking. Lily is a DV survivor.'

'I had no idea that these things existed.' Bridey clasped her hands on the scarred kitchen table. She'd lived in the bubble of the New Lord's making for too long.

'It can be an evil world out there, hon. Given the circumstances these women and children were found in, we've been granted special permission not to send them to a detention centre. The wheels can turn very slowly in Immigration. In this case, thanks to the reforms to visa applications, we've been able to apply for witness protection visas for Kirana and the girls, and we'll work hard to ensure they're fast-tracked.'

Bridey reached for the water jug in the middle of the table and poured water into five glasses, distributing them before answering. 'Those are just words to me. I don't know anything about visas or how the law works. Tell me what I need to do.'

TJ smiled. 'Don't worry, Lily and I will be there to help any time you need it. What it means though is that, because you stepped in and offered a place to stay, we can list the farm as a safe haven while the girls are processed through the system.'

'I'm not sure how safe it is here.'

'We can help you make it safe. Under our contract, we can pay you rent for the accommodation you provide. The women and children will receive a living and food allowance from government support services that will help you feed them. They also receive an allowance for clothing and toiletries, so most if not all essentials are covered. As their case managers, Lily and I will ensure that they have access to health care, counselling, interpreters, and anything else they need.'

'Those are all useful things but how do we keep them safe on a property I don't own yet?' The rent would help with the legal fees, and the allowances would help feed and clothe the women and children, but one real threat remained if they couldn't stop the New Lord from coming to steal them away again. 'Those security men out there won't be here forever and nor will the police. There will come a time when we're alone out here.'

'Mark is working on the case, and you can rest assured that he will not stop until he has the people or person behind this in custody.'

'There is a lot you don't understand about my world and the Children of the New Lord. There is a lot I didn't know until I became part of your world. If I am to right the wrongs that were done to these people by Thom, my first job is to know they're safe. Walls and doors don't keep demons out, they don't stop people getting hurt and fires being started that destroy these safe havens you talk about. Tell me how I keep them safe.' Frustration gave her voice an edge and made her want to thump her fist on the table but that would scare her children because they had never seen their mum angry before. Bridey took a deep, calming breath as TJ reached out a hand to cover hers.

'There is a lot we can do. First, we do a risk assessment. Lily already has that underway. Then we create a safety plan that will tell you step by step what to do if you're in danger, simplify it for you to teach to the children, so they know what to do too. Next, we install security cameras, alarms, screens, and locks. If that still isn't enough to make you feel safe, we will issue you and the other women a personal safety device that will be monitored by emergency services. All you have to do is press a button and someone will respond.'

Still not satisfied, Bridey withdrew her hands from under TJ's. 'And when the danger has passed? What happens then?'

'Once their visas are approved, Kirana and her people will have the chance to make a new life. Either here in Moonie River or somewhere else. They will be well-equipped to start over.'

'What about the children? Kirana and the other women aren't their mothers.'

'We can find foster homes for them.'

Bridey shook her head. 'No. I don't know what your foster homes are, but I grew up in a grooming house with children and handlers who weren't my real family. I know now that the things that happened there were bad. Unbelievably bad. I don't want that for Kirana and these children.'

'Lily and I do thorough background checks and home visits before releasing children into care. All our foster carers are required to have police clearance and Working with Children checks.'

Bridey pushed back from the table and stood. 'If there is one thing I have learned since Thom died, it's that evil is everywhere. I know how I've lived and, all my life, I accepted that's just how it was meant to be. I see it from a different angle now. I've seen kindness and care from strangers that is in sharp contrast to what I'd experienced before. I want to make sure that these people have a life that is hugely different to what mine was like.'

TJ remained seated at the table. 'We want to help you achieve that, I promise.'

'Then please start by arranging that security you talked about.' She gathered the boys close. 'I need to see to my children.' Bridey walked across the kitchen, stopped at the door into the corridor that led to her bedroom, and turned back to TJ. 'I will speak to Kirana once everyone is settled and, between us, we will work out a plan. Then we will discuss the possibilities with you and Lily. I know you're trying to help, and I appreciate that, but once you know the whole story, you'll understand.'

'Hon, I'm not liking what I've seen so far. Right now, I'm as eager as Mark and Cole are to put the people behind this in jail for good. Unfortunately, for us, this fight is ongoing. We put one lot of people smugglers behind bars, and someone else just takes over their operation. They have total disregard for humanity.'

'I see that now in a way I never understood before Thom died.' Bridey glanced out the kitchen window as a car pulled up in front of the house. 'Gus is here with the food. Once all the children are fed, bathed, and settled for the night, we can talk this over. I'll get the boys bathed first if you could please help Gus with the food.'

'I can do that.'

'Thank you. I appreciate what you and Lily are doing to help, and I want to do what's best for Kirana and these people.'

'Then we'll be good friends.' TJ smiled.

Bridey returned the smile. 'I have no idea what it's like to have a friend, but it sounds good.'

It sounded like something she wanted to be but couldn't until all the bad things that had happened on the farm could be erased and a new life could begin.

～

Cole did one last sweep of the farm's perimeter, checking for signs of entry and noting the need for fences to be repaired almost everywhere on the property. The remoteness of the property surprised him. How could a place so close to town be so isolated? Was that why Clifford Camden or whatever his real name was had the place in his sights? The women and children had arrived here and gone unnoticed until Thomas McCaffrey's death. They might have left or stayed unnoticed too had it not been for their captor's suicide.

Dinner at the house had been a silent affair. Cole had scanned the people huddled inside the kitchen. The children had all sat around the table, poking at their food, cautiously tasting the hearty beef stew and rice Gus had prepared. The four women they'd rescued had watched the men warily, as if expecting to be grabbed and dragged away at any time. Kirana's baby had slept peacefully in a body sling, close to her heart.

And Bridey, watching and checking, helping the younger ones eat, placing a comforting hand on skinny shoulders when any of the children showed signs of distress. Was this what her life had been like growing up, taking care of stolen, abused children? Care came naturally to Bridey considering the trauma she'd experienced herself.

She'd glanced up and caught him watching her. A smile had softened the look of concern on her face. Bridey had been in her happy place, taking care of the people she'd chosen to make her family. And his heart was slowly talking him into becoming a part of her family even when his head objected.

Cole manoeuvred the SUV along what once would have been a firebreak, eager to return to the house and Bridey.

Mark had kissed his wife goodbye and followed the forensics team back to Perth, armed with evidence and a sample of Bridey's DNA for identification. With some pushing, they'd get it rushed through the lab.

Cole passed the site of the McCaffreys' last resting place and parked outside the back verandah. The police tape and sorting tables had gone, and the trapdoor had been dropped back into place. He made a note to lock it in case the boys, or anyone else, decided to go exploring. He'd never look at another shipping container in the same way again. The secrets the steel containers on the farm had revealed weren't ones he ever wanted to come across in this lifetime or the next.

Cole got out and closed the door of the SUV. He locked it, waved to the security guards at their posts, and climbed the back stairs. The house was silent as he entered through the laundry and mud room to find Bridey standing at the kitchen bench, her face strained and her hand rubbing at her bruised ribs.

'Are you okay?' He dropped his keys into his pocket.

Bridey nodded. 'I'm fine.'

'Ribs hurting?'

'A little.'

He walked over to her and tipped up her chin so he could see her face. 'A lot, I think. Have you taken your painkillers?'

'They make me sleepy and my head fuzzy.'

'They're supposed to so you can get some rest.' He smiled at her before turning to put the kettle on. 'Why don't you sit down while I make you a cup of tea? What's that in your hand?'

'A liniment made from eucalyptus, ginger, curcumin, orange, and lavender for the bruising, but it hurts to twist, and I can't reach around to my back.' Frustration mixed with pain in her words. 'Lily and TJ are settling the girls for the night. I didn't want to disturb them to ask them to apply it for me. I can wait until they're done.'

Cole turned back to her. 'If you trust me, I can do it for you.'

She stared up at him, indecision ruling her expression.

'Your choice, Bridey.' He cupped a hand to her cheek and stroked her soft skin with his thumb. 'I will never hurt you. Not intentionally.'

Still, she hesitated. 'I'm not afraid of you. I'm ashamed.'

'Of what, honey?' Confused, he dropped his hand back to his side.

Bridey placed the tub of liniment on the table, turned her back to him and lifted the edge of her shirt to reveal a glimpse of her back.

Dark purple bruises marked the area where a boot had connected with her ribs, but it was what the bruises covered that sickened him.

Raised welts, some old scars, some a little fresher, crisscrossed her back.

Cole swore under his breath as he lifted the shirt tail from her fingers and raised it a little higher. 'Who did this to you?' He tried to keep the anger from his voice but failed.

Bridey flinched as his fingers traced the scars. 'Thom, the New Lord.'

'They whipped you?'

Bridey nodded. She loosened the buttons on her shirt and eased it from her shoulders.

Cole's throat grew tight as he studied the map of punishment Bridey had endured.

'My eyes are wide open now, Cole. I don't want the

New Lord just to be punished. I want him dead so he can never do harm to anyone again.'

Right now, Cole would happily have finished the job for her, but more violence wouldn't fix this. He had to believe in the justice system he'd sworn to serve.

He reached for the jar of liniment and unscrewed the cap. With gentle fingers, he applied it to her bruises, spread it with his palms as she stood stiffly under his hands. When he was done, he pulled her shirt back up over her shoulders, turned her around and buttoned it up, before drawing her into his arms. He tucked her head under his chin and held her against him, loosely enough for her to break free, firmly enough for comfort. He ran his fingers over her hair, removing the hair clips that held it in place, freeing it to fall down around her shoulders.

For a long time, they stood, silently drawing on each other's strength. Cole held her a little tighter, one arm around her waist, a hand cupping her head against his chest, as he tried to convince himself that he was providing solace and not losing his heart to this tiny, fragile, brave woman who'd endured too much.

His hand followed the trail of hair down her back. She sighed, an inhale and exhale that had her relaxing into him.

Cole pressed a kiss to the top of her head and fell deeper. There were so many sides to Bridey

McCaffrey. He'd seen vulnerability and strength, terror and bravery, the caring side, and the side of her that needed a degree of revenge on the people who had brought harm to her, Kirana, and countless others like them. In so many ways she reminded him of Carrie, but there were other traits that set them so far apart.

As he tipped up her chin, wanting to kiss her, waiting for her permission, he knew she would taste different to Carrie. He'd sampled that before and found himself becoming addicted to Bridey.

Bridey drew her arms from around his waist and reached up to cup his face in her hands. She stretched up on her tiptoes, their bodies brushing, starting a fire inside him that he tried to reduce to a slow burn. The last thing she needed was for him to go rushing in and taking it to a level she wasn't ready for. His heart knew the next move needed to be hers, even while his head argued with his body to slow it down.

Bridey drew his lips to hers, tasted his mouth with a hint of hesitation. Cole accepted her kiss, deepened it, his hands finding her hips to hold her closer. His heart beat faster, his body demanded more but he steeled himself to let her do the taking, allowed her to set the pace.

Her hands explored his body, a slow touch that made the fire inside him burn hotter, and the difference in their heights a hindrance. In a slow movement, he lifted her up into his arms, waited a moment for her protest. When all she did was press her lips to his neck and hold on tight, he carried her outside to the sofa and sat with her in his lap.

Cole drew the blanket up around them as her fingers loosened the buttons on his shirt and hands slipped inside to leave a trail of fire on his skin. He ran his palms up the silky soft skin of her legs, stopping at the top of her thigh. She lifted her head, and for a long moment they simply studied each other.

'I like kissing you, Cole.'

He chuckled and kissed her forehead. 'I like kissing you too.'

'I don't know how to please you. I have only ever been taken before.'

Her comment brought his head back to earth with a thump. He held her closer. 'It's not about pleasing me. It's about us, enjoying a growing relationship with each other, a place we need to both be comfortable in. I will never take you against your will, Bridey. If we go anywhere with what we have between us, then we go there together. All in, willingly, and in complete agreement whatever the final outcome. And we will only take the next step when you're ready for it.'

She reached up to kiss his cheek. 'Thank you. This is another new world for me.'

'And I'm more than happy to hold your hand along

the road.' He moved on the sofa until they were laying down next to each other, tucked the blanket in around them and held her close. 'And this is far enough for tonight.'

With a long sigh, she settled into his side, her head pillowed on his chest. Long after Bridey's breathing settled into sleep, Cole lay awake.

Chapter Twenty

Bridey walked into the kitchen just before dawn to find Gus already there prepping for breakfast. Around midnight, she'd left Cole to sleep on the sofa outside and gone inside to where her boys had slept huddled together in her bed.

'You're in early, Gus.'

Gus grinned at her. 'I hope you don't mind? I came back here after the pub had closed and I'd locked up. Camped in the back paddock under the stars near the ridge. The fresh air out here is good for an old city bloke like me.'

'You're welcome to camp out any time. I thought you'd prefer the sea air though being a sailor at heart?'

'Had more than enough of that in my younger days. It's not too far to travel to the coast if I need a taste of the sea, so I'm quite happy out here in the country. Besides, we have a lot to help you with today, so I wanted to get an early start.'

Bridey pulled plates out of the cupboard and began setting the table for the children to have their breakfast. 'I appreciate your help.'

Once they had more space to work with, everyone would feel more settled. She could only hope that the rooms above them were liveable. She understood now why Thom had kept it boarded up. He must have done that after the death of his parents. What secrets would they uncover when the panels blocking the stairs came down?

Kirana walked in, tired, and dishevelled, looking like she hadn't slept a wink. Gus reached for the coffee pot on the cooktop, poured some into a mug, added milk and sugar, and handed it to her.

'Have some of that, love. I'm sure you could do with some caffeine.'

'Thank you, Mr Gus.'

He smiled. 'Just Gus. How's the baby?'

'She is sleeping now. I have called her Jayachandra. It means *the One who Won*.'

'That's a beautiful name. And perfect for her. Now why don't you sit down and have some breakfast? You need to keep your strength up.' Gus pulled out a chair for Kirana near the head of the table. 'I have some oatmeal ready now and then later, there will be fresh bread with bacon, eggs and tomato.' Gus pulled out the chair Bridey normally sat in. 'You sit too, Bridey. You nibbled at your food last night, my son tells me. I'd like to see you eat a good meal this morning.'

Bridey sat as Gus dropped spoons of steaming oatmeal into bowls, drizzled it with honey and topped it off with berries before placing it front of them.

'Thanks, Gus. Smells good.'

Her tummy grumbled. A simple meal that reminded her that it had been a long time since she'd last sat down for a meal herself before she'd been blindsided by Thom's death and the Pandora's Box it had opened up. That thought brought her back to earth with a thump. This was a lull, the calm before the storm, because no one was safe until the New Lord was dealt with.

They ate in silence for a while, picking away at the food in the bowls, both just enjoying the luxury they seldom had time or opportunity to enjoy.

Her belly warmed by the oatmeal, Bridey moved her bowl aside. 'Kirana, we need to talk about the children. Has TJ spoken to you about foster care for them?'

Kirana nodded as she dropped her spoon into her half-full bowl of porridge. 'I will take care of the children. And the others. No foster homes. No more harm.'

'We agree on that then. With the help that TJ and Lily can arrange, you and the girls can stay here for as long as you want to.'

'Thank you. Please, Bridey, we don't want to go back to the villages. It won't be good.'

The fear in her eyes tugged at Bridey's heart. 'I will do everything I can to help you. This is your home for as long as you want to stay. But we need a plan in case the authorities choose for you and force the children into care.' In that way, the real world was no different to the one she'd been raised in.

'I am a teacher.' Kirana played with the cereal bowl, turning it in her hands. 'I can be the teacher here so they can stay. In my village, when I was younger, we had missionaries come to teach in our classrooms. This is how I learned English and how to be a teacher.'

'Then we have our first step in the plan. I've home-schooled my children here at this table, but it's too small for everyone. Before we found you, I was cleaning out the old farm office. It's big enough to make into a classroom. If you can tutor my children too, I can work with Melati, Amisha, Sari and Sinta to get the fields planted and growing again.'

Kirana smiled. 'I like this plan.'

Bridey smiled back. 'Then we have a lot of work to do.'

'Maybe the two of you should eat all that porridge

first so you have the strength to put that plan into action.' Gus chuckled as Cole strode into the kitchen. 'And here is another hungry belly to fill. Sleep well, son? Hungry?'

Cole sat down beside her. 'I could eat a bull. Must be the country air.'

'All quiet on the western front?' Gus cocked an eyebrow at Cole as he placed a bowl of oatmeal in front of him.

'Not even a mouse moving out there. I've just been chatting to the security guards before their shift change. A quiet night.' He turned to Bridey as Gus moved away. 'Sleep well?'

Bridey's cheeks warmed as she nodded. Cuddled close to Cole, warm and safe, had been the best feeling in the world. A place she could get used to. A world where fear and harm didn't exist, where love, care, and protection flourished. But there was a lot of work to do before she could believe that a life like that could be hers to keep forever.

Jolted out of her daydreams by the phone ringing on the wall, Bridey stared at it for a moment, the shrill sound foreign in the comforting atmosphere that had fallen in the kitchen. The phone never rang. It had seldom rung before Thom died, and when it had, he'd answered the call, chasing them all out of the room. Pushing back her chair, Bridey rose to answer it.

'Hello?'

'Do you think I don't see you? I warned you, didn't I? Did you think that by surrounding yourself with guards and the police, you're safe?'

Goosebumps raised the fine hair on her arms as her heart pounded and the New Lord's voice rose along with his rant. Threats and promises of harm fell across the line, gathering stones to throw at her in a rage that bordered on demonic.

Flashbacks pummelled her mind as his cruel words brought back memories of being subjected to that rage, on the receiving end of his harsh lessons. Frozen by the terror of knowing that he could make every spoken threat a reality, Bridey stared at the peeling wallpaper behind the phone, clutching the receiver, praying the vitriol would stop. Wishing she could hang up. Knowing she couldn't because hanging up would make the end punishment worse.

Warmth covered her back, as Cole pried the receiver loose from her frozen fingers. His arm came around her and he held her close as he placed the receiver to his ear.

Bridey turned to press her forehead to his chest, inhaled the now familiar scent and comfort she'd come to associate him with. Buried herself against him to draw from the strength he radiated, so different from the brutality she'd been exposed to in the past.

She felt him shift as he hung up the phone, the warmth and comfort as he drew her closer with both arms, the added weight of his chin on the top of her head.

'When will it end?' She whispered the words into his shirtfront, but he heard them.

'Today. It ends today.'

~

Cole left Bridey with Gus and Kirana fussing over her to call Mark. Outside, he walked the wraparound verandah from the back door of the kitchen to the unused front porch. The security guards had seen nothing, yet Camden had ranted over everything he'd seen. From the arrival of the girls to Bridey and himself cosied up on the sofa until midnight.

As he pressed the icon that would summon Mark to answer, Cole studied every inch of the farm he could see and paced the verandah. Barren fields stretched to the trees that bordered the ridge and hid what had once lain behind them. Gus had camped up there last night. He would have known if he'd had company. His dad could sleep with one eye open thanks to his Navy training.

'Perfect timing, Delaney.' Mark's voice interrupted his surveillance.

274

'He's escalating.' No point wasting words when they were on the same page.

'No shit. The team I sent out to his last known location came back with nothing. No trace of him or his flock. Just a bunch of empty buildings and random stuff they didn't have time to take, and they left in a hurry. I suspect these people live light, ready to move when given the signal. We're running the prints they lifted out there through the database now. So far, these people are ghosts.'

'Bridey just got a nasty call from the guy posing as Camden. Still no leads on who he really is?'

'Like I said ... ghosts. But I'm working on it.'

'Need to work a bit faster, mate. I can tell you he's here. Or somewhere near here because he can see everything that goes on at the farm, including the arrival of the girls. He's either the master of disguise or damn good at a game of hide and seek. And he's showing up too frequently to be too far away.'

'Fuck.'

'Pretty much what I said.'

The sound of fingers tapping out a two-fingered rhythm on a keyboard clicked through the phone. 'Send me a list of all vacant or abandoned properties in the area within a hundred-kilometre radius.'

'I'll get Sam onto it. We can't keep this quiet anymore.'

'Yep, time to put out a BOLO. If nothing else, we've got enough to bring him in for questioning. I'll extract the image we have of him from the hospital security footage. You'd better make some room. I'll be back down there with a team by nightfall.'

'He's not going to like the attention. I want everyone in this town safe, Mark. I want this to end. We both know how fast the casualties add up when these cases escalate, and we have enough bodies on our hands already.'

'Bloody oath we do. Don't forget I have valuable collateral down there on the farm with you too. I want my wife back safe, thank you. FDV is not a road I want her to have to travel down again. I'm moving as fast as the red tape and reports will allow me to ... trust me. Took me long enough just to get a warrant for the search of the church's compound. If these things moved as fast in real life as they do on those crime shows on TV, we'd wrap up cases a hell of a lot faster.'

'Agreed.' Frustration chewed at his gut. Sometimes he wondered if people who broke the law had more rights than those who tried to enforce it. There were days like these when his faith in the justice system wavered. 'Any news on Bridey's DNA? Too soon?'

'Email's in my inbox. It helps to have friends in the right places. We got it rushed through the lab last night.' Another few clicks of the keyboard and Mark's brief silence had Cole's nerves stretched to breaking point. 'Bingo! We have a match. And well, fuck me, another cold case to reopen. Damned if you moving to the country has added a shit ton to my case load, thank you very much. So much for a quiet life.'

'Does your beautiful wife know you use such colourful language?'

'You're not my wife and I wouldn't use that language around her, but I love you like a brother. Do you want these results, or did you want to come around and wash my mouth out with soap instead?'

'I'll take the results.' Cole began pacing the verandah again, more to prepare himself than to continue searching the landscape for something he couldn't see. Yet.

'Your girl's DNA matches that of Asha Reid. Her parents were killed in a car crash on the Brand Highway near Gin Gin. John and Norma Reid. There were signs of tampering with the vehicle and a child car seat in the back, but no trace of the child who would have been maybe two or three at the time. All leads ran cold. No next of kin.'

'Were they members of Camden's church?' Cole didn't bother arguing that Bridey wasn't his girl. After last night, it very much felt like she was, and he'd protect her in a way he hadn't been able to protect Carrie.

'That will take a bit more digging. I'll recall the cold case and evidence from the archives. Finding Asha Reid means we can reopen the case. And now we know where she's been which all points to a crime. Tell me about the phone call.'

Cole relayed what he'd heard. 'I'll get more from Bridey, but it's enough to apply for a restraining order, especially after the attack on her.'

'Two things holding us back there. A — to serve the restraining order, we'd need to find him first. B — you can't serve a restraining order on a man who's been dead for God knows how long, so we need to know who he really is before we can do that.'

'Why are you still talking to me? Get to work.'

Mark chuckled. 'Put some beer in the fridge. I'll see you tonight. Keep this between us for now. At least until I have what I need to put out that BOLO. Then we can tell Bridey.'

'Agreed.' Cole hung up and called Sam to do the vacant property search.

'Will do, Sarge. By the way, Elle's arcing up again. Given her love for the bottle, I'd say it's withdrawal. With some help from the CWA, they've cleaned her place up as best they can and she's back there now, so there's nothing to stop her from popping out to the bottle shop and going back to where she started.'

Cole rubbed at the tension building in his neck

and thought about the fifteen women and children already under Bridey's roof. Could he add another two seats at her table? At least if she and Sunshine were here at Mindaleny Ridge, there'd be someone to keep an eye on them. And since Camden or whoever he really was appeared to be working alone, there'd be a certain amount of safety in numbers. With Mark and his team arriving tonight, the idiot wouldn't be dumb enough to follow through on his threats.

'Let me speak to Bridey. Maybe we can make room for Elle and Sunshine here at Mindaleny. Some hard work might do Elle some good. TJ and Lily can add her to their list to talk to Social Services about.'

'Yep, let me know, Sarge. I checked up on Chewy. She's not eating. Not even a nibble at the roses. I think she's pining for you.' Sam laughed.

Cole eyed the one and only paddock with a solid fence. 'I'll talk to Bridey about bringing Chewy to the farm. She can mow the weeds.'

'The children will love that. Want me to pack a bag for you too? Sounds to me like you're moving in,' Sam teased. 'I call dibs on your house. Although I might let Nick rent a room.'

'You're dreaming, Constable Mayne. It's not like that.'

'Sure it isn't. My eyes don't see what your words

are saying, but I'll go with it. For now. I'll get back to you with that report.'

'Don't forget to log it as overtime. Otherwise, I'll get into trouble with payroll for making you work on a Saturday and not paying you right.'

'Goes with the job, Sarge. Take care of Bridey. She's a nice lady. Call me if she needs anything picked up from the IGA. I'll come around after I've done this report and give you a hand out there.'

'Thanks, Sam.' He hung up and went back inside to ask Bridey if he could take a shower. He needed the space and quiet to plan and think because if he couldn't protect the people in his care, he'd have failed in his duty. Failure wasn't a word he wanted in his vocabulary ever again.

Chapter Twenty-One

Bridey stood in front of the boxed-up staircase, debating on her decision to give Kirana and the girls a home in a place that attracted never-ending evil and danger. How many more times could she be kicked and broken before she couldn't stand up and fight anymore? How long could she ride the crashing tide of hope versus despair?

Her heart wanted to believe that Cole, Mark, TJ, and Lily could fix this. That they could make the New Lord go away. But, in her heart, she knew that freedom and peace were a long way off and what lay between could bring more pain and loss.

Who was Bridey McCaffrey anyway? A meaningless name bestowed on her by people under the influence of the devil himself. How could she give a home to strangers when she was one herself? A home she may not even be allowed to keep. What would happen to Kirana and the others then?

'I can hear the wheels turning in your mind.' Cole's presence warmed her back, fresh from the shower and smelling like her homemade soap and shampoo. 'Want to share your thoughts?'

'There are so many going around in my head right now. If we break this down, I have no idea what we're going to find up there. I don't know if it's liveable or not, or how long it's stood empty. I don't know who I am or what the future holds for me and my boys. Can I really take care of Kirana and the children? Will I have control over that when I find out who I really am? How much will life change when I know?'

Cole placed an arm around her shoulders and drew her to his side in a comforting hug before releasing her again. 'That's a lot of questions. Let's start with answering the first one.' He lifted the crowbar at his side and held it to her. 'How about you have a go at removing those boards? Put these on first.' With his free hand, he produced a pair of safety glasses from his pocket and placed them on her head.

Bridey accepted the crowbar, dropped the glasses over her eyes, and stepped towards the hidden staircase. She wedged the flattened end between the board and the wall to pry open a gap. Rusty nails popped loose, hastily applied plywood cracked under the pressure.

Cole pressed a hand against the board to stop it from falling. 'You're doing great. A couple more goes, and it should come off.'

'I thought it would be harder to do than this.' Bridey moved to the other side of the staircase and pried that side of the board loose.

Together they lifted it away and placed it to the side against the wall. In front of them, a narrow staircase stretched upwards between the wall and a peeling painted banister, curving left into the dim light beyond. Trepidation gnawed at Bridey's senses as to what lay at the top of those stairs.

'We're in this together, honey. You're not alone anymore. Let's get these last boards down, the ones attached to the banister. We'll have more light on the stairs if we do. I'll hold it up while you pry the ends loose.'

As they moved the boards away, light from the downstairs windows shone on the worn brown carpet that covered the stairs. Cobwebs decorated the walls and ceiling, but the paint seemed in good repair. Nothing a little scrubbing wouldn't fix. Bridey crossed her fingers that whatever lay beyond had been just as well preserved and hadn't had enough time to decay too badly.

'Ready?'

She looked up at Cole as she slipped her hand into his and held on tight. 'I'm ready.'

Together they navigated the stairs, testing the sturdiness of each step, not knowing how long the staircase had been covered up or what condition it was in.

Reaching the landing at the top of the stairs, the musty smell of dust and neglect teased their noses as they paused for a moment. Decaying curtains were drawn across windows that stretched the length of what was long and wide enough to be a seating area but was devoid of furniture or anything that might have made it feel like a home. She remembered how all their homes had been like that. Minimalistic shells that could be evacuated at the New Lord's signal. Shafts of sunlight found a way through the gaps, shining on dancing dust particles in the air.

Bridey imagined opening those curtains and letting in the warmth of the sun. The view that lay beyond would be of the fields that stretched towards the trees on the ridge. If they'd been allowed up here, would she have seen the lights of the vehicles that had brought Kirana and her people to Mindaleny?

Cole's hand tightened on hers. 'There's a part of me that wants to tell you to leave this place and the pain it holds for you so you can start afresh. The wrongs are not your burden to bear, Bridey. You were wronged too. But then there's this other side of me that wants you to stay and fight for what you believe in. To make this the happy home it deserves to be.'

Bridey turned to him, placing her hand over his heart. 'I trust you to do what you need to do to keep us safe, Cole. I've lived in the dark for too long. I've suffered what Kirana and her people have suffered, and so have many more. If I can stop this from happening to anyone else, it's what I need to do. Whatever the risk.'

'Then let's get started so we can get everyone settled in. We'll do a quick run through of the rooms to see what needs to be done and then we'll gather our resources for the clean-up. Where do you want to start first?'

Bridey took in a deep breath and let it out, fear of the unknown seeping into her bones as she gripped Cole's hand tighter. 'Let's start at the other end and work our way back towards the stairs. I think that's a bathroom at the very end. We're going to need that if the plumbing still works.'

An eerie sense of abandonment hung in the air as they passed darkened rooms with the doors only slightly ajar. Four in total, five if she counted the bathroom. Cole pushed open the door to the bathroom, both unsure of what they would find.

Light beamed in through a frosted glass window high up on the wall above a bathtub. An old-fashioned, round shower head reached out from the wall, suspended over the tub, partially hidden by the shower curtain. The old porcelain toilet paid testament to the age of the farmhouse. Other than the film of dust that covered the vanity and basin, the bathroom appeared to be usable.

Bridey let go of Cole's hand to flush the toilet and test the taps. Brown water ran down the basin and the old pipes protested against years of abandonment. She shivered against the groan of the pipes.

'That will stop once the pipes are in use again.'

Cole's reassurance warmed the chill in her spine. She nodded. 'Yes, it will. Let's move on.'

The door next to the bathroom revealed a neatly made double bed, plain brown slippers carefully placed on the faded Persian rug next to it, as if Mrs McCaffrey would step into them at any moment from a night of restful sleep. Feeling like an intruder, Bridey stepped into the stark room that held little to identify the people who had once slept there.

An old wardrobe stood tucked into the corner near the curtained window. She reached for the door handle, opening the door to reveal a hanging row of pressed denim skirts and white blouses with lace collars. Seven in total, one for each day of the week, all they were allowed. Red cotton triangle headscarves lay folded on a shelf next to a container of bobby pins. Staid lace-up Oxfords lined-up with military precision on the floor of the wardrobe, next to an old tin of brown shoe polish.

The other side of the wardrobe revealed the uniform she knew to be that of the Fathers. Khaki shirts and pants, brown leather belts that were often used on their wives, and sturdy brown work boots with steel caps that did as much harm, if not more, than the belts. The urge to rip the clothes from the hangers and burn them had Bridey firmly closing the doors.

'All this can go. I don't want to see anyone dressed in these clothes.'

'No disagreement there. I'm sure the local op shop can make use of them or maybe TJ and Lily can take them back to Perth for recycling.' Cole's hand at her waist guided her out of the room. 'At least the rooms are uncluttered. It won't take much to clean up.'

The next two rooms revealed unmade single bunk beds, three to a room, and empty wardrobes. A linen closet in the hallway held folded bedding that would need little more than a wash and airing. A shelf in the middle of the closet had nausea rising in Bridey's throat. Children-sized robes sat sorted into piles according to age, the sight of the crude brown Hessian outfits and rope belts raising an itch on her skin as buried memories resurfaced at the sight.

She closed the door, her heart aching in her chest. 'They were preparing for an intake and initiation.'

'If that's what you believe they were going to do with those clothes, then we'll be making a bonfire with the robes tonight.' Cole steered her away from the closet. 'One more room to go.'

His arm around her shoulders and holding her close, Cole led her to the last door. Bridey prayed for no more nasty surprises. A prayer that went unanswered as they stepped inside the nightmare she'd known deep down would be inevitable.

~

Cole stared at the anger that Thomas McCaffrey had inflicted on the walls of his bachelor bedroom. Hate-filled words etched into the walls, a smashed mirror, an axe buried deep into the door of the wardrobe where he'd ripped apart the khaki-coloured uniforms that matched his father's. A stained mattress, torn to shreds, the insides chopped apart, a discarded kitchen knife tossed down at the foot of the bed. Cole could almost feel Thomas's rage still present in the room.

Bridey stood stiff and straight beside him, rubbing at the goosebumps on her arms, no doubt feeling the horror too. He didn't want to think about what might have happened if Bridey or the boys had been in this room when Thomas McCaffrey had let loose on his deep-seated frustrations with his life.

A blood-stained notebook lay discarded on the floor, the pen used to write in it tossed away to gather dust. What secrets had Thomas written in that book?

'Did you want to go downstairs, honey? I'll need to deal with this.' Another crime scene, another episode in a never-ending nightmare for Bridey.

She shook her head. 'No. I need to know what made him do this. I need to understand what made him the monster he was, so I can forgive him. We all suffered at the hands of the New Lord, but nothing that resulted in a rage like this.' She turned to look up at him. 'I want justice. I want to throw open the curtains in this house to let the sunshine in that will chase away the shadows and know that he isn't out there watching, waiting to cause more harm. Right now, I want him dead, even if I have to kill him myself.'

Cole stood silent. How could he disagree when he wanted the same thing she did? But revenge and more blood on their hands could not be the answer when so much damage had already been done. He had to stand by his oath to protect and serve and deliver justice through a conviction. No harm in wishing though that, when caught, this impostor who believed he was God would be at the mercy of the worst of the worst in a prison cell, where justice was served up with equal lawlessness. Let the law do its job then let the inmates do the rest.

He stepped away from Bridey, leaving her in the doorway, pulled out his phone and dialled Nick's number. 'I'll need gloves and evidence bags.' Studying the brown blood-like stains on the axe lodged in the door, he said, 'We may have a murder weapon.'

'On it, Sarge. Sam's about to leave now. I'll send everything through with her.'

'Good. Tell her to fire up her smudge stick. This place is going to need it.'

'I thought you didn't believe in all that woo-woo stuff she plays with.'

'Mate, if you were seeing what I'm seeing, you'd start believing in it too. She'll want to give this room a damn good cleansing before she even steps through the door.'

'That bad, huh? I'll pass the message on.'

'Cheers, Nick.' Cole hung up. No point calling Mark again when he would be at the farm in a few hours anyway and they could process the evidence together. 'I think I need a strong coffee.'

With an arm around her shoulders, Cole guided Bridey from the room, closed the door firmly, locked it and placed the old-fashioned key in his pocket. He sure as hell didn't want anyone stumbling in on what they'd found.

Cole followed Bridey down the steps, back to the part of the house she was familiar with, knowing how shaken she would be. Her boys waited for her at the bottom, peering up into the void. Thank God they hadn't ventured upstairs. Not yet. Bridey said nothing as she sat down on the bottom step, gathered them close and held them tight.

'You're squishing me, Mum!' Caught between his brothers, Garrett's protest was muffled.

Alex reached up to touch her face. 'Why are you crying?' He cast a furious stare at Cole. 'Did you hurt my mum?'

Bridey smoothed a hand over her eldest son's hair. 'Sergeant Delaney hasn't done anything wrong, Alex. He is a good man. He would never hurt any of us.'

Cole descended, stopping on the step above where Bridey sat. 'Your mum is right, boys. I want you to know that I will never hurt you in any way. That's a promise.'

'Then why are you crying?'

'Because I saw something upstairs that made me really sad, and today is the last time I ever want to be sad in this way. We're going to change a lot of things around here on the farm, so that everyone who lives here will be happy.'

'We can't be happy all the time!' Shaun scoffed. 'That's impossible.'

Bridey laughed as she hugged them collectively again. 'Nothing is impossible, Shaun. Together, we're going to make it possible.' Releasing the boys, she stood up from the step. 'First, let's get you all ready. We've got a lot of work to do today.'

'Like what?'

She shepherded them ahead of her towards her bedroom. 'Do you remember how we were cleaning out the office and you were sorting out all the old magazines and things for me? We're going to help Kirana clean that up so that she can use it to start a school.'

'Will we be going to her school?' Shaun tugged on her skirt.

'Would you like that?'

'I'm not sure because I want you to teach me, just like you always did. And if you're not going to be teaching us then what will you do?' Alex stopped walking to deliver Bridey a glowering look.

'I will be working on the farm, getting things to grow again. And when everyone has finished their lessons for the day, then Kirana can bring you all out into the fields to help. Does that sound like fun?'

'I think I'd like that.' Garrett's face lit up.

'But we're not allowed in the fields. We'll get into trouble '

Bridey turned to her eldest son, determination visible in the stiffening of her spine. 'No one will tell us we can't work in the fields. Not anymore. We're going to make this our farm, Alex, and we're going to take care of it and anyone who needs help, like Kirana and the girls. We're going to learn everything we can about growing crops, selling them at the markets, and making a living for ourselves.'

'And what if that man comes back to hurt us again?' Tangible fear hung in the silence that followed Alex's frustrated shout.

Cole moved to kneel on one knee in front of the boy, placing a comforting hand on his bony shoulder. 'That's my job, Alex. I will find him, and he will go to jail for a long time. I will make sure that he never hurts anyone again.'

'You made that promise before. Now I'll never have another sister or brother.'

Pain struck his heart as the words left Alex's lips with a wisdom far beyond his six years. Cole hung his head for a moment. How could he argue? 'I lost a little baby too. For a short time, I had a wife and a daughter, and now they're both gone. I understand what it's like to lose someone, Alex. If I could change anything in this world, I would turn back time so that my wife and baby would still be alive. They didn't deserve what happened to them. Your baby brother or sister didn't deserve what happened, and neither did your mum.'

'What happened to them?'

How did you explain to a six-year-old the horror of having everything you loved ripped away? Cole glanced back over his shoulder at Bridey, witnessed the sadness on her face as she nodded her consent for him to tell Alex how he'd lost what he'd lived and breathed for. Turning back to Alex, he took a deep breath. 'Some very bad men came into my house and hurt them.'

'Did you catch the men?'

'Yes, I did. I caught them and now they've gone to jail and they're never coming out again.'

'Never is a long time.' Alex nodded. 'I want the man who hurt my mum to go away for a long time. I want him never to come back, just like my father.'

'I want a dad like Gus. He makes us pancakes.' Garrett grinned at Cole.

Cole stood and ruffled the boy's hair. 'Gus makes the best pancakes. I wonder if he'll make us some for breakfast?'

'I'll go ask him!' Garrett prepared to launch towards the kitchen, but Bridey stopped him.

'Wait! Change out of your pyjamas and brush your teeth first, please.'

'Yes, Mum.'

Shaun paused to slip his hand into Cole's, looking up at him with a seriousness in his eyes no kid that age should have. 'I want a dad like you. A police officer. So, we'll always be safe from the bad people.'

Cole cast a glance at Bridey who had her hands covering her mouth and tears on her cheeks. He looked back down at Shaun's tiny, serious face and lost his heart a little more to Bridey and her boys. 'I promise that as long as I am the policeman in charge in this town, I will do everything I can to keep everyone safe from the bad guys.'

'Come on, Shaun! Let's go,' Garrett urged.

Shaun released Cole's hand. 'I believe you.' With a grin, he followed his brother down the corridor to the bedroom.

Alex pushed past him to follow his brothers. 'I don't believe you.'

How sad that a child so young had had his life built on the foundation of violence and mistrust. He'd carry the burden of his father's sins for a long time. Cole's heart ached for the boy as he stopped in front of his mum.

'I'll take care of you, Mum. I'm the man of the house now.' Alex threw his arms around Bridey's waist as she hugged him close before he disappeared into the bedroom.

'He doesn't mean it, Cole.'

Cole moved towards her. 'He's hurt, scared, and angry. I get it.'

'I'll talk to him. Ask him to apologise for disrespecting you.' She looked up at him, her eyes still shimmering with tears.

He cupped her face in his hands and brushed away her tears with his thumbs. 'No. He doesn't need to apologise. I need to earn back his trust.'

Chapter Twenty-Two

Bridey covered Cole's hands with hers and pressed them to her cheeks. 'Thank you. For everything you've done. Promise me one thing?'

'Anything.' Cole moved his hands away from her face to intertwine his fingers with hers, standing a little closer.

She caught his gaze searching her face, a frown between his eyebrows. Unable to hold his stare, she dropped her chin and channelled her gaze to over his shoulder. 'If anything happens to me, please take care of my boys. Make sure they're safe and happy. In a place where they won't experience growing up the way they have so far.'

He let go of her hand to tip up her chin. 'Nothing's

going to happen to you, Bridey. I won't let anything happen. Not on my watch. Never again.'

'You can't save everyone, Cole. There will always be bad people out there like the New Lord. You catch one and another will take his place, maybe just in a different form.'

'That's my job. It's what I swore to do. Deliver justice where needed.'

He traced her lips with his thumb, making her shiver at the pleasant sensation that ran through her. If only she'd met Cole first, had lived a different life. She couldn't change a thing about her past, but she could change her future.

Standing on her tiptoes, she pressed her lips to Cole's, testing the waters of the feelings she had for him, and how so different he was to all the harsh authoritative types that had influenced her world until now.

Cole was as strong and authoritative as his job demanded, but Bridey didn't doubt for a second that when he cared for someone, he cared deeply. And kindly. As his arms came around her to hold her closer, she felt that as he kissed her back. Enough pressure in his hold and the press of his mouth that she never felt trapped or in danger. Enough that he allowed her to set the pace, to call the shots, to either invite him in or close the door. No harm, no regrets, no force. Just enough.

Soft chatter reached her ears from the lounge room where her unexpected house guests prepared to face the first day of their new lives. As Cole lifted his head, Bridey reluctantly let go of the fantasy that all was safe in their world. The road ahead was still littered with obstacles they needed to clear.

Cole brushed her fringe from her forehead and placed a kiss to the scar she knew he'd find there. 'Before we get this show on the road, I have a favour to ask.'

'What is it?'

Cole smiled. 'How do you feel about adopting a goat?'

'A goat?'

'I inherited a goat with a penchant for eating flowers. I figured Chewy could help you out with cleaning up the fields. He's a little lonely out at my place. What do you think?'

Bridey shrugged. 'Why not? This is a farm, right? I think the children would enjoy having a goat.'

'Thank you.' He moved away to take her hand. 'And one more favour?'

Bridey smiled up at him, her heart lighter than she could ever remember it being. At last, there was a glimmer of sunshine on her horizon, a promise of a better way of life. 'Go on.'

'You've heard me talk of the Donnellys, Elle and Sunshine? Any chance we can squeeze them in here with the others? Elle has had a rough time and both she and Sunshine are a little ... neglected. Elle has developed a drinking problem since her partner abandoned her and Sunshine. I'm worried that the cycle will continue if they don't get the help they need.'

Bridey chewed on her bottom lip. The goat she could deal with but having another alcoholic in the house presented a different challenge. Her children had lived through the horror of having an alcoholic father. Was this a responsibility she wanted? How would it affect Kirana and the others who had experienced so much already? And then there was still the danger that lurked in the shadows.

Her thoughts ran to the room upstairs that held the canvas of her late husband's anger, the fruits of his rage, the memories of the consequences that came from him burying himself in a bottle. They came full circle to the knowledge that if she'd known how to help him, known what to do, things may have been different. If she could help Elle, she could help Sunshine and save them both from living the horror she and so many others had lived.

Damping down on the doubt and anxiety that the prospect of two new lodgers brought with it, Bridey nodded. 'I'll take them in. I'll need help to get rid of all the alcohol Thom had hidden around the house. I don't want Elle or anyone else finding any.'

'I can help you with that.' Cole hugged her close. 'Thank you.'

She looked up at him with her heart in her eyes. 'The way to thank me would be to end this nightmare so we can all be free to move on.'

'One hundred percent with you on that one.'

Stepping away from Cole, Bridey led the way back to the kitchen. Gus spooned porridge into bowls, Kirana drizzled honey over it and Sari handed it out. Bridey's gaze swept around the room. She'd need a bigger table and more chairs. The large dining room she dusted every day came to mind. It had not been used in a long time, perhaps never. With a little reconfiguration, she could fit in a few smaller tables rather than the monstrous formal table that was in there now. A cosier dining space where everyone could sit together, talk, and laugh like a happy family. Dare she dream?

The women and children they'd rescued whispered amongst themselves in a dialect she didn't understand. Although less terrified today than they had been yesterday, Bridey could understand their subdued behaviour. They had no idea if they would be better off under her roof than they had been before.

TJ's and Lily's voices drifted in from the loungeroom, their words muted in conversation, a buzz in the background amidst the whispers in the room. The hum of male tenor and bass in the conversation between Cole and Gus mixed with the sound of pots and dishes being scraped and cleaned, as Cole got stuck into helping his dad clean up.

Could this really be her new normal? She cast a look around the table, counting heads, making sure everyone was accounted for. Her eyes fell on the twins, heads close together, and moved to find Alex's chair empty.

Panic tightened a hand on her throat. Bridey moved to place her hands on the twins' heads, her touch light on their soft, downy hair. 'Shaun, Garrett? Where's Alex?'

Surprised, the boys turned to the empty chair, lifted up the table cloth to see if their brother was hiding under the table.

'Maybe he went to the toilet?' Garrett suggested.

Could it be as simple as that? Maybe she was being too paranoid. 'Stay here with Gus and Cole. I'll be right back.'

Damping down on the fear that stuck like cold porridge beneath her sternum, Bridey went in search of her eldest son. When all the usual places he might be showed no sign of Alex, panic replaced the fear in her belly. He knew all the rules. Never wander off alone. Don't talk to strangers. Frantic, she raced up the staircase, ignoring the pain as her elbow caught on the banister where it curved upwards.

'Alex!'

Had he just gone exploring with the curiosity of a six-year-old? She tried the door that hid Thomas's hatred. Still locked and no sign of Alex. As she raced back down the stairs, and turned the corner into the front hallway, she saw it. The front door they never used stood wide open, leading out onto the front verandah. The toy truck Alex had taken a liking to from the box of toys Mrs Lee had given them lay abandoned on the dried-out decking boards. His favourite book lay spine-up forming a triangle on the weed-covered pathway that led to the broken front gate.

Silence hung in the early morning air like a heavy mist, weighing on Bridey's chest. Nothing moved on the abandoned fields to show that he may have gone exploring. Ice-cold terror gripped her spine, burned her throat.

'Alex!'

~

Bridey's scream struck the fear of God into his heart. Cole raced towards the sound. He found her on her knees on the overgrown pathway to the gate, clutching a toy truck and a book to her chest; face pale, eyes filled with terror.

'Alex is gone!' Her teeth chattered around the words.

Cole took her elbow and helped her up, her skin icy cold to his touch. 'We'll find him, honey. He's probably just hiding somewhere.'

She shook her head. 'No! He doesn't go anywhere without his book.'

Cole looked around. Where were the security guards? Why wasn't there anyone on watch? 'Sam is on her way here. I'll get Nick out here too. We can all search for Alex.' He placed a comforting arm around her shoulders and guided her back into the house. 'We'll find him.'

All eyes landed on them as they entered the kitchen and Cole pulled out a chair for Bridey to sit. He kept a hand on her shoulder as he prepared for the barrage of questions.

'What happened?' Lily rushed over.

'Alex is nowhere in the house.' Cole did a quick headcount in the room to make sure no one else was missing. 'Did anyone see where he went? Did he say anything to anyone?'

Murmurs and headshakes answered his questions. Dread filled his gut as he recalled the threats Camden had made on the phone to Bridey. Would he be crazy enough to carry out those threats with the focus on him right now?

He dragged a hand through his hair. Fuck! 'Gus, I need you to stay here. Lock all the doors. Stay away from the windows. No one goes outside.'

'But I need to go to the bathroom.' Garrett's young voice fell into the silence that followed. 'The toilet is outside.'

Cole ruffled Garrett's hair. 'Good point, young fella. Gus, there's a bathroom upstairs. It hasn't been used in a long time, so it will need a clean and the pipes flushed out. Close all the bedroom doors.'

'I'm on it.' Gus located the cleaning products under the kitchen sink and dropped them into a bucket with some cloths.

'Anyone who goes up there only uses the bathroom. No one goes alone.' Satisfied with the murmured responses and nods, Cole called Nick. 'I need you here. Alex is missing.'

'On my way, Sarge.'

He hung up and turned to Lily. 'Call the security company and ask them where their guards are. They're not at their posts.'

Lily had her phone in her hand before he'd finished his sentence.

I need everyone to stay here with Gus and listen to what he tells you to do. I'm going to find Alex.'

'I'm going with you.' Bridey pushed back her chair.

'Bridey—'

'He's my son.'

The determination in her voice stopped him from arguing. 'You stay close and listen to everything I tell you to do.'

She nodded as his phone rang. Cole hesitated to answer it. He wanted to get going with an urgency that gnawed at his gut. Glancing at the screen, he saw Elle's number on the display. Damn it, why was she calling him and not Nick or Sam? Ignoring her would be ignoring his duty. What if she was in real trouble?

He hit the answer icon. 'What's up, Elle?'

The deep-toned chuckle that drifted over the line wasn't a pleasant one and it didn't belong to Elle. 'You know what the problem is with small town cops, Sergeant? They're slow. And security companies? Even slower. Those two dummies you had out the front? All I had to do was bribe them with a drink and they left your front door wide open.'

Cole's stomach dropped as he recognised the voice. 'I know you're not Clifford Camden. We found his remains.'

'See? Slow. Look how long it took you to figure that out. Small towns are where cops go to die. Where their brains turn to mush while they rescue drunken whores and damsels in distress.'

'What have you done to Elle and Sunshine?'

'Ah ... Elle ... She was a beautiful girl once, you know? But she'd do anything for a drink. She was useless to me as a handler. No damn discipline and couldn't stay out of the bottle. And that spawn of hell she calls Sunshine? Useless. Stubborn as a goddam bull and the daughter of the devil. Little bitch bit me. Probably gave me rabies. But she'll pay for that. Later.'

Cole fought off the battering of memories of Carrie and how bastards like this one had made her pay. He needed to find them. All of them. Fast. 'Where's Alex?'

'That, my friend, is the million-dollar question. Wouldn't you like to know?'

Cole bit down on the anger that began a slow boil. 'What do you want?'

'How about ... I let you know ... later.'

The line went dead, and Cole hung up to dial Nick. 'Change of plans. I need you to do a welfare check on Elle and Sunshine. Camden says he has them, and Alex too, but we need to be sure he's not keeping them all at Elle's place. If anything looks off when you get there, back away. If he's as smart as I think he is, I don't think he would've stayed around in town with them. He's on the move.'

'Sure thing, Sarge. I'll head over there now. See what I can find out. I'll ask around town if anyone has seen anything suspicious. Mrs Lee always has a keen eye on things.'

Frustration had him dragging his hand over his face as Cole hung up from the call. He needed more hands on deck for this than his small-town police budget allowed for. Things like this weren't meant to happen in small towns. Their budgets didn't factor in fanatical, murderous lunatics running church scams to cover for illegal trafficking to serve the sex and drug trade.

He looked down into the terror on Bridey's face, her eyes wide and filled with fear for her son. How many more times could he promise her it would end without making that happen? None.

Lily tugged on his sleeve. 'Mark's on his way with a team. He says to tell you he has intel that will be useful.'

Cole nodded. 'Thanks.' The two-hour wait for him to arrive would be agony, but they needed the reinforcements, and he had two missing security guards to find.

'I can't sit here and wait while the New Lord has Alex.' Bridey fidgeted with her hands.

'Camden mentioned something about Elle being a lousy handler. Did you know she was involved in the church?' Cole went down on his haunches beside Bridey, balancing himself with one hand on the table and the other on the back of her chair.

'No. I don't know Elle or Sunshine. The only person I was allowed to talk to was Mrs Lee, and that was to ask for the mail. I would go in, get the mail and the groceries, pick up Thom's whiskey, and come straight back. Thom was extremely strict about that.'

TJ opened the kitchen door to let Sam in.

'Nick says you've had a bit of trouble.' Sam dropped a folder on the table. 'The list of vacant properties you asked for. And I brought Chewy down with me because I figured you won't be home again tonight to feed her. She's in the fenced paddock next door. You owe me a new seat cover. She chewed her way through it on the way here.'

'Thanks, Sam.' Cole picked up the folder and flipped through it. 'What can you tell me about Elle Donnelly's ex-partner?'

'Elle told everyone he was a fly-in-fly-out worker, but he was much older than her and didn't seem like someone who worked on a mine up north. His hands were too soft. I mean, like no callouses or dirty fingernails, no Pilbara suntan. You can't work up north and not get red dust in every crevice. That shit just doesn't come out. I did a stint in Port Hedland. Took me months to get the red dust out of my hair and ears, not to mention my car.'

'We can share our experiences in Port Hedland later, Sam. Right now, I need to know about Elle's partner.'

'Sorry, Sarge.' Sam shivered. 'He was a creepy sod. Made my skin crawl. Mean, shifty. He had cold eyes, like his soul was dead inside and only his shell existed. I think everyone in town was pretty happy when he took off. '

Bridey's sharp intake of breath had them both focusing on her. 'What did he look like?'

Sam shrugged. 'Maybe late forties, early fifties by now. He took off and we never saw him again. That was just before I joined the force and came back home as a cop. Chubby around the middle. About 182 centimetres tall, salt and pepper hair, cold blue eyes. He wore hi-vis shirts when he was in town, the orange and blue ones with the reflective tape, but I never saw them dirty.'

'Name?' Cole's demand came out harsher than intended. The answer had been under his nose all the time, yet he would never have connected the two if Camden had not become desperate.

'Neil Romanovitch.'

'Call it in to Mark. Tell him we have another alias to go on the BOLO. Bridey, do you recognise this man from Sam's description?'

Bridey sat with her hands pressed to her mouth, white as a sheet. 'Yes.'

Chapter Twenty-Three

Bridey's mind spun as deeply buried memories returned in vivid scenes, like the ghosts of restless souls needing to tell their story.

Snippets of conversations she'd overheard her handlers having about how much things had changed since the New Lord came to replace the old. How much worse everyone's life had become, and the escalation in punishment. The disappearance of leaders who dared to disobey, and the growing number of cleansing rituals when more and more bodies of the disobedient were placed on the pyre. The growing fear in the eyes of the adults in charge, too afraid to go against the New Lord's will. Her own journey to becoming Thom's wife. Knowing what Elle and Sunshine might have endured in their years under his control, and what their fate would be if the New Lord had taken them as well as Alex.

She searched her mind, willing her younger self to remember more as she gathered the twins close and drew on her fear and dread for her eldest child. She couldn't lose anyone else to a devil who thought himself to be the saviour of souls.

Closing her eyes, she allowed scattered memories to resurface, even the ones she'd worked so hard to block out. The ones that made her scars burn like new wounds. The ones that instilled a terror in her that made her want to hide under a bed like her five-year-old self once had, only to be dragged out by her feet to face her punishment for being disobedient.

Two people — strangers — in a car. She could feel their fear, hear urgency in their tone. Bright lights through a window, blinding light that made the car swerve, and screams before the silence. A child crying. A house somewhere. More strangers. A gathering of people and a mass move, like ants seeking a new nest.

The sounds around her faded as she held the twins tight to keep them safe. Thom talking on the phone on the wall. Snippets of his side of the conversation. Abandoned compound. An old mission. Yes, he knew where that was.

Bridey's eyes flew open, searching for the folder Sam had brought with her. She looked up to find Sam and Cole gone. Releasing the twins, she reached for the folder and searched through the listings until she found it.

A facility abandoned for years with no plans to redevelop. Twelve twin-share rooms, six single rooms in the main boarding house, all with shared facilities. Three houses with four bedrooms and one bathroom each, and a chapel on the property. A forgotten state-owned asset with a sad and troubled history as disturbing as the New Lord himself. A ghost of the past nestled deep in the country, surrounded by gum trees and overgrowth, with loose surface roads that hadn't been maintained and didn't encourage visitors. The perfect place for the New Lord to build his following.

Was that where he'd planned to place Kirana and the girls? It explained what they'd found upstairs and what the McCaffreys were preparing for before their demise. With the property only twenty minutes down the road, they would have been in the perfect position to host new arrivals for initiation before they moved to the compound for training.

Bridey tried hard to quell the rising panic that seized her breath. She needed to find Alex. If this was the place he'd been taken to, how many others were at the compound already? The longer she waited, the worse the harm for her boy.

Cole's world of justice remained foreign to her, and it moved too slowly. She'd heard TJ and Lily discussing the possibilities of jail time for the New Lord when he was found.

There'd been talk of how easily bail could be granted and sentences that were too weak to protect the victims. The numbers of incidents of family domestic violence that continued to grow when offenders were given sentences that were too light, or bail that allowed them to re-offend. How, too often, reports made by victims weren't taken seriously until it was too late.

They'd used words she knew nothing about — like restraining orders that never worked the way they were intended to. All things foreign to her without the modern amenities of television, mobile phones, and Internet. She understood now why the New Lord had banned those things from use. Because with modern technology came enlightenment that would have exposed him for the devil he was.

Her anger grew as buried memories resurfaced, a boiling volcano growing with heat, bubbling to the surface ready to spill. He wouldn't stop. He couldn't be stopped. He would continue to kill and harm and brainwash until age and end of life caught up with him.

The New Lord had been evading authorities for

years. That's why they'd always been on the move, lived like paupers with little to carry when they were forced to leave. He'd always have chosen their new destination ahead of time, and they'd moved in the darkness of the night.

She placed her hand on her empty womb, a twinge of pain reminding her of the life she'd lost, both at his hands and by the boot of his foot. She thought about those who'd lost their lives to his sacrifices. Those who'd tried to run, only to be dragged back and punished. Elle and Sunshine, whom she didn't know but had heard enough about to know the pain they would have endured. Kirana and the girls they'd found, prisoners and slaves to the New Lord's whims. Thom and the cruelty she'd experienced at his hands. The McCaffreys — dead — murdered, either by their own son or at the hands of the New Lord.

Her anger grew hotter. A monster like that did not deserve to live out his life in a jail cell with a chance of parole and a sentence that might free him to commit his crimes against humanity again. Cole's law failed to protect victims, time and again, because of the rules that bound their hands. In her world, those rules meant nothing. This time, she'd make the rules.

Gathering the twins close again, she kissed the tops of their heads. 'I need you two to stay with Gus. You need to listen to him.'

'Why, Mummy?' Garrett's exaggerated whisper was loud enough to be heard, so she stood and shepherded them into her room.

'I've got to run an errand, and I'll be quicker if I go alone. I'll be back before you know it.'

'Where are you going?' Shaun tugged at her skirt.

Bridey reached up to retrieve the shotgun from the top of the wardrobe, felt around for the box of bullets, and shoved it into her skirt pocket. 'I'm going to bring Alex home.'

∿

Cole searched the property for the missing security guards with Sam, dread growing. Two strong, grown men simply didn't disappear to leave the door open for a child under protection to be snatched.

Alex was a scrapper. He'd proved that with his distrust of strangers and protectiveness over his mum. But he was also only six years old. Powerless against a man driven to rage as his illegal schemes unravelled like a ball of twine, leaving him exposed when he'd prefer to remain hidden. Beside him, Sam shivered.

'I'm not liking this, Sarge.'

'I'm with you on that one. Here's a question for you ...' Cole dropped down to his knees to shine his torch into the space under the house.

'Yep, go ahead and ask.'

Coming up empty, he stood and dusted the sand from his jeans. 'Why didn't Romanovic take Elle and Sunshine with him when he left town? Why leave them here?'

'Maybe she just wasn't what Romanovic was looking for?' Sam shrugged. 'Elle and I were at school together. She was always a bit of a hellcat, always in trouble and didn't quite fit in with the crowd. Came from a broken family. Her mum died from an overdose when we were in year eleven, her dad just kept sending her money so she could stay here in town. He had some dodgy connections in Perth until he got himself shot and killed in a turf war. To be fair, Elle had to learn how to take care of herself from way too young. She didn't exactly have steady role models.'

'And Romanovic's MO is clearly to seek out what he would see as purity and submissiveness. I think you're right in thinking that he was using her to find a new place to settle his followers. Two bodies in a buried sea container, a church pastor found dead after almost fifteen years, the women held prisoner over that ridge, and a man driven to suicide. We're talking about a killer who doesn't like to leave witnesses behind. Why let Elle live?'

'I'd like to think that maybe he had some feelings for her, but that's unlikely, isn't it?' Sam scoffed.

'Maybe he didn't see her as a threat? She wasn't going to tell anyone what he was up to. He would have seen her as the outcast in town. The only person she interacted with was the pub owner because Sunshine wasn't allowed to buy her booze.'

'And she might have seen him as her ticket out. She either didn't know what he was really up to or didn't care, as long as he took care of her needs.' Cole shook his head. 'And once he found what he was looking for, he didn't need her anymore.'

'Elle was used to not being needed, so she didn't make a fuss when he buggered off. She just carried on with her life. I'm surprised Romanovic didn't take Sunshine. She would have been useful to him with his set up. Especially since she wasn't his kid, and Elle doesn't exactly want her either, which is sad.'

Cole gingerly lifted the edge of a blue tarpaulin covering what could be more bodies or a pile of wood. He dropped it down again with a sense of relief, even though that feeling would be short-lived for sure. 'How did they meet?'

'At the pub. He was in there having a drink in his fake hi-vis clothing when she came in drunk and wanting to get more drunk. He took her home, promising to get her there in one piece and the next thing we knew, they were an item. He'd come back every couple of weeks and play house. When he left,

Elle would come in to the pub with a black eye and bruises to drown her sorrows.'

'She was a soft target.'

'Locked in a cycle of abuse and neglect. The truth is, Sarge, the law doesn't do enough to protect victims like Elle. Police, lawyers, judges ... we all need to get tougher on the perps and take victims more seriously. The red tape has gone soft on justice and hard on rights when it should be the other way around.'

On that point, Cole could agree. 'Was Elle offered any help? Maybe from an NGO? Any attempts made to issue a seventy-two-hour Police Order or encourage her to apply for a restraining order?'

Sam laughed. 'Come on, Sarge! You might as well wipe your arse with those seventy-two-hour orders. What's a piece of paper going to do? By the time you catch up with the perp to issue it, there's your three and a half days gone. It's not like they stick around waiting for the cops to show up with a piece of paper to tell them to stop being arseholes. Nick told me he'd lost count of the times he'd asked Elle if she wanted to make a report. She always said no. Because she knew that if she did make a report, the next time her boyfriend came to town, she'd be dead.' She kicked at a pile of junk lying near the stairs leading to the back verandah. 'She knew it was pointless. He gets a slap on the wrist from a judge for being a naughty boy, and she gets to nurse broken ribs and a fractured eye socket with a bottle of grog. Where's the fairness in that?'

He'd seen it too many times in Perth. Police would be called to a home for an incident of FDV by concerned neighbours, the victim would decline filing a report or bringing charges for fear of the consequences. Or worse, he knew of colleagues who hadn't taken those reports seriously, had not taken action, and the cycle continued until the victims ended up on a cold slab in a hospital basement.

Protocol and paperwork did nothing to stop it from happening, even when the perpetrators were known to police. Action from the authorities and well-meaning organisations often came too late for the victims because they were bound by red tape and the human rights of offenders who didn't deserve those rights when they stripped innocent victims of theirs. The powerlessness of it all frustrated him. Bridey, Elle, Kirana and the others — none of them had deserved to be treated the way they had been.

'I see nothing here that indicates that the two guards met with foul play near the house. Their car is still parked out back, so they haven't left the property. He must have lured them away from here.' Romanovic wouldn't have wanted to risk drawing attention from anyone inside if there'd been a struggle. Cole had hoped to catch them having a nap out here, but that was wishful thinking. He just hadn't wanted his gutfeel to be right.

'Nothing wrong with ruling out the obvious first, Sarge. Where to next?'

Cole studied the landscape, his gaze falling on the packing shed and old office where Bridey had called him from on the day they'd found Kirana and the girls. Every minute they spent searching was another minute Alex was in the hands of the devil, and a lifetime of torture for Bridey. He owed it to her to find her son fast. Safe and unharmed.

'Romanovic knows this property like the back of his hand. He'd know all the hiding spots. He'd want to get rid of the guards fast, without a fuss, so he could snatch Alex and make a quick getaway. The best way to do that would be to lure them far away enough from the house to deal with them but be close enough to make his move. Let's check out the packing shed.'

They moved up the overgrown path to the packing shed. Cole pulled open the door to the office. Empty. They moved in under the open roof where sorting and packing equipment had lain unused for a long time. Too open to hide in. Cole turned to view the door of the cold room. He remembered bolting it and putting the padlock on it to stop the boys from getting too adventurous and going exploring in there.

The padlock lay discarded on the floor with a pair

of bolt cutters beside it. Cole's heart sank as he reached for the cold steel handle to open the door, his gut knowing what he'd find inside. He looked at Sam, her face set, and her jaw clenched. She knew too.

'Ready?'

She rolled her shoulders and took a deep breath. 'Ready as I'll ever be, Sarge. For the love of God and all that's holy, let this not be another incident report that resulted in death.'

'I'm with you on that one.' Cole heaved open the heavy insulated door.

The men lay in a corner, hands bound, their uniforms stained dark red, slashes criss-crossing their bodies, and a discarded machete lying beside them. Cole didn't stop to name the range of emotions that plummeted through him as he searched for, and found, weak pulses on both men.

'They're alive. Just. Get an ambulance out here. Fetch Gus and tell him we need water and something to slow the bleeding until the paramedics get here.'

'On it, Sarge.'

As Sam set off at a run, Cole called Mark. 'How far away are you?'

'Forty-five minutes with lights and sirens. Why?'

'We have two more victims.'

'Fuck. I'll be there in thirty.'

'At this rate, you might as well just move the whole

damn unit down here. I'm leaving this mess in Gus's hands. Sam and I are going to find Alex and take this bastard down. Nick is out canvassing in the town to see what information he can find.'

'Small town grapevines work faster than BOLOs, for sure. Get moving. Did you get a list of those properties?'

'Yes. We have the file, but we had to prioritise and find the missing guards first. Thank God we did. He messed them up good, and then left them to die in the cold room. Any longer in here and they wouldn't have made it. Probably what this evil bastard was hoping for.'

'Find out where he is. Make sure you let Lily know where you're heading, and we'll get there as fast as we can to back you up. And Cole? Don't do anything I'll need to suspend you for. I don't want to have to investigate you for excessive use of force. Dot those Is and cross those Ts. Close all the loopholes that this bastard might find to jump through.'

'It will be my pleasure.'

Hanging up on Mark, Cole reassured the men that help was on the way, unsure of whether or not they heard him. He stood, walked to the edge of the packing shed, forging a plan of approach in his head.

If Romanovic could take down two burly security guards on his own, he had three extra vulnerable victims in captivity. With Romanovic's sick penchant for violence escalating, that scared the shit out of Cole.

He looked across the distance to the house as the old Valiant's engine sputtered to life and skidded backwards in reverse. It lurched forward as it gained speed and traction down the driveway towards the road. White hot fear streaked through his blood. He didn't need a visual to know who was behind the wheel.

'Fuck!'

Chapter Twenty-Four

B ridey drove as fast as she dared in the opposite direction to the town. The old street guide map she'd kept tucked away from the time she'd tried to escape with the boys had come in handy to locate the road the mission was on. It wouldn't take Cole long to figure out she was gone or where she was headed.

The twenty-minute drive felt much further as the narrow country road wound deeper into the distance between the tall gum trees. She passed paddocks with herds of cows and hay bales, a field of bright yellow canola, a tractor cutting a fire break along a fence line.

How could life carry on as normal when her child and others were undoubtedly being subjected to a cruelty beyond anyone's imagination? The tranquil landscape represented a peace and innocence that didn't exist. Within the beauty of God's creation of earth, an ugly truth lurked behind closed doors and walls. Today she would end it.

Bridey slowed the car as she approached the turnoff that would lead her to the mission. According to the map, it lay another ten kilometres down Orchard Road. She turned onto the road and drove under a canopy of trees until she reached the faded sign indicating she had reached her destination.

She stopped the car. No signs of life beyond the sandy patches of land scattered with hardy scrub and gumtrees. The odd grass tree thrived with green hair-like fronds spiking out from the top of a thick black trunk. Screened by palm trees, so out of character on the natural landscape, a bold white cross marked the spot of the mission chapel. While the New Lord didn't believe in the traditional forms and representations of religion, his ego would dictate that he take possession of the chapel. An impostor who thought he was God.

Reaching for the shotgun, she loaded the bullets the way she'd seen Thom do it at their kitchen table, her movements mechanical, her soul dead inside. The New Lord had taken her child, her baby, her heart. He'd ruled her life with his violence and teachings for long enough.

She knew the harm he could inflict, had felt the lashings of his fury. Now was not the time to feel anything other than hatred for a man who had killed and harmed for reasons that existed only in his twisted mind. If she let him walk away again, he would never face the justice he deserved.

An eye for an eye would make her a criminal when she'd been a victim all her life, just as Elle and Sunshine were. She would do this for them, for her children, and Kirana, and all the girls the New Lord had harmed for far too long. If she didn't, it would never stop. The laws that ruled be damned.

Protection orders, gun laws, emergency housing, counselling, all the charities in the world, all the things Lily and TJ had discussed with them ... none of the good deeds mattered unless the law that Cole believed in drilled down and dealt with the source of the problem. The powers behind the guns, the whips, the fists, and the chains that ultimately led to death when a cry for help went unanswered.

Placing the rifle across her lap, she put the Valiant into gear and slowly negotiated the rough track — full of potholes and grooves — that led into the mission grounds.

In the stillness of the countryside and abandoned property, he would hear the engine of the Valiant approaching, and that was fine. She wanted him to know she was there. She needed to look him in the eye and remember all the lives he had taken, all the harm he had done when she pulled the trigger. She couldn't risk letting him walk away again.

He waited at the entrance of the chapel as she drew to a halt a safe distance away. Bridey knew how fast he could move. She wouldn't risk not having the rifle in her hands and her finger on the trigger if he rushed at her.

Turning off the engine, she gripped the rifle and got out of the car. Safety off. Lifting the butt of the rifle to her shoulder, she held it the way Thom had.

Romanovic laughed. 'Put that thing down, girl, before you hurt yourself. You probably don't even know how to use it.'

'Where are they?'

'Who? That worthless, drunk piece of shit and her rabid offspring? Or your precious boy? He's pretty. I could use him when he grows up. He'd be a great lure for the girls.'

Anger and disgust had Bridey pulling the trigger, the backlash bruising her shoulder as the shot hit the wall behind Romanovic.

Not fazed, he smirked. 'So, you *do* know how to use it. Might need some practice though. You'll be out of bullets before you hit me. Or maybe you think your cavalry will arrive in time to save you?'

Bridey took a step towards him, blanking out the burning pain in her shoulder. 'I don't need a cavalry.'

Romanovic threw his hands wide. 'So, you shoot me. What then, Bridey? You go to jail. Your offspring go into foster care. And guess what? They end up in a foster home where daddy likes little boys, and mummy beats up on them because she's jealous of the attention they get. Does that sound like a solution to you?'

'Stop talking! Take me to my boy.'

'Why? So, he can watch while his mother murders a man? What a role model you'll be. You know, your mother was just like you. Thought she was a warrior, a saviour of women. She convinced your father to run, to seek freedom. So, they ran. Right off the road and into a tree when their brakes failed. Leaving me with you.' Romanovic shrugged. 'They didn't die straight away. I had to finish them off.'

Bridey swallowed bile. 'Did the McCaffreys run too?'

Romanovic laughed, a guffaw that made her hand jerk on the barrel of the rifle. 'Ma and Pa McCaffrey ... My mistake was allowing them to move to that farm. I thought it would be a good place for them to host our new recruits, close to all this.' He waved his arm across the span of the abandoned mission. 'The perfect place for me to start over. But they'd spread the same poison your parents did amongst the followers. Tried to convince Thom I was evil when all I'm trying to do is change humanity for the better. Bring the sinners back in line.'

'By beating them and burning them on a pyre when they don't obey you? Murdering them and dumping them in a pit under a potting shed? Locking up and starving innocent women and children in a shipping container? Using them, treating them like slaves to perpetuate your own beliefs? You're not a saviour. You're the devil himself.'

'I didn't kill the McCaffreys. Thom did. He needed to prove his loyalty to me by removing the disobedient. Prove to me that he didn't share their disregard for their New Lord.'

The smug look that lit his features made Bridey want to pull the trigger again. An eye for an eye. It would be so easy to put a bullet where his heart beat only to keep him alive, because he sure as hell had no soul.

'You drove Thom to violence, murder, and suicide. You made him hold women and children prisoner. Women and children who were taken against their will and brought here illegally for the purpose of pairing them with the violent men you recruited to be their husbands.'

'Thom should have stayed out of the bottle. He was just like his real father. Clifford Camden liked a drink. He was a lush, a weakling. He had no control over his followers. He wanted to create a Utopia where everyone was equal and women were strong, warrior goddesses. The fool. As for those women you're harbouring in Thom's home? Whores. All of them. Outcasts in their village for their loose ways. The village leaders couldn't wait to hand them over. Women need to know their place. It is because of man that they live, yet they have betrayed man since the beginning of time with their beguiling ways.'

'Don't spout that bullshit at me! I've seen the truth now. Everything you have preached is a lie.' Bridey's finger trembled in the curve of the trigger as she stepped towards him, rifle poised to shoot.

Romanovic laughed. 'You stupid girl! Do you really think those people you've surrounded yourself with are your friends? That they care about you? When all this drama you've created blows over, they'll go back to their boring lives in their tiny, small-minded town, and forget all about the Widow McCaffrey. You'll lose the house you're squatting in, the farm, and you and your offspring will live in poverty until you die from hunger sleeping in the Valiant in a park at night.' He took a step forward. 'Come on, girl. You don't know their way of life. You wouldn't fit in. You're better off back with the people who raised you. You can have one of these houses. I'll even fix it up for you. We can find you a new man. One who will know how to manage you.'

She couldn't let him get inside her head. That wasn't the life she wanted to go back to. 'Stop talking! Take me to my boy.'

Romanovic threw up his hands. 'He's over in the main house with the other two useless oxygen thieves.'

Bridey swallowed her anger, refusing to fall for his taunts. Once she knew Alex, Elle and Sunshine were safe, she'd deal with the New Lord in the way he'd dealt with others. A single bullet wouldn't be enough punishment. He needed to feel the pain he'd forced on others.

'Move!'

'Don't shoot me in the back.'

'I wouldn't waste a bullet. I want to look you in the eye when I pull the trigger.'

Romanovic laughed as he turned and walked towards the nearest house. Broken windows and graffiti, the remnants of a rose garden, a sweet-smelling Daphne rose hanging onto life in the barren soil. A square without imagination, warmth or personality with a blue tiled roof and brown brick walls, and a derelict sadness she felt from afar. The mission had not been a happy place. No wonder the New Lord had chosen it as the place to settle what was left of his following. He thrived in the darkness not in the light.

The front door opened at the shove of Romanovic's hand, the rusted hinges squealing in protest, the wood swollen from the rain and neglect scraping against the worn linoleum of the entrance hall. He led the way through the broken bottles, discarded beer cans and litter left behind by urban explorers with destruction on their minds. Thom had chased a few of those from their property when they'd thought the farm abandoned.

Romanovic stopped walking and turned to face her. 'You know Thom killed his father, don't you? Shoved a bottle of whiskey down his throat and watched him drown. Thom knew, like I did, that Camden was leading the church down the wrong path. That's when I took him under my wing.'

'And made him a carbon copy of you?' Disgust tasted sour on her tongue. The evil that emanated from him was almost palpable. 'Keep walking.'

'I didn't need to make Thom do anything. He was a willing student. I had big plans for him.' Romanovic moved on.

The corridor opened up into a dilapidated kitchen. Mustard-coloured benchtops, stained with time and misuse, old pine cupboards with doors hanging askew, dark green tiles forming a splashback behind a gas cooktop covered in filth. Three people tied to chairs, blind-folded and gagged, their chins sagging towards their chest.

'What have you done to them?' Terror made her

hands shake. She breathed to steady them, blocking out the stench of rotting food and God knew what else that filled the space around her.

'They'll be fine. A little of the stuff I had Thom making for me before he screwed everything up. Keeps them calm. I couldn't risk those two hellcats going wild on me.'

The bruises on Elle's and Sunshine's jaws showed they hadn't taken the drugs without a fight. Everything inside Bridey urged her to shoot the bastard and be done with him, but that would only reduce her to his level.

'Why did you set the shed on fire?'

'Thom did a stupid thing by shooting himself. He did what I'd trained him never to do. He brought attention to us, to the church and to progress. And you, my dear, perpetuated that by bringing in the cops and that doctor you always run to for every little bruise, so I had to get rid of the evidence. I would have set the house on fire too if that little moron in that chair hadn't come out to pee. I almost had him then, you know, but he's quick. He was lucky. He got away that time. This time, he wasn't so lucky.'

Anger bubbled to the surface. Bridey willed herself to stay calm. If she allowed her emotions to take over, everything she'd planned would unravel.

'Untie them.'

'Are you crazy? Why would I do that?'

'Because it's the end of the road for you and your fake church.'

'What, and one little girl with a gun is going to stop me?' His laugh echoed through the abandoned house, the sound making his three captives jerk their heads up. 'You idiot. I am so looking forward to dealing out the punishment you deserve.' He walked toward her, forcing her to take a step back. 'You're weak! You won't shoot me. You don't have the guts to pull that trigger again.'

'She might not, but I do.'

The sound of Cole's voice brought a rush of relief as Romanovic froze in his advance on her. Over his shoulder, Bridey saw Cole and Sam had come in from the side of the house through the missing sliding door.

'Your cavalry's arrived.' Romanovic held up his hands in mock surrender. 'Just in time to see you die.'

He lunged at Bridey at the same time as she pulled the trigger, the shot drowning out the charge of Cole's Taser and the metallic sound of a knife falling to the floor.

She ignored the shouts as Cole and Sam rushed into action. She didn't care if Romanovic lived or died. All she cared about was her boy. Pushing past them, she dragged off Alex's blindfold, pulled out the rag that gagged his mouth, freed him from the rope that bound him and collapsed to the floor with him in her arms. She rocked him back and forth, her tears falling on his face.

'You're squishing me, Mum.' Alex's words slurred through his drowsiness, reaching her ears through the noise Romanovic made protesting his arrest.

She hadn't killed him. More the pity. 'Are you okay, baby? Did he hurt you?'

'I have a bruise on my arm.'

'We can fix that, sweetheart.' Bridey hugged him hard.

Cole dropped to his haunches beside her. 'Are you hurt?'

'No. The New Lord?'

'The Taser got him before your bullet did. The shot missed.'

'I refuse to regret that.' She slipped her hand into her pocket and drew out a mobile phone, handing it over to him. 'Everything's recorded. You can turn off the tracker now.'

Cole took the phone, shaking his head. 'I think I'm going to have my hands full with a whole bunch of you staying on the farm.'

'Kirana knew what to do. She showed me how to start the recording and activate the tracker.'

'She told me. I'm also really happy that you had the sense to tell someone where you were heading.'

Bridey held Alex closer as he dozed off against the effects of the drug he'd been given. 'Can I take Alex home and get him settled before you arrest me?'

Cole pressed a kiss to her temple. 'I'm not laying any charges against you, Bridey. But we will have a chat about how you should never scare me like that again. I think I aged ten years in ten seconds flat.' He stood and took a sleeping Alex from her arms as Mark and his team arrived on the scene. 'Let's go home. Mark will take it from here.'

'Yeah, right! Thanks, mate. Call me when all the action is over and then leave me to clean up the mess, why don't you?' Mark nudged Cole's shoulder as he passed them by. 'You okay, Bridey?'

She looked up at Cole. 'I will be. Can we take Elle and Sunshine home too?'

'I think they'd appreciate that. Sam, when you're done here, can you please bring the Donnellys to Mindaleny Ridge? I'll take Bridey and the children back in the Valiant.'

'Sure thing, Sarge.'

As Bridey took Cole's hand to stand up, she cast one last look at the monster lying face down and cuffed on the floor and said goodbye to the horror of her past one last time.

Chapter Twenty-Five

B ridey handed Cole his coffee mug, the brew strong and hot. Across the newly fenced off field, Amisha and Sari worked with their teams to bring the farm back to life.

Over in the sorting shed office, Kirana had gathered the children for their lessons. It resembled nothing like the old dark, dank, and depressing place it used to be. Colourful drawings adorned the freshly painted walls alongside posters with the alphabet and times tables donated by Mrs Lee. Wooden tables and chairs had been arranged at one end, in front of a wall painted with chalkboard paint, all carefully crafted thanks to the local Men's Shed.

The transformation over the past few months had been nothing short of a miracle. The girls' protection visas had been approved, and Bridey's application for adverse possession had been approved, thanks to the letters of support from just about everyone in the community. She'd bet she had Mrs Lee to thank for that too. Every day Bridey watched as the smiles on the girls' faces grew broader, their hearts grew lighter, and their confidence blossomed.

'Am I doing the right thing here, Cole? Or am I just creating another version of what I grew up in?' Doubt crept in.

'Look at them, honey. They're singing, laughing, glowing even. They're free to leave whenever they want to, but they stay because they like it here. Because they love you and appreciate the freedom you've given them.'

'I had plenty of help. I didn't do it alone. I couldn't have.'

'Have you considered TJ and Lily's offer?'

'Yes. I've accepted it. They have signed the lease for the farm to be a safe house. And with Gus buying the old mission to renovate into a farm stay, he'll be creating more jobs and overflow accommodation for any others we host here.'

'I haven't seen my father this excited since I told him I was joining the force. It's given him a whole new lease on life.' Cole placed an arm around her shoulders and drew her close, pressing a kiss to the top of her head. 'How are things going inside the house?'

Bridey smiled up at him, her heart full. After all the pain and heartache, he was her light at the end of the dark tunnel. A polar opposite of Thom. Kind, caring, gentle. The twins adored him, and even Alex had started to let his guard down again. It would take a little longer for her eldest boy to trust anyone again. She believed that — given time and nurturing — their new, loving way of life would heal his soul.

'Good. The last of the painting is almost done thanks to the men from the Men's Shed. Mrs Lee is cleansing all the rooms with her rice ritual and making sure everything is positioned properly for good Feng Shui. The house feels much happier and brighter now.'

'And you? Are you happy?'

Bridey put her arms around his waist and hugged him tight. 'I don't remember ever being this happy and content. Thank you.'

Cole chuckled. 'Honey, the pleasure is all mine.' He tipped up her chin to kiss her lips.

For a long moment, Bridey lost herself in everything Cole. The way he made her feel safe, loved, wanted. The light touch of his hands, how he never made her feel trapped or afraid. And, when he lifted his head to search her soul, the way he saw her and loved her for who she was, not who he thought she should be.

Resting her head against his heartbeat, she sighed. 'I got a call from the coroner's office this morning.'

'Look at you getting used to using a mobile phone,' Cole teased.

She looked up at him, a little sad. 'The McCaffreys are ready to be laid to rest. I've arranged a place for them in the memorial wall at the church. I didn't think it was right to bury them with Thom after what he did.'

'I think they would have liked that.'

'I thought so too. How's Elle doing?'

'As well as can be expected. I've never been so grateful for a judge who could see the victim's side of the story, and the ongoing threat that Romanovic poses if he's given bail or any leniency at all. She threw the book at him, so he'll be away for a long time.'

'And if he applies for parole?'

Cole shook his head. 'With all the charges against him, Elle's being the final one, the judge imposed a non-parole period for the remainder of Romanovic's life. She wasn't taking any chances that he'd see the outside again.'

Bridey let out a sigh of relief. 'When Elle gets back from the city, she'll have a place here with Sunshine.'

'I think she'd like that. Is Sunshine behaving herself?'

'Kirana has taken her under her wing. Sunshine is showing promise of becoming an excellent teacher. She's enjoying reading to the kids and helping them with their homework. I've even seen her smile a few times.'

Cole laughed. 'I bet Nick and Sam will be happy to hear that. She's been a bit of a challenge for them for a while now. I guess it's all worked out fine then.' He dropped his arm from around her to take her hand. 'Which reminds me ... I've got something for you. Mark dropped it off.'

Bridey frowned. She couldn't imagine what Mark would have had to give her. If anything, she owed him and his team for their thorough investigation that would lock up a monster for life.

Cole led her into the kitchen. A cardboard box sat on the table, the lid askew. 'Mark set aside a few things for you that weren't needed to be kept as evidence. Go on, open it.'

Hesitant to know what she'd find, Bridey lifted the lid from the box and set it aside. Old books, a diary, a copy of a birth certificate and a couple of old passports. She reached in to pick up a passport. Opening it to the details page, she ran her finger over the name and photograph. 'John Reid. My father?'

'Yes.' Cole picked up the other passport and opened it. 'This is your mum.'

Bridey took the passport from him, her fingers numb as she held it to study the photo. In it, she could see her own resemblance. 'Norma. John and Norma Reid.' The names felt foreign on her tongue. 'I wish I could remember them.'

'You were only a toddler when the crash happened.'

'Who were they?'

'They emigrated here from the UK. From your mum's diary, we figured out that they met Clifford Camden on the plane over. He offered them a place to stay at his commune until they found their feet. Camden's vision for the commune was a vastly different one to Romanovic's. When Romanovic took over, people started to leave. They wanted out. Most of them never made it out. Your parents were leaving when the accident happened. They wanted to keep you safe from Romanovic. Your mum's last entry in the diary on that day was that they were heading west from New South Wales.'

An ache filled Bridey's chest. 'Things could have been so different if they'd lived.' She placed the passports on the table and reached back in for the birth certificate. 'Asha Reid. That's my real name?'

'Yes.' Cole moved closer, his warmth and presence comforting.

'It's a pretty name.'

'Is that who you'll be from now on?'

She shook her head, sadness weighing on her chest for a girl who would never be. 'It's who I was, a name on a piece of paper. The New Lord changed that too long ago. I am Bridey, the woman he and his followers made me, and Thom perpetuated. I will never be Asha Reid.' The paper fluttered back into the box as she let it go.

Cole turned her around to hold her close. 'Bridey is the woman I fell in love with. She's strong. A fighter, a warrior, a wonderful mum ... a kind-hearted person who cares for others despite what she's been through herself.' He tipped up her chin. 'I'm hoping that when she's ready, she'll say yes to being Bridey Delaney. Not a wife, but a partner, an equal in everything we do together.'

'Even when I'm cranky from burning the midnight oil studying farming methods while running a women's shelter and raising three kids?' She reached up to put her arms around his neck, his hands resting on her hips.

'Even then. Because you won't be doing it alone. I'll be right there beside you all the way.' He rested his forehead against hers.

'I think I got lucky, Sergeant Delaney.' Her whisper touched his lips.

'I think I'm the lucky one.'

Their whispers fell silent in the kitchen as a

sunbeam filtered through the window, bathing them in its warmth. In Cole's arms she'd found peace, freedom and love, a nurturing she'd never dreamed possible. As she shared his kiss, she promised herself she'd never give up the fight to bring the same happiness to others who found themselves victims of cruel hands and minds.

THE END

This book has been written and edited using Australian / UK English grammar and punctuation conventions because the story is set in Australia. For more information on the differences between UK and US language and punctuation, please consider reading this article: https://tinyurl.com/56tkbh6a

If you enjoyed this book, please consider leaving a review on BookBub, Goodreads or the platform you purchased it from. If you would prefer to email me, please visit the contact page on my website at https://juanitakees.com/contact/. I do love to hear from readers and welcome your feedback.

Kind regards, Juanita Kees

Exposed, Tagged, Silenced and Shattered (Unfinished Business series) can be purchased from your favourite bookseller. If they don't have it, ask them or your local library to order it in for you.

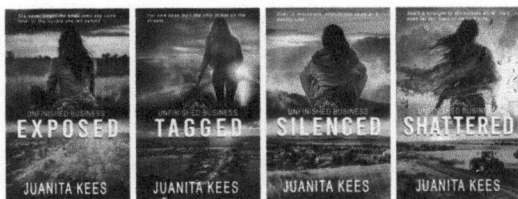

Other Books by Juanita Kees

Wongan Creek Series

Whispers

Secrets

Shadows

Unfinished Business

Exposed

Tagged

Silenced

Shattered

Bindarra Creek

Home to Bindarra Creek

Promise Me Forever

The Calhouns of Montana

Montana Baby

Montana Daughter

Montana Son

Contemporary Romance

Finish Line

Paranormal Fantasy

The Gods of Oakleigh

HOME TO BINDARRA CREEK
A Bindarra Creek Romance

JUANITA KEES